DRAGON CLAW CHRONICLES

Legend of Eliza

MAGUIRE & CUMMINGS PUBLISHING HOUSE

MAGUIRE & CUMMINGS PUBLISHING HOUSE

First published in Great Britain in 2020
By Maguire & Cummings Publishing House.
Legend of Eliza

Paperback edition
First Publication

ISBN 978-1-8381546-9-1

MAGUIRE & CUMMINGS PUBLISHING HOUSE
www.maguirecummings.co.uk

For Jemma Bunce,

Thank you for being patient with me while Eliza took over *my* life.

For Michael Cummings,

Thank you for being patient while Eliza took over *our* lives.

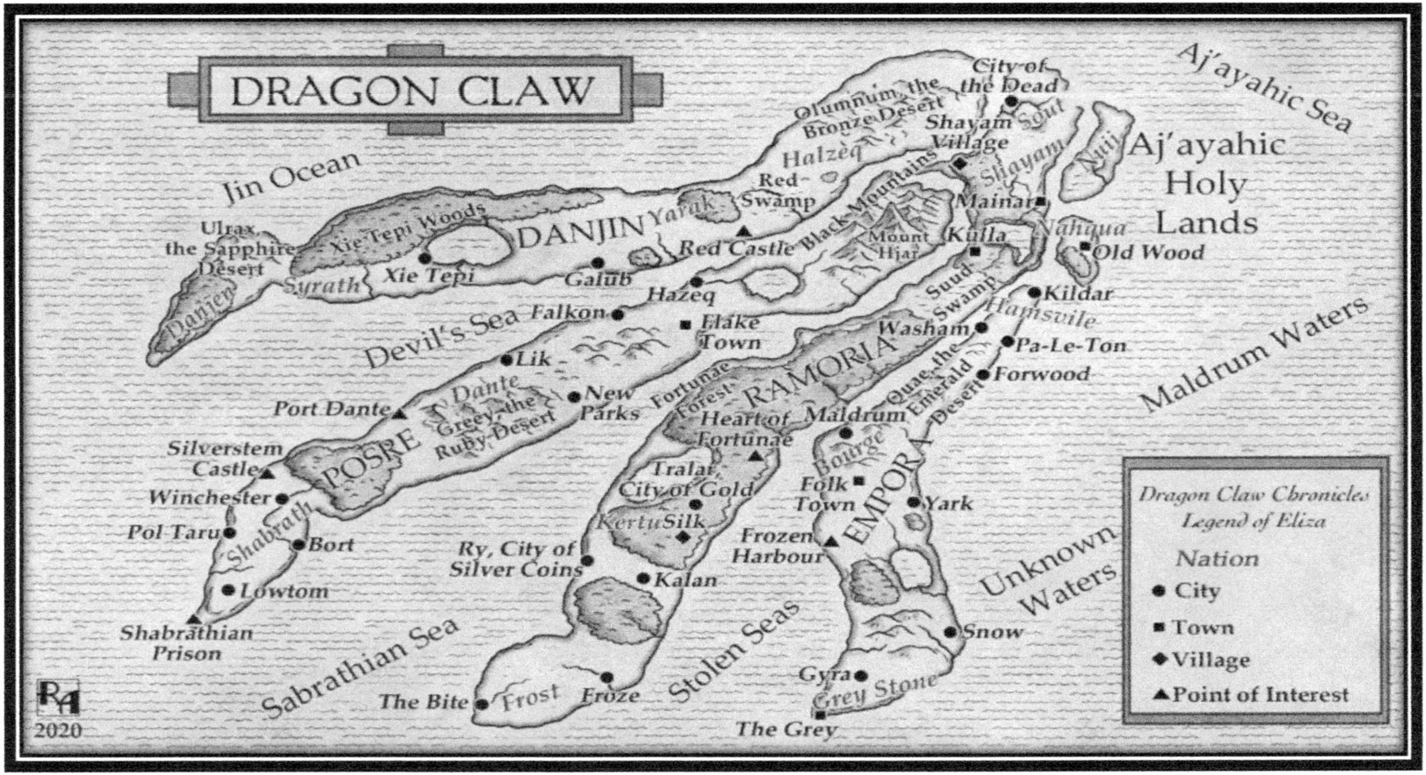
DRAGON CLAW
Jin Ocean
Aj'ayahic Sea
Aj'ayahic Holy Lands
Ulrax the Sapphire Desert
Danjen
Syrath
Xie Tepi Woods
Xie Tepi
DANJIN
Yarak
Galub
Red Castle
Red Swamp
Halzeq
Olumnum the Bronze Desert
City of the Dead
Shayam Village
Sout
Shayam
Nuii
Mainar
Black Mountains
Mount Hjar
Kulla
Nahqua
Old Wood
Hazeq
Falkon
Devil's Sea
Flake Town
Suud Swamp
Kildar
Hamsvile
Washam
Pa-Le-Ton
Forwood
Maldrum Waters
Lik
Dante
Port Dante
New Parks
Greey, the Ruby Desert
POSRE
Silverstem Castle
Winchester
Shabrath
Pol Taru
Bort
Lowtom
Shabrathian Prison
Sabrathian Sea
Fortunae Forest
RAMORIA
Heart of Fortunae
Maldrum
Quae, the Emerald Desert
Bourge
Tralar, City of Gold
Kertu
Silk
Folk Town
Yark
EMPORA
Frozen Harbour
Ry, City of Silver Coins
Kalan
Unknown Waters
Snow
Stolen Seas
Gyra
Grey Stone
The Grey
The Bite
Frost
Froze
2020
Dragon Claw Chronicles
Legend of Eliza
Nation
City
Town
Village
Point of Interest

Contents

Part Three: Man, Monster and Magic

Epilogue:

Additional:

An Introduction to Dragon Claw

The story you are about to read is not told in chronological order. It is written in a non-linear style, including many assorted tales of Dragon Claw's past.

You will meet wizards, witches, wolves, vampires and many more interesting characters. Alongside the stories of Ella-Rose, Michael and Finn, you will also follow tales of war, love, hate and the opening of a crooked world.

Similarly to that of Earth, folk across Dragon Claw have their own religions, ideas on politics and experience the four seasons: winter, spring, summer and autumn.

Prior to the eruption of an infamous volcano, Dragon Claw had always been divided in two. Half belonged to the *Aj'ayah*, the other to the *Luminous*. Between the lands stood the vicious monster with one molten eye: Mount Hjar. The beast was worshiped by both lands and for millions of years Hjar, in return, remained tranquil. Unfortunately, a monster's anger will always erupt.

The Luminous and the Aj'ayah were broken by the lava and separated into four lands; empires, each led by monarchs of either the race of man, monster or magic.

The Aj'ayah managed to retain small, broken holy islands in the aftermath of Hjar, hovering east of Ramoria and rumoured to be cursed to any whoever dared take rule.

The Four Lands/Empires:

RAMORIA
EMPORA
POSRE
DANJIN

The Four Emperor Names:

RAPTURE: This family name holds Ramoria, strong and vigorous men.
SYRUS: This family name holds Empora, honourable and dutiful men.
FALLEN: This family name holds Posre, artful, clever mages.
TRAJAN: This family name holds Danjin, intelligent, yet deadly monsters.

The Four Thrones:

ORCA: At the Siren Palace within Ramoria, held originally by the RAPTURE name.
ELEPHANT: At Castle Snow within Empora, held originally by the SYRUS name.

BEAR: At Silverstem Castle within Posre, held originally by the FALLEN name.
DEVIL: At Red Castle within Danjin, held originally by the TRAJAN name.

You can find more information about the families within Dragon Claw in the Glossary.

Legend of Eliza

Prologue

The Crooked Cabin

Buried deep within a thick mound of snow, the crooked cabin sat peacefully amid the path of emerald trees, held together by only dead wood and ice. Whoever foolishly thought to have chained its door so powerfully must have taken ill to the mind; for where there ought to have been windows, were only the welcoming entrances for frost to dive in.

Only a sorcerer, who dared to, could enter the cabin. Nevertheless, in order to explore the strange magic stored between those walls, one must have first given their mind passage to enter into the crooked world in which it resides. The cabin was no homely place. Far from it in fact. Yet, in tranquil meditation with only a small, leather book atop his lap, the old man sat quietly inside, focussing his mind on one thing only. For years - more so than he would have liked - he had used the space in training to reach the consciousness of a girl through his own, failing at every given moment.

He had to try.

How could he not when all the lands of Dragon Claw depended on it? It had become a vicious cycle of hammering the same message over and over again, torturing the poor girl's mind. All in hope that it fulfils a prophecy, he wasn't sure even existed. Recently, however, there seemed to have been a small change in the wind. The old man, at long last, began to feel her mind's presence inside the cabin.

'*Ella-Rose?*' he whispered out to the emptiness. *'Ella-Rose do you hear me? Dear girl, hear me now and hear me well. The answers you seek lie deep within Fortunae. Hurry. Please hurry!'*

Around the old man, a perfectly drawn chalked circle closed on him like a trap. A prison it seemed, formed by his own hand. Four brightly flamed candles were placed carefully surrounding, illuminating the nothingness of the room that could once have been claimed a kitchen, given the constant smell of rotten cabbage. Thankfully, the scent of burning wax soothed. He wore only stained, torn rags, though no matter how low the temperature dropped, the frost dared not to disturb.

Cold is pain and pain lives only in the mind, his brother once taught him. *Allow your mind to escape the world, because a mind that ceases presence will feel no pain.*

Perhaps the snow had just become a familiar friend over the years. Else, could it have been the efforts of an inexplicable sorcery, summoned from between the walls of the crooked cabin itself? Curiously, neither and yet both were true. Frost was always far from friendly, and the spiritual, boundless creation of the small, damaged lodge was not something to be abused. Power from the cabin was enough to drive anyone to insanity. Surpassing all nuclear, electromagnetic and magical forces of Dragon Claw's lands, only those, who owned the rare ability of sorcery, could enter. And only those, with a mind strong enough, could harness its power.

Not to be mistaken with the average, standard use of magic involving silly little spells to cause mischief, sorcery holds power enough to change the axis of the world. When such power is combined with the energies trapped within the crooked cabin, an indescribable force would soon form, strong enough to destroy all of Dragon Claw, if so desired.

Most who tried to control the power of the cabin ended up destroying themselves through greed, while others feared and steered clear of it. There was one, however, who believed he could control it. Years ago.

Emperor Lozari Rapture manipulated the cabin's power by creating an imperishable means of destruction: soldiers of the undead. Thrusting its energy into the forgotten souls of war, Lozari, second son of Parra Rapture, raised the darkest army Dragon Claw had ever known. His soldiers stole the lands of Dragon Claw for years before the Gods must have decided they'd had enough and disallowed such a mockery of their work. The misguided emperor – thought to be the last of the sorcerer's bloodline - soon choked on the bitter taste of defeat, forcing his army to return from whence they came.

Dragon Claw had taken a turn for the worst, however sorcery, at long last, was thought to have become extinct. At least, that was what most believed. Only few held true knowledge of the secret relationship between Lozari Rapture and Savanah Fallen and even fewer knew that Savanah had passed away giving birth to the second of her two children: Zagan and Thanisis. Many suspected that the race of sorcerers was not yet through, but it had never been confirmed.

Meanwhile, the crooked cabin infinitely remained, hidden in a broken world, accessed only through the mind of a sorcerer.

***

The old man gave no heed to the snow fighting its way through the smashed windows. Instead, he closely spied the mysterious, cloaked figure nearing towards him through the holes of the broken oak. Along the pebbled path, protected by rows upon rows of emerald fir trees at each side, the figure slowly drifted closer. Still, the blizzard attacked mercilessly each second. It was only when the mysterious figure reached the writing, carved deep into the wood next to the chained door that the old man began to shudder.

In all his seventy-two years, he never knew who had written those words, nor was he interested in ever finding out. He never doubted that it had been placed there for a reason far beyond his own understanding. The words were scraped unevenly into the cabin wood by either knife or claw. At one time, the message would have read:

Only upon a full-mooned, star-filled night,
And by the hands of summer's tilted, grey bite,
Will it be true, Eliza sets to fight.
Tell me true and tell it now, can peace be sought through war?
Or would pain and suffering just forever be restored?
The medallion is split, yet its power burns throughout a crooked world.
So, is it so, or is it no? Can peace be found in the lands?
Or is it that love and peace are illusionary slaves of Dragon Claw?

Only now, the scars of the charred wood ruined most of the words and the message shared something different. Could it have been the words of a prophecy? Or was it merely just a marked piece of wood?

Only
by the hands of
Eliza
can peace
forever be restored
throughout
the lands
of Dragon Claw

The old man could practically hear the mysterious figure's mind so arrogantly reading each word. Suddenly, three loud thuds raged against the door! Chains rattled, rats scattered. The first few pounds to the cabin were deliberately ignored. It was the following four alongside the mysterious figure's sharp screaming that at last relieved the old man of his mind; guiding him back into the unsalvageable depths of his consciousness. He tried as best he could to stand, dropping at every instant. His physique had weakened, his legs disobeyed his brain's every instruction and on top of that, he had developed a most awful cramp in his stomach.

He managed to crawl and pull himself up, holding tightly to the chains of the broken door. Though he may be old, it was not his age that caused the weakness in his legs. More that he had transferred all of the strength his body had left to offer to his mind. His only focus had been to telepathically send his instruction to Ella-Rose. Had it at last worked? He could only hope.

The next bang to the door forced an aching, involuntary mumble from the old man. 'Prove yourself,' he muttered. 'Prove yourself, else I'll kill you I swear it!' He continued to pull himself up with aid of the door's chains, taking more effort than he would ever wish to admit. None would be able to comprehend the struggles and pains flowing through his mind in the fifty years he had locked himself away there. He would never forget the day he had said his goodbyes to Dragon Claw, accepting he would never get to see its beauty again. After all, it was on that day he had been forced to entrust the prophecy involving a girl who wasn't even to be born until thirty-five years later. Alas, Ella-Rose does live, now at the trying age of fifteen with no idea of her frightening days to come. Nothing - not one thing would stop the old man from fulfilling his duty.

The mysterious figure poked one eye through the gaps of the wood. 'It's me,' she said. 'It's Nyla.'

Nyla? The old man could see more clearly now. Meeting her fierce stare through the holes of the wood, he spotted a woman, seemingly older than himself, wearing only a dark cloak.

'How can I trust you?'

As if to answer his question, the cloaked woman pulled a small, golden chain and dangled it; a broken piece of medallion fell between her bony fingers. Once, the medallion would have possessed the delicate design of a ladybird, only now, half of its golden body was crushed and ruined and the other half was missing.

'Who gave you that?' He didn't wait for a reply; he already knew the answer. A throaty cough, followed by nauseating anxiety soon took the old man's entire body, attacking the limited strength he had left. 'You shouldn't have come here!' His voice was hoarse. 'Don't you understand what would happen if *she* finds you? Fifty years I have slaved to keep this prophecy in line. Your being here risks everything. It's not safe, dammit. Not—' His breath was soon exchanged with a beastly fit of coughing. Hastily, he took to the barred door, hauling off the chains to drag open the black wood. It proved a tougher enemy than expected with the iced hinges hugged to its frame. He studied her grey eyes. Examined them even. 'Quickly now, I suspect we have little time.'

Inside the crooked cabin was dark, dingy and drab. There was no sitting-room nor bedroom, no kitchen nor bathroom. Of course, the old man had no care of its state. Mainly, because he could only see half of it. He had lost his left eye at a young age. Many legends were told, absurd stories that shared he was born with a disease; a virus that healers could rid only from the eye. Others insisted it was through the talons of a great monster set upon him by his own brother. Though, after all the pains and torments of his life, even he had forgotten truth's worth.

Nyla gave no mind to the crooked cabin's state either. Not the rotten smell that chased up her nose, nor the foot-sized rats, feeding on their new-born in the corners. She gazed at the old man with enhanced admiration. Worship even. 'Only now can I see that it was no lie. It truly is you, Zagan.' She hugged him like an aunt would a nephew. 'You were expecting me.' It wasn't a question.

'I believe so. It was Coccin himself who told me you would come.' *Warned me perhaps?* 'Nyla, your being here risks all,' he repeated, this time firmer. 'I'm sure Eliza will soon be aware of your presence here.'

Nyla winced at his words. That was the first time she had heard the name of her sister in years and although her ears must endure it, she would never allow the name to pass through her lips. 'I don't doubt it,' she said, 'but that *demon* – I daren't speak her name - holds no power without the complete medallion.' Nyla held out the broken piece once more. 'That's why I was sent here, was it not? I have one piece, you have the other. Together we can combine them, force the strength from within this cabin into the medallion and destroy this crooked, broken world once and for all. Never again will its power affect Dragon Claw.'

Although Zagan heard her words, he made no effort to reply. Instead, he raised one shaking finger to the medallion piece and said: 'That damned ladybird,' and let out a small *humph* of a laugh. 'Back in our youth, a ladybird was actually a symbol for the word *secret* in the Dihne Alphabet.' He laughed to himself, lost in his own words. 'Things may not always appear what they seem...' he trailed off.

Nyla fell in closer, examining the scars buried deep into his face – and his mind. 'I remember,' she said, 'but you and I both know it now holds a much deeper meaning. The deepest secret everyone of Dragon Claw holds onto these days: *evil.*' She could not refrain herself from searching into the white nothingness of his left eye. An emptiness longing for answers to questions too abstract to even be heard. 'The Ladybird is the mark of the demon; the mark of…' Nyla shook her head, she could not bring herself to say her name. 'Tell me where the other piece lies.'

Zagan caught her grey eyes staring at the leather book he had left amid the candlelight. 'The other half is hidden,' he answered. 'In plain sight believe it or not, yet safer than you and me.' A harsh wind struck him as he peered from an empty window, gazing upon the malformed moonlight mists and frozen lakes. Thoughts of Dragon Claw swam through his mind once again. 'You shouldn't be here,' he hesitated for a spell. 'I suppose you already knew that—' he cut his voice in half, quickly limping to blow out each candle; an irrational task to lower their risk of exposure. 'The demon. If it manages to find the complete medallion, war upon Dragon Claw will be the least of our worries.'

'They're saying the war is over. That Dragon Claw is introduced to a newfound peace.'

'It's all a lie!' Zagan roared. 'This war isn't over. It is only just truly beginning. While the demon lives and the gates leading to this crooked world, this— this haunted cabin, remain open, Dragon Claw will never know peace.'

Nyla considered his words.

'Mysterious are the ways of the Claw,' he continued. 'Now, it is your turn to trust me.' Zagan took the woman's thin, fragile wrists into his hands, harsher than he wanted. It appeared his strength had sneakily returned. 'Give it to me,' he said. Almost screamed. 'The medallion piece, hand it over now!'

'I— I will not,' she said, pulling her arms free.

'Nyla—'

Her eyes dropped into her hand. 'No, the medallion stays with me. You're supposed to give me the other half! The prophecy— th-this was not part of the plan.' Her voice darkened.

'But it was part of *my* plan!' Zagan warned, and with a powerful, unseen force, the medallion flew from Nyla's wrist and landed comfortably into his hand.

'No, Zagan, please, you must give it back. You said it yourself, right? If that piece were ever to fall into the wrong hands, war will be the least of Dragon Claw's concern.'

'Aye, it is the reason I have taken it.' Zagan looked once more into her grey eyes and this time saw nothing but hate. 'You didn't honestly believe I wouldn't know who you truly are, did you?' Then, as he swiftly grabbed the small, leather book and broken medallion piece, Zagan disappeared into thin air, leaving behind only a thick mass of black smoke. His last words called out once more for Ella-Rose and this time, he knew she'd hear them. This time, he knew the prophecy was true.

'The answers you seek lie deep within Fortunae. Hurry. Please hurry!'

PART ONE
Old Books, Older Tales

'Magic?' Michael rudely mocked. 'Force? Pfft, a book isn't full of anything but a bunch of silly words and that's that. What in the world would make words so magical?'

'Why, we do,' Caesar chortled. 'How about I let you in on a little secret, ay lad?' he grinned, leaning in nose to nose. 'Books bake bigger brains, boy!'

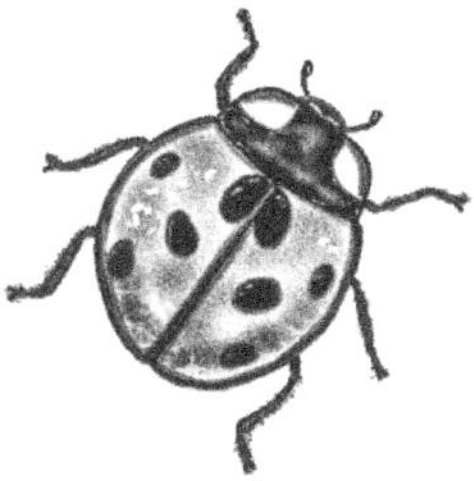

Chapter One

Ella-Rose's Nightmare

The sun had only just began to rise and already the day felt strange. Sara Azerius, a small, middle-aged woman with ears pointing wherever they felt fit and the largest of glasses squished tightly to her head, covering her face almost entirely, (without which, her eyes would have been nothing but stones,) could feel it. Was today the day she had dreaded for fifteen years? The day her whole world would change forever? She wished to shake the thought but knew there would be no way. Today *was* the day, there was no denying. The day she would regret for the rest of her life.

Sara struggled to open the front door. She juggled a cup of coffee in one hand and a bacon sandwich in the other. She rested her teeth lightly around the two slices of bread to allow herself to pull the Daily Scoop from her mailbox.

THE WAR IS OVER!

The headline screamed in big, bold letters.

'Hey, do you believe any of this, Joe?'

Josef Jacobs called back from the next cottage down, 'I'm a paper-man!' tapping on the silver-envelope-logo sewn into his unwashed-for-three-days shirt. 'Ain't be knowin' much for pol'tics. I thought t'war was over years ago.'

Sara shook her head. 'It had quietened, yes, but it was far from over,' she clarified before taking another bite of heaven. 'I think we were just always lucky to live so far away from it all.' She took a deep breath that sounded more like a sigh and started to read the top line of the Scoop. '*With Khosi Trajan at last slain by the Emporan Army, Empress Divina Syrus now sits firmly atop the Orca throne and the four lands of Dragon Claw are wholly introduced to a newfound peace."*

Nobody really knew much of Divina Syrus, except that she was the granddaughter of the famous Kraal Syrus and daughter of Wyrell. With Khosi Trajan dead and every other monarch murdered by the war, it was up to Divina to rule the lands of Dragon Claw and restore a civility as best she can. Some thought she had simply taken the role by default. Others thought it fate.

Joe listened as best he could to Sara's thoughts. Or, as best he would to show no offence. 'It's only a newfound peace because e'ryone else is dead!'

Sara smiled from cheek to cheek. 'Not everyone.' Then, as she started to make her way back through the front door, a dark thought crossed her mind. *Not yet.*

The sun fought valiantly with scorched red swords against the knight blue skies, hardly reserving itself when exaggerating an unbearable heat throughout Ramoria; the land well-known for its passionate temperatures. Yet, not even the hottest day of the year could interrupt the fixed routines of the Shayam

Village folk. Mr Sheldon would certainly be tending to his garden of daffodils, (or daft-odils as the local children often labelled, since they resemble more of a toucan than they ever did a flower,) fashioning that most awful burgundy dressing-gown. By now, Mrs Lyons would surely have led those poor drenched joggers up the stony path and thrice around White River.

The scent of fresh linen vacuumed up Sara's nose as she entered into the kitchen. She pulled open a drawer, shoved the newspaper inside and took an elastic-band to force down the broken lever of the kettle. "*Hernández; it's the best brand in the business*," Ms Adamou from next door had assured. The crazy old hag. The stupid handle had broken after the first month.

As Sara sat to enjoy her second cup of coffee of the morning, knowing it would certainly not be the last, a loud thumping and grinding from the other room caught her attention. There was no way Ella-Rose could have awakened so early. Impossible. The lazy thing was never awake before nine o'clock. Besides, there's only one person who could make such an awful racket and that was Ella-Rose's twin brother, Michael.

'Morning Aunt Sara,' the boy smiled with a gleam in his eye, still stamping and thumping his feet along the hall.

He was already dressed for the day and heading towards the front door, before Sara rapidly swiped in front of him.

'Hold up, hold up.' She stood at the tips of her toes. 'My, don't we look handsome today?' She licked the tips of four fingers and stretched her arm high to play with the blonde curls in his hair. It would have been much easier to give the woman a stool to stand on. 'Oh Mikey, please do be careful today. Yes, I know, I know *you always are*, but—but—' *the day feels strange*. 'Just be extra careful, okay?' *Today is a bad day, I know it.*

Michael looked at her like he would a crazy woman.

'Mikey, are you listening to me?'

'Um, yeah sorry, okay. You *do* know I'm just going to Caesar's right? He said he's got something exciting to show me that just can't wait.'

'Oh? He's not mentioned anything to me.' A lie.

'All that could happen to me there is that he bores me to death with one of his old stories.'

'Michael!' She shook her head, but found she couldn't stop herself smirking. 'You didn't happen to see if your sister was awake, did you?'

Michael ignored the question with his usual I-don't-care shrug.

'Oh, for goodness sake,' Sara rolled her eyes and said her goodbyes, then turned and headed straight for the closed door down the hall. She glanced at the clock. Nine-fifteen. 'Ella-Rose! Rise and shine!' Sara called through the wood. 'Ella Rose do you hear me?'

'The answers you seek lie deep within Fortunae. Hurry. Please hurry!'

Ella-Rose leapt from her sweat-soaked sheets with a start and frightful shiver. The tormenting nightmare had again returned; a fantasy she once thought so trivial, screaming through her unconscious. Why she continued to allow these cold, dark visions to take her imagination, was far beyond her understanding. She knew immediately: *'I need to stop reading Professor Caesar's dreaded old tales before bed.'*

Nightmares were just scary stories inside her head. She tried to shrug it off, but this time felt different. This time she couldn't get her mind to leave that crooked cabin.

Beneath her feet, Ella-Rose could feel summer's heartfelt touch as it dodged through the curtains. She was quick to rise in rescue of the remaining brightness, captured behind its thick prison. She almost ripped the curtains down with her tug. Summer had again birthed a sun, streaking the sky with its bright yellow. Ella-Rose tied the hangings aside, allowing space for glistening emerald leaves to spring forward towards the window pane; performing a well-rehearsed tango with the relaxing wind. A curious swaying branch prodded its tiny fingers in request of invitation. Almost instantly, she opened the window, triggering a fresh bloom of jasmine to burst into the room. How wonderful it was to have the enchanting Fortunae Forest for a back garden.

'The answers you seek...'

Ella-Rose shivered. As she synchronised her vision with the sunlight, she could not help but feel scrutinised by unseen eyes, watching her from amongst the trees. As she began to edge in closer for a better look, she was suddenly interrupted from the sound of a small middle-aged woman's footsteps creeping up behind her.

'Good Morning,' said the half-scraped words imprinted on the cup between Sara's fingers. 'Oh my goodness! I can't believe my eyes. Ella-Rose, out of bed before ten o'clock in the morning? Never in my life did I think I would ever witness something as crazy—'

'Alright, alright, I get it.'

Sarcasm was always one of Sara's favourite hobbies. She just wasn't very good at it.

'Honestly, you're usually such a pain to wake-up of a morning.' With an aching, grimacing chuckle as the hot droplets of coffee trickled between her fingers, Sara Azerius set the cupful of a *Good Morning* down on Ella-Rose's dressing table - a coaster essentially itself, having been completely covered with ring stains.

Ella-Rose shut the window and took to the coffee almost immediately. 'You know me,' she slurped. 'Just a usual girl living in an unusual world.' A wild smirk grew across her face. 'Or was it the other way around?'

Sara noticed Ella-Rose's smile thinly fade away and shuffled along the bed to sit beside her. She lay a warming hand on her thigh and offered a comforting raise of her eyebrows, as if to say, *'Come on. Out with it. What's bothering you?'*

'I had that same dream last night,' she began. 'Really, it's quite frightening. They spoke again about this broken medallion and a creepy, old woman Nyla—'

'Medallion? You mean like in that Ladybird tale from Caesar's Book of Great Legends?' Sara interrupted, pulling the book with her foot from under her bed. 'Darling, don't you think that maybe you've been spending too much time reading the professor's old fantasies?' She smiled, pushing her magnified eyes into her face. 'I wouldn't read too much into it. *Literally*. Just another nightmare is all.'

'No!' Ella-Rose forcefully blurted. 'No, I've had nightmares. Goblins and ghouls, mummies and monsters. You don't understand, this felt—' she heard the silence in the room before she was actually aware of creating it. How could she even begin to explain that her dream had somehow felt real? 'Oh, what am I saying?' she continued with a light chuckle. 'Of course, you're right. Yes, just a nightmare is all.'

***

Sara Azerius left to the sitting room to begin her own early morning routine – clean, clean and then clean what's clean – a routine Ella-Rose and Michael would often disturb.

Although they were twins, Ella-Rose had always prided herself on having not many similarities to her brother - both personality and looks. With her hair fashioning a lengthy, elegant chestnut brown, his was shaped a short, wispy, messy blonde. While her face was covered in tiny freckles, his would usually be splattered with dirt.

Ella-Rose gulped the last of her coffee and leapt from her bed to ready herself. Today was the first in weeks she would see her best friend, Finn.

'Do see that you're careful today,' Sara called from down the hall – the famous combination of both sweet and firm took over her voice. 'I know how adventurous you children can be. I have no doubt you'll find your way into Fortunae, but this is no time to be straying from the forest paths. Dark creatures have been spotted beyond those trees, do you hear me? Steer clear.' Just as when she had given a similar speech to Michael, Sara's voice was again met with silence.

Ella-Rose brushed her hair and threw on a summer coat. No matter how much heat the sun shared with Ramoria, she would always be made to wear her coat in case of a drastic change of weather. As Sara would often say, *you can't assume the sun will always shine.*

'Ella-Rose are you even listening to me?'

No. Well, not entirely anyway, she was far too busy preparing for her upcoming adventure. Too long had she awaited Finn's return to Shayam Village from his visit to Hamsville.

With aid of a devious, conniving wind, Ella-Rose slammed the bedroom door shut, smacked a great sloppy kiss on Sara's cheek and headed for the front door. 'Oh, you do worry too much,' she rolled her eyes. 'We'll walk as far as Caesar's and no farther. Besides, I'll be with Finn the entire time.' Her beaming smile grew.

'Ah yes, how very reassuring,' Sara dubiously smirked. 'Just, do make sure you—'

But before Sara could let her words meet their natural halt, she was suddenly interrupted by an unpleasant bang. Ella-Rose's unique style of closing a door. The small woman pushed her glasses up from her nose to her face and turned to see that the girl had already left.

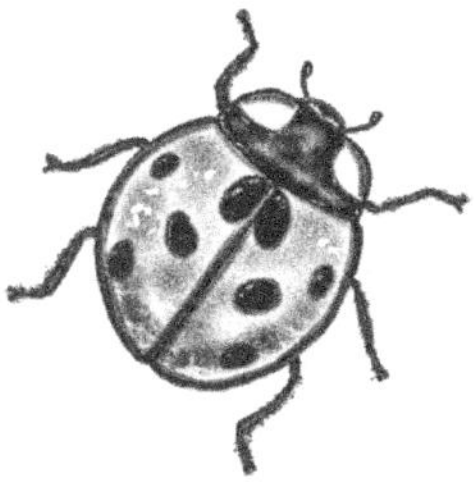

Chapter Two

Old Books, Older Tales

Michael uninterestedly watched as the professor dug his way through hundreds of worn, dusty books atop the shelves. How odd it seemed to see so many dead particles resting upon those he unequivocally used most. It was far beyond Michael's comprehension to understand how such decorated pieces of dead tree could entertain anyone and yet, there he found himself, listening to the soft touch of Caesar's fingers as he cavalierly stroked by timeless classics as, "Dead Black Seas", "The Book of Great Legends" and "Killer Gods: *A Translation by Sarajai Sharjal.*"

Michael could not recall a time the professor had never a book upon his lap, else a story in his mind. A wise man he was; writer, poet and above all a grand, old family friend.

After massaging the bald atop his head, Caesar brushed his fingernails through the thin strands of hair drooping past his ears. Though, the arthritis of his arms had turned even the simplest of tasks into a challenge. 'I'm sure it is in here somewhere,' he muffled past a long, exhausted moustache. 'How could I have misplaced it already? It was only earlier this morning that the book was left outside my door.'

'Someone left it at your door? Who?'

'Oh, an old friend.'

'Hmm, sounds suspicious.' Michael didn't realise that someone as old as the professor could have any friends. 'Wait a minute, you told me yesterday that you had something to show me. Now, you're saying you only got it this morning. And how come you've never mentioned this "old friend" before?'

Caesar searched his mind for answers. 'Well, he has been away for quite some time. Fifty years, I think. I believe it is my duty to read this book to you, while your dear sister, uh Eliza—'

Eliza? 'You mean Ella-Rose.'

A regrouping pause. 'Ah yes, my boy. I do ask that you excuse my muddle of a mind.' Ever since passing the age of one-hundred, the poor professor had become so old that his memories had started to morph into a bowl of mush. He could share seven assorted tales as one, unknowingly jumping from one story to another. It was always so difficult to keep up. 'What was I saying? Ah, yes. While dear Ella-Rose completes a quest of her own.'

'Quest? My, you sure have lost it.'

Caesar rested his face onto his arm and unleashed a loud and throaty gruff, (the type all old folk must perform at least once every hour.) He turned back to his bookcases and, shortly afterwards, called out a joyful 'Hazar!' when drawing what appeared to be a small, leather book. He blew its front with the little wind his lungs had to offer, covering Michael in a light blanket of dust.

'Cough! Cough! Watch it, man!' the boy wheezed. 'Books are so boring. Can we not play a game instead? We could play *Enchantments*! Oh please let us.' He started to chirp up, jumping from the armchair everyone knew to be called *Caesar's*

Good Arm. In all his fifteen-years, Michael couldn't recall never having his collection of Enchantment Picture Cards in his pocket. Each one displayed a unique mystical creature of Dragon Claw's four enchanting lands. From the Elves of Windy Hills, to the Dragons of Mount Hjar. 'Who knows, professor?' Michael smiled. 'Maybe this time I'll let you win.'

Caesar collapsed onto his Good Arm with a mighty thump, forcing the boy back. 'Nope,' he smiled. 'Nope, nope, no *chanties* today, dear boy.' He mended his thick, orange-framed glasses with a wiggle and a wipe. 'Instead, you are going to hear a couple of tales from this special book.'

'Special book?' the boy scoffed. 'A book is just filled with pieces of paper with no purpose.'

'Well, that truly is nonsense had it ever before been heard. A book is nothing less than a mysterious chest, filled to its rim with a bewildering magic. See, when closed, the chest conceals its deepest and darkest secrets only for itself to hear. It is only when one finds the courage to lift open its lid, a force, much more powerful than you'll ever know, will begin to reveal itself.'

'Magic?' Michael rudely mocked. 'Force? Pfft, a book isn't full of anything but a bunch of silly words and that's that. What in the world would make words so magical?'

'Why, we do,' Caesar chortled. 'How about I let you in on a little secret, ay lad?' he grinned, leaning in nose to nose. 'Books bake bigger brains, boy!'

'Boh buh babbeh what?'

'Precisely,' he joked, bonking the book off the boy's bonce. 'Now, where were we? Ah, of course. Do you know what this is, lad?'

To say the ancient piece of leather was physically impaired would have been complimentary to its defeated state. The book's thick skin was badly beaten, though the silver markings shining across its spine - in a language unknown to the boy – and the peculiar, golden symbol of a ladybird upon its front – were both completely unscathed.

'I don't know, a deceased tree?' Michael smirked with pride. 'Hey, that's strange. Caesar, this book has no title. It has all this strange, shiny writing over it, but no name. Why would you want to read this one?' He began to study the book with an eager eye and all thoughts of Enchantments soon vanished.

The old professor simply snickered and shook his head. 'Contrary, my boy. This book has been given many a name since its birth. Written by the hand of a great and powerful sorcerer.'

'Sorcerer?' Michael couldn't help but howl with laughter. 'Now I know you've truly lost your marbles, professor. Sorcerers have been extinct for years. Lozari Rapture was the last of its race and when he was slain, every book and document with knowledge of the power were forced to burn before the Trajans. What was that word you taught me again? Uspuru? Usperper?'

'Usurper,' he giggled.

'That's it, the usurper Trajans.'

'Dear boy, it is music to my ears knowing you have finally been listening to my stories. However, I'm afraid there is still so much more to learn. Michael, this very book contains stories of The War of Four. Tales from Dragon Claw's lands having once four monarchs to it now having only one.' Caesar glanced at the copy of his Daily Scoop atop his coffee table. "*With Khosi Trajan at last slain by the Emporan Army, Empress Divina Syrus now sits firmly atop the Orca throne and the four lands of*

Dragon Claw are wholly introduced to a newfound peace."

'Deadliest war in the entire history of Dragon Claw, you're aware?'

Michael nodded.

'Then let's put that noggin of yours to the test. When did the war begin?'

'Years and years and years ago?' Instead of the word *years*, Michael insisted in howling his made-up word *yearios*. 'They thought it was over back when Benjamin Syrus killed the last sorcerer. Now, they're saying it's over again.'

'Good lad,' said the professor. 'Can you tell me how many thrones there were at the beginning of the war?'

'Easy! At the start there were four; one for each empire. Now there is only one. At least, there is only one that anyone cares about. The Orca Throne.'

'What makes you think the Orca is the only throne of importance?'

'Well, since all others were pretty much destroyed, whoever sits on the Orca is basically the ruler of Dragon Claw, right?'

'I'm impressed.' Caesar knew it was now time to catch the boy out. 'Can you name all those in rule of the empires when the war began?'

Michael nodded, once more with confidence.

'I'll ask you to start with man, then monster, then magic.'

Michael grinned and rubbed his hands together. 'Right! Here we go! Kraal Syrus was mortal. He lived in the cold land, Empora, sitting on the Elephant Throne at Castle Snow. It was believed that Kraal had a scar above his left brow in the shape of a jackal.'

Emperor Kraal Syrus of the Emporan Empire was said to be a killing machine in the war, fighting in battles all over the lands before being cut down at the Battle of Quae by a strong, fearless knight named Joje Sebastian. Kraal had two children; his eldest, Benjamin took on the role of Emperor at Castle Snow after Kraal's death. When Empora was overrun by Lozari Rapture's deadly army, Benjamin fought hard to get their land back, and succeeded in doing so. No-one knew how he managed it, but he slayed Lozari, supposedly ending the sorcerer's race for good.

Years later, when Benjamin died, through what his council said to be due to his own stupidity, Castle Snow was overrun and destroyed by Emporan rioters. Kraal's second son, Wyrell was forced to take over. However, with no throne at Empora and no Raptures left to fight against, Wyrell went straight for the Orca. He ruled Dragon Claw with his most trusted adviser at his side, Khosi Trajan.

But, a Trajan is never to be trusted.

Khosi betrayed the Syrus name and took the Orca for his own, forcing Wyrell's only daughter, Divina to stand up and rebel. Divina Syrus built an army in secret, enough to take back what she felt was hers.

'Clever boy,' said Caesar. 'And though the Syrus army were mere men and women holding no special powers, their strength, for a time, prevailed.'

'Emperor Khosi Trajan was the monster in the land of Danjin,' Michael continued to list the four emperors at the beginning of the War of Four. 'He first sat on the Devil Throne at the Red Castle… before it was destroyed, I mean.' Michael now glanced at the headline of the Daily Scoop himself.

Khosi Trajan… Slain… Divina Syrus… Newfound peace.

‘He lived to be one-hundred and thirty-six,’ Michael gasped, squinting to read the article. ‘He was murdered only a couple of days ago by Divina Syrus, wasn’t he Caesar?’

Murdered. The word went through Caesar’s every nerve. Could something take the claim “murder” if it was committed for the good of Dragon Claw? ‘One-hundred and thirty-nine years of age.’ He decided to correct Michael’s misreading instead of addressing his terminology. ‘You must understand, Khosi Trajan was evil.’ *Then again, you wouldn’t really understand, would you? You’re just a child. Children don’t truly understand the difference between good and bad until they’re given a sword and forced to fight.* ‘It always has been my belief that one is never too young for politics. After all, young people often do have the clearest of minds and loudest of voices. In time, you will learn of the Trajan family,’ he said, gently patting the cover of the book resting on his knee.

Michael took a long, confused pause before finally deciding it time to continue with his teaching. ‘I’ve given you man and monster, next comes Raylan Fallen, the mage. Not to be confused with a sorcerer, of course. In the land of Posre, he sat atop the Bear Throne at Silverstem Castle. All I remember of Raylan was that his face was never clearly seen because of the long, dark cloak he would always wear. Then, finally, um —'

'Yes, yes, that's three. What of Parra Rapture? Great Emperor of Ramoria; he who sat atop the Orca Throne at the very beginning of the war! How is it that you'd forget him?'

'I didn't forget. I just don't know where his name lies. Man, monster or magic? The Rapture family were always the race of men before Emperor Parra discovered he held the power of sorcery,' Michael stopped. 'I mean, that was how the war began, was it not? Because Khosi Trajan found out he was a sorcerer and plotted to destroy him.'

Caesar considered this for a spell. Only those belonging to the Dragon Councils knew the specifics of how the war truly began, while the lesser folk seemed blessed with the undeclared duty of spreading speculated gossip.

The title: War of Four, coined formerly during Gregor Pirioni's rendition of *L'Opéra D'un Millier D'îles*, was considered ill-named in the beginning, given that Posre's armies, in the early days, remained withdrawn from such "child's play," as was written so bluntly in Dr Chloe Kiln's *Meditations of a Shattered Dream.*

Regardless of its commencement, years after the blood-filled battles had begun, three of Dragon Claw's lands were practically ruined by an imperishable means of destruction: soldiers of the undead. Though, one land always remained orderly: Ramoria. Not that it didn't endure dreadful battles causing ruin and devastation. It was more the fact that the Orca stood strong throughout. The lands had since recovered over the years and life has grown stronger once more across Empora, Posre and Danjin. However, with the castles and thrones destroyed, he or she who took the Orca ruled all.

'Most believed the initial instigation of the war arose the moment news of Syrus's betrayal to the Ramorian/Emporan alliance was confirmed,' Caesar taught. 'The Syrus family held peace with the Raptures ever since the start of the war, but when rumours surfaced of Emperor Parra's true race, Trajan influences soon swayed Kraal Syrus, just as they previously had Raylan Fallen. Three lands united against Ramoria. Trajan, Syrus and Fallen signed a secret treaty of an alliance at Kashmir; an alliance that later became known as United Dragons. Little did they know, Trajan would betray them all in the end, taking the Orca for his own.'

'What happened to all of the original emperors?' Michael asked.

'An excellent question, my boy! Parra Rapture mysteriously disappeared, leaving his son, Lozari, to take charge—'

'Hold up - I don't understand – how can somebody just mysteriously disappear?'

'Patience, my boy. All will be revealed soon enough. As you know, Kraal Syrus died at the Battle of Quae, passing Castle Snow to his eldest son, Benjamin Syrus; Khosi Trajan survived up until a couple of days past; Emperor Raylan Fallen of Posre was murdered early on during the war, and though his daughter, Savanah Fallen never showed much interest in opposing and fighting for claim of the Orca, she secretly kept her claim of Empress to the small village folk and broken cities of Ramoria. Adamantly, she declared for the claim of her name to forever be unchanged, but it was believed she died months after, during childbirth. Are you following, boy?'

'I think so.'

'This is where things get a little tricky. You see, when Parra disappeared, Lozari took the Orca throne, but he did not hold it for long. He was drawn towards something much more powerful.'

'More powerful than an empire?'

'We will go into that a little later, dear boy,' Caesar assured.

Michael rolled his eyes.

'Now, where was I? Ah yes! The four original emperors died. When Lozari was slayed by Benjamin and Benjamin was killed by, what his council claimed to be, his own stupidity, it seemed that only Khosi Trajan and Wyrell Syrus survived the War of Four. Which meant—'

'They could take the Orca.'

'Precisely! Wyrell Syrus lived on for years and it was agreed that he would take the Orca throne.'

'But, why Wyrell?' Michael interrupted. 'Why didn't Khosi just take it there and then?'

'That, Michael, is still something I wonder to this day. You see, not many know what Khosi was up to in the time he served as Wyrell's advisor. It is still something I am yet to discover. What you must understand is that there was never any denying that the Trajan family held most power across Dragon Claw, regardless of who sat atop the Orca. They're a very religious family. Their laws, as well as their questionable morals related firmly to the third Testament of the Book of Aj'ayah.'

'Book of what now?'

'Dear, oh dear, do you not listen to any of my tales? The three Testaments of Aj'ayah own the diverse origins of race and belief. Each book shares its own laws for the races of man, monster and magic. Thankfully, when the Testaments were discovered, most folk understood that the laws were too ambiguous to be enforced absolutely. They created governments instead to teach folk how they ought to live. Khosi Trajan, however, managed to radicalise his army to believe that sorcery was a sin.' Caesar twisted the edges of his moustache. It was a conditioned trick he would always perform when noticing Michael's attention drifting away. 'After discovering Emperor Parra Rapture's secret,' he continued. 'Khosi never did hesitate in conniving for the Ramorian/Emporan false alliance to continue. Allowing Parra to believe that the Syrus armies would fight for them.'

'So, you mean to say the Syrus family were spies?' asked Michael. 'They were just pretending to like the Raptures, when really, they fought for Trajan?'

'Aye, of sorts. Kraal Syrus sent a servant boy to Ramoria's Palace – or Siren, as it became known - to spy on Parra Rapture for many years, later resulting in the misguided death of Parra's firstborn son, Thaddeus. It was then that Dragon Claw all went—'

Michael imitated the sound of an explosion bursting out from his hands.

'Exactly. Not long after, Parra Rapture disappeared. Of course, blame was handed on a plate to the United Dragons.'

'Which is when Parra's second son took rule of the Orca,' Michael added, pulling out his Enchantment card of Emperor Lozari Harlam Rapture. 'Look Caesar! It's the strongest card I own.'

'As it should be. Lozari was a strong, passionate man, but a very dangerous sorcerer. It was said, had he continued in his ways, he'd have soon brought an end to Dragon Claw.'

For a short moment, silence filled the room. 'Caesar, did you fight in the war?'

'Me?' the professor laughed, queerly. 'Oh, I had a very special role, lad, but I'm afraid that is a tale for another day.'

Chapter Three
Finn Alfred Reginald Hampson

The walk to Finn's Cottage took all of seventy-two and three-quarter steps - the three-quarters Ella-Rose would count as the broken door sill upon which she'd stand to tap the silver angel knocker. His path was made of cream-coloured stone, with pink roses along each side. Vines of green ivy spread itself from brick to brick across the front wall, so much so that there was no telling what the original colour of the cottage truly was. She raised the angel's halo high and at its release, it sang a soft melody through the mahogany and into Mr and Mrs Hampson's hallway. Ella-

Rose's face beamed when the door creaked open, revealing an unusually-sized boy behind.

Finn Alfred Reginald Hampson, so named after their family's pride for related soldiers who so valiantly fought alongside the Raptures in the war, had the longest name Ella-Rose had ever heard. The name Finn had been passed down for several years. His father was a Finn and his grandfather was a Finn. Alfred came from his Great Great Grandpa. Alfred Hampson was the first man to win the Medal of the Dragon, although he never did get to wear it. He was awarded the medal for his sacrifice at the battle of Quae where he so bravely threw himself into a burning building in rescue of a young knight. The name Reginald came from his uncle, a courageous man who sailed all the way to Danjin in search of intelligence on the Trajan's operation. Intel that aided in the rescue of Lozari Rapture, after the sorcerer was taken. Locked away by Raylan Fallen, long before the war had even began.

Since birth, Finn had lived with an unfortunate condition; even great healers across Ramoria could not treat the disproportionate restriction of his growth. His spine would allow him to stand only as low as two feet, three inches while his arms and legs would refuse to catch up with the rest of his body. *Dwarfism*, they claimed it. Regardless, Finn had by far the biggest and sweetest heart Ella-Rose had ever known. He was one who could find beauty in even the darkest of places.

As soon as the boy arrived at the door, he was met with the largest of hugs and an explosion of kisses at his cheeks. 'Oh Finn, I can't even begin to describe how much I've missed seeing your little face. It's so dull when you're not around. Come on, come on, we have to leave for Caesar's at once,' Ella-Rose insisted.

'Huh? What's at Caesar's? I thought we were going to Mainar Town for some ice-cream.'

Ella-Rose shrugged. She knew Finn was not aware that *the answers she sought were deep within Fortunae.*

After sharing several greetings, the two left hurriedly before Mr Hampson would change his mind. It had taken twice as long to convince Finn's concerned pap to allow his leave than it had for Sara. After all, awareness of the village folk had hit a red alert quite recently; ever since that cold night Ms Val Adamou, the village butcher, came trampling back from Fortunae after conducting her weekly search for legendary, glowing quartz flowers, (said to only show on a starless night), screaming frighteningly of a monstrous *masked clan.* The out-of-the-ordinary expression she had given had burned violently through everyone's minds, especially of he who found her – Mr Hampson. Not to mention the peculiar way she started to act ever since. Rumours spread, professing a crazed turn in Adamou over the following days. She would lock herself inside her closet for hours a day, chanting the most peculiar things. Val had never been one much too fond of religion; just as most other Shayam folk, she would visit the church only for celebrations and festivals, no more and no less. Days later, Mr Sheldon, tending to his daft-odils wearing that most awful burgundy dressing-gown, had heard haunting screams, wildly escalating from her home. Upon rushing in, he found her, locked inside the closet, accompanied only with an uncontrollable shiver. The tips of her fingers painted red from having dug her nails, thick into the wooden flooring. No-one could quite tell what the carved message had read, the best they could make out was the small symbol of a serpent skull below. Not long after, she was arrested with charge of insanity. Everything soon normalised. Though, still to this day, folk cannot rid their minds of that crazed, out-of-the-ordinary expression.

***

Secretion of sweat poured chillingly as Ella-Rose and Finn arrived at the gaping jaws of Fortunae. For a moment, they stopped to steal taste of the freshly-grown berries, forming a whirlpool of flavour bathing in their mouths. Fairies flew high, pixies hovered low. Wood elves danced with the wind, while the water nymphs swam against it.

Fortunae was filled with millions of glorious, enchanted creatures. Often, folk claiming themselves *biologists* risked deeper travel into the different forests of Ramoria, chancing the meet of an entirely new and enchanting species. It was, however, a danger most never dared take.

The trees played puppeteer to the performing shadows of the sun, waving a warm welcome to their new guests. Sky-blue sparkles gleamed from the waterfall ahead, diving into the chilling White River. Fortunae certainly had a mind of its own; the splashing droplets cooling the children's toasted skin almost seemed an intentional gift.

Ella-Rose raised her eyes to the sky, watching the fairies dance below a thick sheet of emerald leaves, truly appreciating the natural beauty of the forest. 'Magical,' she accredited, swallowing the wind through her nose. It always was the small things that took Ella-Rose's eye: the shout of a breeze, the footsteps of a sprinting river, it was all just so…

'…Magical,' the old man whispered, following her hand-made dream catcher with his eyes as she dangled it from between her fingers. Golden from the wood of the forest, scarlet from the feathers of a finch. 'My, how very magical,' Caesar spoke with his usual loud and gruffly noise - the type of noise all old people make at least once in their day. 'Do you know what makes it so magical?'

She shook her head.

'Beauty.'

'Blue tea?' she repeated, giggling. 'Are you sure, Caesar? That sounds awful silly to me.'

'Dear, not blue tea, but bea-uty. Beauty is the essence of life. A secret, hiding itself only in the eye of the beholder. And for that— yes, for that, beauty is a most powerful magic, El-...'

'...la-Rose!' Finn called out, throwing her from straying thoughts.

'How strange,' she muttered in reply.

'What?'

I've just remembered something, but strangely, I don't think the memory belonged to me at all. I'm having someone else's memories… was what she wished to say, but all that her lips would allow was to say: 'Nothing.'

Finn rolled his head and something caught his eye. 'Hey look at that!' He pointed upwards, towards a waterfall, where a light array of multi-colours arced a rainbow before their eyes.

Staring deep into the illuminated eye of nature, Ella-Rose listened as the colours spoke to her. Of course, not with words, but with a transparent allure, so strong that it took hold of all her thoughts.

Beauty truly is a most powerful magic.

Morning turned to noon sooner than they realised, mixing the summer skies into a yoghurt of peach and apricot. The path beneath disappeared where they walked, transforming into a trail of beaten ground; a creation of both foot and paw. They reached the foot of a Grand Torque, one of the largest trees growing in the forest, standing higher than six-hundred feet tall. Apparently, the Torque was the oldest of all the trees, older than Professor Caesar himself, but not even Ella-Rose would believe that. Caesar must be over one-hundred and fifty years old, surely.

Finn was first to stop and take rest. The trunk was rough against his soft, smooth skin. A feeling so familiar, it caressed almost comfortably.

'Well?' Finn opened.

'Well what?'

'Aren't you going to tell me why we've come this way?' Finn's voice, less like his physique, was high. 'You and I both know that the path to Caesar's is miles that way,' he pointed southward. 'We're not supposed to go this far into Fortunae. As my pap says, "Dark creatures lie beyond the paths."'

‘Oh, come on, you don’t really believe all that nonsense, do you? Nothing bad ever happens in Fortunae Forest. These horror stories you read in the Scoop, they’re all just tales of politics and war. Look around you, how could a place so magical home anything dark and dangerous?’

‘I, um, yeah I suppose you’re right, but you never answered my question. Where are we actually going?’

Ella-Rose frowned ‘Well, you wouldn’t believe it if I told you. You wouldn’t have come. You remember I’ve told you about those recurring nightmares?’ She stopped for a taste of breath. ‘Well, do you remember those legends Caesar would tell us when we were younger? Of emperors and sorcerers, gods and spirits.’

‘Yeah, but what has that got to do with—’

‘What if… oh, I don’t know, what if they were all real? What if they’re not just stories – not just dreams, but something else? Agh, it’s all such a shamble in my brain.’ She bit the inside of her lip and lowered her gaze. ‘We’ve come here because I think I’m supposed to find something.’

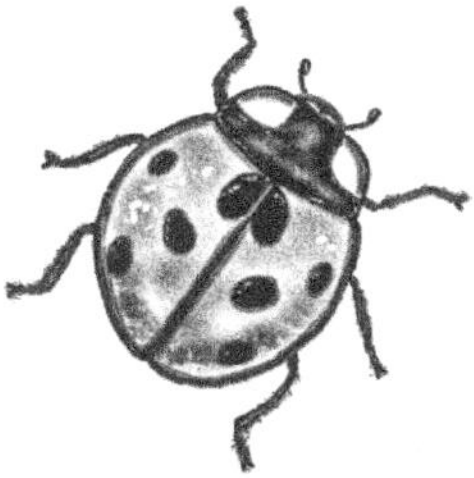

Chapter Four
Dangerous Power

The song of Caesar Azerius' throat crackling up phlegm was not nearly as distasteful as the rhythm in which it was swallowed. 'Michael, my boy,' he gargled, holding up the small, leather book once more. 'This book is a closed chest with many a secret, I assure you.' Turning over its worn, brown cover, Caesar Azerius began to read a tale from years and years ago.

Like most great things in life, the silence was both beautiful and dangerous. Overpowering respect emanated from the Throne Room as the clean-shaved man marched across its sapphire carpet. His eyes were grey, his lips were thin; common traits for a man of Sebastian blood. The rugged and worn armour held tightly against his body assumed zenith position of knighthood, for the metal from which it had been forged appeared no less than dragatus trum; a rare iron, considered illegal use by any status less than a High Knight. He reached the foot of the seven steps leading up towards the Orca, towards Emperor Parra Rapture; steps he once feared.

'Sir Joje,' a tough muffle through a forest of hair. 'Long have I awaited your return—'

'Dead!' It was all Sebastian's dry lips could allow when capturing the emperor's burning charcoal gaze. The eyes of a bear, just as he remembered from childhood. Joje's voice, once vigorous, taken now by monotonous strain. 'For four days and four nights, crucified till asphyxiation, arrhythmia, hypovolemia,' he continued. 'Ought I to go on? Or is it that the death of my father has at long last opened your eyes?'

Had it been any other to so impurely address a Rapture, they undoubtedly would've been granted ticket to Death's Door and certainly, any who find themselves sailing to those Shabrathian Dungeons, (as Death's Door was formerly named,) were forced to face the remainder of their days locked inside a windowless, steel-rusted cell. Not that a life there had much sustainability; folk tend to wither away when beaten on an hourly basis and fed but once a week. The longest lasting prisoner recorded was one named Shai Kalee, punished for the crime of being born the wrong race. When reports were shared of the witch's "immortality", riots soon followed. Violent protests arose, demands of an enforced death, or "cleansing" as they would so mask it. Kalee was toyed by her mortality for two years before granted freedom by whatever gods she held. Shabrath was nothing but a door carved by Death himself; a place whose inhabitants would find themselves begging for the darkness to come and steal that which they once valued most.

'I warned you this would happen,' Joje went on. 'Warned you ever since those cursed Aj'ayahic Testaments were discovered from Danjin. These monsters fear that which they do not understand.'

The broad, black-bearded emperor shuffled upon his throne trying his best to not get stuck; the first time had been embarrassing enough. 'Aye, your father, Sir Yakub Sebastian, was a fair man. Not a good one, I'll admit. But fair.'

'Dammit Parra, you know better than any I have no love, nor will I feel sorrow for my father. The fat old bastard was a constant reminder I was one day to become bald. But you – even as my brother by law, you have been a better father to me than he ever was. I expect Khosi has his suspicions of you. He will kill you too when *he discovers the truth.' And as if once was not enough, 'Kill you, Parra!'*

Even prior to marrying Joje's stunning sister Korine, the knight had always been a most loyal friend and teacher to the emperor.

'For once, Sir Joje, you are wrong. Just look at this power, this... sorcery,' exclaimed Parra forming a strong energy at the palms of his hands. 'You say they'd fear me. If the folk across Dragon Claw saw just a sliver of what I can do, they would worship me a god.'

'Worship? Lord Parra, times are changing! Do not be so blind as to not see it. Darkness is coming,

yes darkness is coming,' he shivered. 'There has been a most dangerous power unleashed throughout the lands of Dragon Claw.'

***

The last words to leave Sir Joje's lips sat heavily on Parra's ears even hours following their separation. Alone, he sat at the long table readying for his fourth lunch of the afternoon, trying his best to drown out Sebastian's voice. Usually, he would enjoy his meals in the company of friends and family, but with Joje's words sunken deeply into his mind, how could he stomach the company? Yes, Parra obviously knew that there had been a most dangerous power unleashed throughout the lands of Dragon Claw.

***

At the beginning of time, it was said that Dragon Claw was only divided in two lands: half belonging to the Aj'ayah, the other to the Luminous. Between the lands stood a vicious monster with one molten eye: Mount Hjar. The beast was worshiped by both lands and for millions of years, Hjar, in return, remained tranquil. Unfortunately, a monster's anger must always erupt. The Luminous and the Aj'ayah broke apart becoming four lands; empires, led by monarchs of man, monster and magic.

The family name, Rapture, held Ramoria, strong and vigorous men; Syrus held Empora, honourable and dutiful men; Fallen held Posre, artful, clever mages and Trajan held Danjin, intelligent, yet deadly vampires. Four rulers for four empires; peace held dominion amongst the lands of Dragon Claw. Of course, sooner or later, even peace must falter.

The Aj'ayah retained only small, broken islands, hovering east of Ramoria, rumoured to be cursed to any who dared take rule. Not all believed in such pretence, but why ever tempt? After all, it were the Wolves of the Aj'ayah who brought peace to the four lands in the aftermath of Hjar. It was believed that an angel named Thomas spoke to them all in a dream, giving them word of three ancient testaments of Man, Monster and Magic, buried deep within the land of Danjin. The wolves allegedly dug out the three testaments and soon after, the testament's rules and laws were enforced. Each text owned the diverse origins of race and belief. Historians, Jacob P. Yeller and John K. Taylor studied the language (symbols, as it were), far too difficult to uncover its actual era, let alone from whom they had been written. First translations were published by Father Kiln Webber and Supreme Hellig Di Nori. Later, translations were written by Khosi Trajan himself. Renditions that caused strong tensions and differentiation throughout the four lands. The Aj'ayahic ideals became known, forcing a most dangerous power to brainwash each race; a power so fierce as to turn the four lands against one another and birth discussions of war. Religion.

***The Testament of Man** held the claim of two Gods present to hold dominion over all lands since the dawning of Dragon Claw. One, they named Peace, the other, Love. Emptiness of Dragon Claw grew lonesome for the two, for what use were Peace and Love without Life with which to share?*

So, Peace and Love began their efforts by shaping Man, Magic and Monster. Love and Peace watched as civilisation developed. Their creation learned to communicate. Communities were built. Castles and temples, forests and swamps started to expand. Life prevailed, forcing Love and Peace to stand aside as secondary instruments. Peace grew callous of Life having polluted Dragon Claw, thus designing a fourth God to imprison Life, one they called Time. Alas what good was Time without an end? Time took it upon itself to create a God of its own and named it Death. However, as soon as the folk across Dragon Claw discovered their days were numbered, they used Death to their advantage, travelling with only a means of pro-creation. Population soon increased across the Luminous and vast variations of interbred species were born, spreading to the holy land of Aj'ayah. This angered Peace, for their creation were making fools of the Gods, proving them obsolete. How could it be a punishment to Live, Love and Die Peacefully throughout Time? What they needed was War. And so, it came to be. However, the creation of War was soon realised to be a mistake, because War manipulated Peace to unleash Evil upon the world.

Only then did the Gods realise that they had all become reckless in their ways. They decided to unite as the single, beautiful and infinite Great One; each power shared in order to remain dominators of the world. Alas, Death, War and Evil disobeyed the Great One, instead standing as one named the Devil. Both cooperatively maintained watch over Dragon Claw with a balanced distinction of good and evil, right and wrong.

***The Testament of Magic** taught its race to believe only in an empirical existence; the rare energy known as sorcery proved strongest across Dragon Claw and the few born with the power were identified by wizards and witches as a superior race. However, those born into a life of magic do not extensively dismiss the existence of a Great One, instead claiming it Matra, (translated into 'Mother' from the Aj'ayahic Tongue); a most powerful being, owning the extremely rare gene to take many forms. It is believed this Matra will one day birth the Ladybird, (translated into 'Demon' from Aj'ayahic Tongue.)*

Opposing the Testament of Man's Devil, the magicians believed only in Death as the Matra's great enemy; an immortal being with such hate in his rotten heart that he takes on the role with a cold and fierce bite.

The Testament of Monster *too believed in a great, infinite being. However, they wrote that the genus of Vampire were peak of the monster's hierarchy, known famously for their cunning intellect, artful skill and deadly ways. The race of Monsters is varied in faith, though there is never any confusion that the majority of monsters hold onto the strict belief that sorcery is a deadly sin. Any to practise such devilry were to be crucified till death.*

Certainly, when it came to the Aj'ayahic religions, there were always species of each race who stood aside the testaments and rebelled against such occult theories. They simply believed that to be was to exist and to exist was to be. Dragon Claw's chains hold tightly onto all and neither Great One, Devil, Matra nor Death could break its inevitable designs.

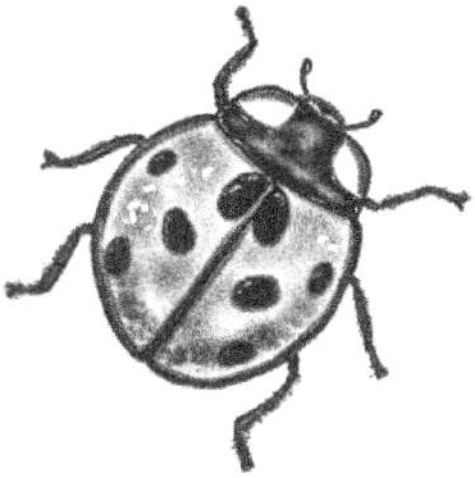

Chapter Five
Mr and Mrs McArthur

'You cannot be serious,' Finn rolled his eyes at Ella-Rose's justification. 'Answers that you seek? To find answers, you need questions.'

Exactly. Ella-Rose would surely have understood had she given questions to begin with, but as far as she was aware, she sought no answers. 'Look, I know how silly it sounds—'

'Silly?' blurted Finn. 'No, it's positively insane! Do you really believe these nightmares are real? The sorcerer, the magical medallion, the Ladybird – do they not sound familiar to you? It's just mythical nonsense the old professor fed to us. You know, like The Tale of Pip and Chip, Adventures of King Chopin, Legend of—'

Ella-Rose froze. Although Caesar Azerius had shared many a story over the years to the children, of all the tales, Ella-Rose had always recalled one more than others… Legend of Eliza.

At the time Emperor Parra Rapture had mysteriously disappeared and Lozari, for a short while, sat atop the Orca, fighting against the United Dragons, something much stranger was happening within a small town called Kulla. When the War of Four began, time seemingly wafted its wings faster than usual across Dragon Claw. The entire fifteen-years it had been since Clementine Hunter, Mr and Mrs McArthur's maid, stumbled upon the blood-covered babe at the door of their lovely, homely cabin had flown by. Sorceress, *was the claim the child's parents branded upon her. Folk across Ramoria shared crude tales of a* demon *who fell from the blooded skies. There were even those who would go as far as to claim her an unnatural flaw in the Great One's plan. Alas, before all rumoured nicknames, the girl was known only as Nyla; the adopted and only daughter of Wallim and Penny McArthur.*

The cabin sat peacefully amid a path of emerald trees, *just the right amount of distance from Kulla Town Centre. Though small as it was, it was the McArthur's family home and they wouldn't have changed it for the world.*

Clementine Hunter, of course not her given birth name, for she would argue, 'Who gives yer parents the right to pick yer own name?' *thereby choosing one to match her ripe, plump exterior and tangerine hair, (Satsuma never had quite fit), had always been the McArthurs maid at the cabin. It wasn't necessarily a job the McArthurs required, as the cabin was small and mostly well-kept. However, Clementine had never been the brightest star in the sky, and being Penny's cousin, Wallim had insisted that they took care of her after her parents died.*

'Now, you hold up there, boy-o,' Clementine had said years earlier. 'I'm sure people won't be too happy finding out you've stole some other's babe. Might just be I won't tell, if—'

There it was. If: the devil's conjunction.

'...If I be taking that there pricey piece of gold that's wrapped around the little one's neck,' she finished, pointing her lengthy claw at the golden ladybird medallion held to the baby's chest.

The last thing the McArthurs had wanted that night was to be burying Penny's cousin in their back garden, but what other choice did they have when the blackmailing began?

And, as the entire fifteen years passed since dear Clementine was buried, respectfully beneath the orange trees, of course, the guilt hadn't surfaced even once for the McArthurs.

Folk be killin' daily in these days of war, *Wallim had insisted.* How could a majority be wrong?

***

At fifteen years of age, the irregularities started small. She would begin a conversation and forgetfully cut her words mid-sentence, followed by demented, uncontrollable laughter. It was not until Nyla's sixteenth year that the changes truly began to occur.

'Nyla, darling,' Mr McArthur spoke in a calm, to-the-point manner. 'What have yer Ma and me said about talking to yerself, now? Yer be,' he gulped. 'Yer be scaring yer Mama out of her head.'

'And what have we *told you time and time again, Papa?' Nyla's voice was sharp, her body unmoved from atop the kitchen table. 'I am not talking to myself. I'm talking to Eliza.'*

'Stop it!' Mrs McArthur screamed, tears flooding. 'Wally, tell the stupid girl to stop with all her crazy. She be frightening me. This Eliza girl ain't rel, yer brat. Oh Great One, why ever did you allow this demon into our home?'

'Wash yer mouth, Penny McArthur. Don't be speaking of our daughter in such a way. The girl's just lonely, is all. Got some difficulties in her head, I reckon.'

'Differenties?' Penny incorrectly repeated. 'I wun't be calling such thing a differenty. You've seen as well as I 'ave what she did to my neck just yest'day.'

'That was not me!' Nyla insisted and as if shaped from nowhere, a demanding cold wind soon took to the entire cabin, sending forceful shivers up the

McArthur's spines. 'I had spoken true, Mama. Eliza did that, not me. Not me! Besides, it was just an accident; she liked the golden necklace you wear is all, the one with the ladybird.'

'You see, Wally? You feel that? She's a witch. A sorceress I tell yer. A damn demon!'

Obviously, Wallim had felt the wind slap against the back of his neck, though never would he believe that his daughter, his special gift from the Great One, had grown to be a witch. The McArthurs had done everything Father Warner taught of the Aj'ayah in keeping the Devil from the cabin; they prayed to the Great One every night and visited the church for all the celebrations and festivals. 'Nyla, honey,' he spoke softly still, budging closer towards the table to sit beside her. 'We think it's great that you finally have a friend, um, Eliza was it?'

'Yes,' she smiled, paying attention to nothing but the father-daughter moment. 'Oh papa, she and I have so much in common. We both have hair as white as the White River and we each share the same birthmark in the shape of a ladybird on our ankle. Isn't that crazy?' Another full-faced smile hit her face. 'Although, we haven't the same eye colour at

all. While mine are grey, hers are the brightest purple I have ever seen.' Nyla didn't much mind Wallim McArthur. He always seemed sweet and kind, even though the frail man never did step up when Penny chastised her for Eliza's behaviour.

Though, had Nyla known that all it would take for the beatings to stop was to choke Mrs McArthur with the thick gold around her neck, she'd have surely done it herself.

'Perhaps we could invite this friend over for lunch one af'ernoon,' Wallim suggested. 'Very much like to meet her, we would.'

Nyla giggled. 'What a silly thing to say papa. Eliza is already here.'

***

Much like the final breaths of a dragon, summer's heat soon died out, readying for autumn. In recent days, there had been little mention of Eliza. Even so, the peculiar happenings became far too much to manage. The crops they grew in their back garden were starting to wither anywhere Nyla would walk; healthy calf at the farm not far from Kulla Town

Centre began to drop at her mere gaze. Something was awfully off with the girl and Wallim McArthur would no longer deny it.

'We ought to kill the brat,' Penny suggested. 'Like we did ol' Cousin Clemmy. Older the girl grows, the worse she gets. Be a public service, would it not?'

'Don't be speaking so stupid, woman.' Wallim knew, to kill a maid, none would ever care bat an eye, but murder the young girl strolling through villages each morn, everyone would lose their minds. 'All those years it took to disguise her as our own and now you speak of killing the child? Our child! Shame!'

'Right, right, not kill the girl,' a slight, insane chuckle fell slowly from the dark patches of Mrs McArthur's lungs. 'But if this Eliza be a demon, I warn yer, we'll need to exorcise.'

***

A combination of black, purple and orange spread wildly throughout the kitchen. The smooth, oaken table Wallim McArthur claimed to have carved himself, (but paid those odd pair of village men to do it, and not necessarily with money,) was pushed to one side. Bright, orange candles attacked the darkness while they sat comfortably around their hand drawn Aj'ayahic diagram. It were the Women of Eld who had first sketched such holy symbols, believing it had the power to summon spirits of Angels in a time of need. The bright, white moon shined against the kitchen window creating a luminous tapestry against the fractured tiled flooring. Wallim had practically begged for the tiles with the pink and yellow flowers. 'Create a loving atmosphere, t'would,' he had pushed, but Penny wouldn't allow such a waste of the little money they owned.

'Great One, oh thou Greatesth Oneth, we honour ye today a most benevolent guest of our here household.' Power took her words when raising both arms high above her head. 'It is in your name that we ask you execute this dem—'

'Whoa, stop!' Wallim called, brushing the bald spot amidst his furry head. 'Execute? We agreed we ain't to kill the girl.'

'Don't be so stupid, Wally! We got to kill the Demon,' Penny explained.

'See, you say that, but I'm finding it hard believing it's the demon yer truly speaking to,' Wallim pedantically directed. 'You need to show more passion in yer speech, more fear.'

'Fear? God damn fear? I'm rightly terrified and you're telling me I ain't showing fear?'

There was a long pause... Then a loud bang.

'Bloomin' shit, did you hear that?'

Wallim laughed, picking up the wooden ladle he had intentionally thrown on the ground to get the reaction. 'Ay, there yer go, now you be lookin' terrified—'

'Wally! For pity's sake! Just fer once in yer pathetic life...' Penny went on like that for four minutes, but what the McArthurs didn't know was that the sound Penny had heard was not actually from the ladle hitting the tiled ground, but was in fact Eliza's sneaky entrance into the kitchen, banging her leg as she hid beneath the table.

'Come on now, honey. One more time, hey?' Wallim McArthur suggested. 'Then, let's grab the girl!'

'Yes, yes, let's grab the girl,*' Eliza smiled, forcing Nyla's consciousness to rise inside herself.* 'They mean to kill you Nyla,' *she said staring at the bright orange candles that the McArthurs had placed around the badly drawn religious symbol.* 'We should burn them now before they're given the chance. We must protect each other, right?'

'Stop it,' whispered Nyla. 'I am not like them. We *are not like them. We will harm no-one, I say.' Her words came out more demanding than she had wished. 'Instead, we will leave. We can't stay here a moment longer. You will protect me though, won't you?' And although Eliza's response was silent, Nyla knew what they needed to do.*

Chapter Six
The Emperor's Guest

Caesar Azerius fixed his glasses, pushing them deep into his face. 'You see Michael?' he said. 'There is so much to be learnt about our history.'

The thought of playing with Enchantment cards had fallen deep into the past. Michael was enthralled listening to the tale of Emperor Parra Rapture, conjuring up his own ideas of how he might have mysteriously disappeared. 'Can I see the book, Caesar?'

'Oh, not just yet, dear boy. You wouldn't want to spoil the ending now, would you? After all, there may be some twists along the way. This story is not yet over, Michael. In fact, it is only now just beginning…'

Emperor Parra Rapture shivered listening to the millions of cold wet daggers, piercing at the Siren Gardens. Surrounded by the song of striking pellets, his memory stirred back to the time he'd once enjoyed the rain's melodies, not feared them. The drip drop that fell from the top. Now, the rain simply played as a bothersome reminder to his teenage years and the abnormality that occurred the morning Yakub Sebastian and he travelled to Ramoria's famous forest.

Yes, he remembered that day very well. Winter had loomed quickly across the south of Dragon Claw, restricting summer's smiling shine from Ramoria. For young Parra's father, Emperor Harlam Rapture, that meant one thing and one thing only: scarcity of crops. It was never in Harlam's interest to take his seventeen-year-old son to the Heart of Fortunae – a great temple where meetings were usually held - but, 'he must learn the ways of the Claw,' Harlam's trusted wife insisted. 'Take

Yakub with you also, Parra would like that. It's at long last they learn about the politics of the Dragon Council.'

Of course, she was right. She was always right.

***

Harlam, and a few Ramorian and Emporan lords spent most of their morning discussing nothing but corn and, (as Parra put it,) the boring stuff. However, it was supposed to be the "boring stuff" the children were meant to be learning. Prince Parra was one day to stand as the Emperor of Ramoria, but indeed, boys will be boys.

The rain fell more ferociously than ever on the afternoon Parra and Yakub snuck from the temple and travelled through Fortunae Forest. Violet flowers offered their fresh burst of lavender. Rabbits danced to songs unheard. Grouped spiders settled beneath webbed shelters.

The boys dipped and dived beneath leafy umbrellas for far too long. The trees tried as best they could to protect them from getting wet, but every cold, wet dart jabbed too fast and too hard; the leaves were unprepared for such a day. Never had the boys known rain to fall so monstrously. Their clothes became so wet that they clung heavily against their skin. The leaves turned moss green, the stoned path was pumpkin orange. How strange that a simple change in the weather could cause such a vast difference to the forest's appearance.

It was not specifically the rain creating the dark nostalgia, but she whom Parra had met when trying to escape it. He had tried and even managed to subdue most of his memories from that day. He vaguely remembered Yakub calling out the words: our gods do piss on us.

It was something Mad Mandi used to say in those Chiller Killer tales by S. J. Parson. Our gods do piss on us, so let's raise a glass. We'll drink from their peeps, just not from their—

But was it Mandi who was all that mad? After all, it was not she who spoke the words, but rather the absurd writing of S.J. Parson. Nevertheless, it put Parra off sticking out his tongue in the rain for a while.

No matter how much he'd try to forget, two things stuck painstakingly in Parra's mind. The first was that strange girl he'd met in the forest, and the second was the number...

'Four,' *the strange girl had somehow whispered through young Parra's entire body.* 'Know it now and know it well. The number is four. Four: the times we both shall meet. Four: the children your seed shall bear. Four: the war you will create. Four: the deaths your soul will face. Yes, oh yes, the number is—

'Father.' There was a mumble. 'Father!' Then, a grumble.

Parra Rapture and his glorious wife, Korine, were blessed with two children.

Thaddeus, the emperor's first, strapping son, did not inherit his father's unusual powers, and for this, Parra was grateful. Lozari, however, was observed carefully under the strict order of the Dragon Council. Various healers were sent from across Dragon Claw to diagnose the strange happenings of the boy.

'Seizures,' *they assured.*

Had the emperor denied, he would certainly need reason and so –

'Seizures,' *he agreed.*

Yet, holding the medication in his left hand and the boy at his right, he could not help but think: What, if anything at all, is the dosage for sorcery? *Thankfully, the matter resolved itself when Lozari reached his fifteenth year, for more tolerant and controlled had his powers become. Alas, there was no way the emperor could keep such a dangerous child at Ramoria. One slip and he could expose the Rapture name, perhaps forcing all to execution.*

Prince Lozari was sent to the city of Kalan in Empora to assist a bookkeeper known as Wilfred the Worm. From then forth, Parra and his loving wife vowed to spawn no more children. Never again would he risk a child to receive the damned gift.

But, no! Four. The number is—

Korine agreed. She loved her two children more than anything in all of Dragon Claw. How understanding she was. How sweet she—

'Oh, for goodness sake, wake up you fat fool!' Empress Korine edged Thaddeus to pour - what seemed at the time - the coldest jug of water over Parra's sweated head, forcing him to rise with a mouth full of whattheheck! *'Our guest is soon to*

arrive, Parra. Let him see you for who you once were. Not…this.'

***

It was due to the underwater decor of the palace that it attained the name Siren. Including state, staff, guests, kitchen, library, hospital, ball and throne, the palace had six-hundred and eighty-three rooms. Dimensions of the Throne Room alone seemed reasonable enough for a small castle; such a wasted space for a chair, most Ramorian folk believed. Only, it was not just a chair, it was the Orca Throne. Held by the Raptures since the eruption of Mount Hjar. Aquatic symbols hung on banners of white and blue. Tentacles of kraken, octopus and squid stabbed out from the walls. Certainly, the most majestic of all the four empires', though, each monarch would surely argue for their own.

Within the hour, Parra was brand new. A full head of hair, falling like a waterfall down to his shoulders. Brows, trimmed. Stomach, tucked. Eyes of a bear.

Still as sapphire seas, the Throne Room sat in a state of tranquillity as the people of Ramoria, standing at all corners, watched the emperor take the Orca and the empress stand gracefully by his side.

Such tranquillity, however, was soon disturbed when a buck-toothed servant boy, known to most as Gross Gabriel, trampled disorderly up the seven steps.

'Lord Parra, son of Harlam, Madam Korine, daughter of Yakub,' his words echoed across the emptiness of the room. 'He has arrived, oh by the Great One, he has arrived! Never, in my years, has a servant boy laid eyes upon—'

The Emperor's hand gesture was twofold: first, forcing Gross Gabriel's immediate silence; second, allowing their guest to enter.

Smoothly across the hall, Sir Joje Sebastian strolled towards the Orca with a Great White Wolf trailing behind in a way that demanded upmost admiration.

'Announce yourself,' called Parra.

''Tis Agarov of Aj'ayah,' the wolf called back proudly, strongly and sturdy held his posture. 'Allu allu, Grand Master of Ramoria.'

Parra stared intensely for a spell, before a wide smile spread across his face. 'Agarov, you old dog, my how long has it been?'

'Too long,' the wolf replied, each word with a fierce growl. 'I fear I come today not as a friend, instead as a messenger.' Interest hit a peak in the emperor's brows. A message worthy of being carried by the Great White Wolf was not a thing to eagerly await. 'Rumours have risen from Emperor Raylan Fallen, rumours of your, ahem—' Agarov was quick to search the surrounding audience, all of which had bent their knee. 'Complications, sire.'

'Raylan Fallen?' Parra let out a heart-paining laugh. 'That little twerp? Who is he other than a puppet to Khosi Trajan? This message may have been written in Fallen ink, but it is Trajan's voice that shall be heard.'

'Then, do you permit?'

'Yes, oldest friend, I permit.'

Agarov shook a cream-coloured cloth from his fur, placed his paw upon it and began to read. 'As the flowers grow and the rivers run,' he read melodically. 'The sun will burn and burn will the son.'

Aubergine rose upon Emperor Parra's cheeks and with a beastly roar, mightier than any wolf, he forced the people of Ramoria to take immediate leave.

'Out! Everybody, out!'

However, the doors to the Throne Room never did reach a complete close, for a slight, but unnoticeable creak sounded from behind the small party that remained within, hiding a most curious, bucktoothed grin.

'A threat?' Parra raged. 'I have broken bread with those damned mages and he returns with a threat?' The thoughts of the past burned into his subconscious.

'I fear there may be a traitor amidst your walls,' Agarov spoke softly now. 'There was an ambush at Kalan. A well-structured and planned capture of your son. I am sorry, Parra, but Raylan holds Lozari in Shabrathian Dungeons waiting only three days before—'

'He thinks he can blackmail me? I am a mighty sorcerer! I will destroy him. Skin him, rip him into pieces!'

Streams of tears ran down Korine's cheeks. 'What reason has Fallen to steal my son?' she sobbed; each word fought against her cry.

'None that is apparent, Empress,' the wolf sighed. 'But rumours - just rumours, mind – suggest the Fallen boy tries to prove his loyalty to Khosi Trajan. They're planning an alliance.'

'Sebastian,' Parra rose from the Orca and beckoned the clean-shaved man forward. 'You'll find our betrayer immediately. They will soon hold the privilege of watching us destroy Fallen and anybody else who dare to conspire against Raptures!'

It appeared that none, apart from Sir Joje Sebastian could identify the evident trap which stood afoot. 'Agarov, you spoke of rumours, yes?' the knight began, turning only enough to show the crystal glisten in the corner of his eye. 'For goodness sake! Tell me true, are you all so blind as to not see how this will end? I mean no offence to any, but ever since those three testaments were brought to be, religion has brainwashed every race across Dragon Claw. Trajan was quick to stand firm and absolute beside these mad principles.' The dry face of Joje's father soaked into his mind. 'Any writings that teach murder and torture of innocents is wrong, wrong I say! What rights have any to hold animosity against those who practice sorcery? Khosi Trajan has filled this Fallen boy's head with hatred, while we sat back and allowed it. How could we not? For none, would dare deny the testaments lest they be claimed a blasphemer. This vampire thrives on authority and control. The Trajans would take Dragon Claw for their own given the chance. Fallen is a mage, dammit! A mage taught to hate sorcery. Is this really what Dragon Claw has come to?'

'This news of treachery has brought to me no surprise, I assure you,' he went on. 'I'll bet the world will have known of your true race for many years. Were it not for your title, you'd have been killed alongside my father.' A haunting silence swam through the Throne Room, quicker than a shark chasing its prey. 'Yes, Raylan has your boy in chains and I agree it is likely that Trajan holds the steel. You need to understand that this is a personal attack seeking a personal defence. Rapture, if you are to go forth in publicly exposing your gifts to the world, excuse me in saying, but surely they will be the ones

to do the ripping. They will steal the Orca while you die as a sinner and blasphemer.'

The emperor refused to look Joje in the eye.

'Are you too so blind as to not heed the true strengths of religion? Its manipulative powers will soon convert the four lands into a battlefield of war. Belief holds a much more intense magic than sorcery ever could. Moulding the minds of the plenty while the few are left shunned. A wash of the brain, a leech on the soul. Do you think they look only for a battle? No, these bloodsuckers thirst for war.'

'Then what kind of man would I be to deny them?'

'You're not a man,' Agarov reminded. 'Parra, you are something much more powerful. They'll see you as a weapon.'

'If Fallen wants a fight, why shan't I obey? Since the explosion of Hjar, Ramoria has shared an alliance with Empora—'

'And with Posre,' Sebastian cut in. 'Raylan Fallen did not think twice before betraying us, how could we ever trust Syrus now?'

'Nonsense Joje! The Rapture and Syrus armies will stand together as they have since the dawn of

time. Hundreds of thousands of soldiers ready at our command.'

The slight uncomfortable laughter that sang from Parra's lips soon ceased at Korine's shout.

'Stop it!' Aghast, rivers flowed down her cheeks. 'Stop it, I beg of you. How is it you can laugh while our son has been stolen from us? Don't be so foolish as to not heed Sir Sebastian's wisdom. I care for Lozari more than any, but we are not about to start a war. We may have a strong army, but they certainly have their dishonourable wits. If this attack at Kalan was planned, I beg you, walk not so freely into Fallen's hands.'

'Korine is right,' Agarov agreed. 'Why break the puppet, when we can simply cut its strings? I know Khosi Trajan as I do the back of my paw. A clever and deceitful being, but a gambler too.'

'I care greatly for my son, but do not mistake his worth when compared to my empire.'

'I'd never expect you to give up your throne, Parra. Of course not. I have reason to believe Trajan's eyes are set on Nuii alone.'

'Nuii?' and again, with rising inflection 'Nuii? How do you... have you spoken with Khosi?'

'Not at all. Khosi would never trust my presence at the Red Castle, but I have met with his son, Prince Yara,' Agarov altered. 'Long before Lozari was snatched, Lord Parra. I assure you.'

'Nuii is nought but a swampland,' pushed Joje. 'As I understand, neither is it truly belonged by Ramoria. Nuii belongs to your *untouched lands of Aj'ayah.'*

Given its name from the ancient tongue meaning, dirt, *Nuii was an Aj'ayahic swampland located a mere boat trip from the north east of Ramoria. The Raptures took ownership of the land in the aftermath of Hjar by the sheer happenstance that the islands lay so close that they almost touched Ramoria's boarder. None ever dared argue against the islands' ownership for fear of being cursed.*

'What needs has Trajan for it?' asked Korine.

'Needs I apparently have not.' Parra stroked at the thick, black bush formed around his chin. 'If it means that our son will be returned, give the damn swampland to Trajan. Shove it up Raylan's arse for all I care. Just bring back my son!' The emperor rose from the Orca and advanced towards the seven steps, addressing only Joje Sebastian. 'There is treachery

within Siren walls. Until found, you will trust no-one!' He turned to Agarov. 'Oldest friend, please wait a moment.'

The wolf stood obediently tall.

'Promise me, if anyone even so touches a hair upon the head of a Rapture, you'll tear out their heart.'

'By the Spirits of the Aj'ayah, I give you my word. It will be my blood ever before theirs.' The White Wolf bowed low, almost ground-touchingly and suddenly his face turned grey. 'Parra, if I may, I feel as though I must share a warning with you.'

'Go on.'

'A caution which struck my attention ever since my arrival into Ramoria. I mean no disrespect, Parra, but there appears a most awful stench lingering around your family.'

Although the wolf's words struck hard, the emperor could not deny it. For, he too had smelled it: the sickening scent of death.

***

When noticing everyone readying to depart, the spying servant boy, by the name of Gross Gabriel, swiftly hid behind the Throne Room doors, stuffing the papers containing all which he had overheard away into his pocket. The sneaky, buck-toothed boy was clever enough to not journey too far from Master Parra. He had danced the same dance enough to know that if he was not waiting eagerly outside, it would certainly raise suspicion.

'Now, leave me alone with my thoughts.' Gabriel heard Parra say, dismissing his party. 'Joje, do send in my servant boy.'

'Which boy, Emperor?'

'Why, our gift from our generous allies of Empora. The buck-toothed one. Gabriel Syrus.'

Chapter Seven
Kulla Town Centre

Finn loved his friend more than anything, but he couldn't deny that Ella-Rose would often delude herself on these fantasies. He needn't have said a word, for the sceptic look painted on his face was more than enough.

They continued through the forest until spotting a sign to their left. The exact same sign Nyla had seen when leaving the cabin in Legend of Eliza:

Welcome to Kulla Town Centre

Nyla thought that the town seemed smaller amidst the winter darkness, not that it was ever so grand in luminance. Every home, inn, market and office was locked up tightly with wooden planks, (for the less-wealthy folk,) and steel chains, preventing the season's smugglers and squatters from smuggling and squatting. The only sound clanking through the empty road was the loud choking from the water tower at the edge of Fortunae Forest. She didn't quite know what was causing it, nor was she eager to find out. With only a sad ladybird medallion for a friend, Nyla hurried along the dead road in search for shelter.

'Perhaps we should go back,' Nyla said to herself.

Thoughts of mistake and regret entered her mind for brief moments, quickly erased by the annoying screech of Penny McArthur, "Filthy rat!", "Miserable shit!", "Stupid bitch!"

She tried her best to not let the cold night air dominate her, though winter's torment came straight from the gods and what chance had she at all against them? The moonlight made an appearance from beneath the thin sheet of lavender clouds, somehow giving the comforting illusion of warmth and safety. She took the small dose of placebo with ease, but the water tower gritted its teeth ever so loudly yet again and reality's painful kick came down on her hard. Without a doubt, she may soon end up as dead as Kulla Town Centre itself.

'Psst!'

The noise came from her mind.

'Pssssst!'

No, the noise came from behind, followed by the high-pitched words: 'You there, come over here!' She turned, swiftly, yet stiffly and saw the upper-body of a boy, (whose bottom-half appeared to have been eaten by the dead road.) 'Come on, quickly now, you'll catch yer death out there. Climb into the sewer, 'fore they get here.' With that, the boy's half-body swooped down to become no-body. Not wanting to wait and find out who "they" *were supposed to be, Nyla made haste towards the stinking, open grid, laying her trust wholly in the sewage boy. She thrust herself through the open hole and climbed down a damp, rusty ladder, luckily landing on solid, stoned ground.*

'Don't fret, missy,' insisted the full-boy, closing warmly in on her. 'These here sewers've been clear of the townie's poops fer plenty of years. Shucks, where're me manners, ay? Allo,' he smiled, almost hitting her as he jabbed a dirty hand towards her stomach. 'Name's Coccin. Friends call me Co if it so please yer. Do be ever so welcomed to me humble abode.' Coccin carefully raised Nyla's white locks, eyes wide in examination, causing the girl to flinch. 'My, I ain't ever seen hair as beautiful as yours,' he smiled, dropping the tickling curls back down to her face. 'So, what's yer name, girl?'

Nyla sat atop the cold stone floor, warmed by the strong smell of excrement which had once flooded the tunnel walls. She had to think for a moment. 'It's Nyla,' she said comfortably.

'Friends call you Ny, I'll bet?'

'I don't have any friends,' she half giggled. 'Coccin, earlier you—'

'—Co, please,' he broke in. 'We're friends now, right Ny?'

'Yes, sorry. Co, earlier you said that "they" *were coming. Who are* they?*'*

'Huh?'

'When you spotted me, you told me to come quickly before they *arrive. Before who arrives?'*

The young boy shuffled into a thin patch of light, allowing Nyla to see his entire face for the first time. He had used dirt and mud to spike up his hair like antennas. His rosy red cheeks shined brightly, boasting the three small freckles at each side. 'Ever heard of a paug, Ny?' he asked.

Nyla shook her head.

'Nasty little things, they are. Scavengers, up there in that water tower,' he pointed up through the manhole from where they had entered. 'Don't much know what they look like, mind. All what I know is all what I hear, and trust me, they don't speak too flattery-like.' Coccin stood and pulled the grid back into place with more ease than a pup tugging at a rope.

As soon as it clanked into place, Nyla almost immediately heard the song of scampering feet, playing above their heads. Superfluously, the boy raised his forefinger to ensure silence. Nyla couldn't quite hear much, only assumed mumbled murmurs of what her newfound friend had called paugs. Numerous questions swam inside her head, she almost forced them out of her mouth at once, but knew it best to resist and await Coccin's voice before risking exposure. After all, the kid seemed to know what he was doing.

After several minutes, Coccin slowly and silently grabbed a small piece of mouldy bread from a rusted bucket and offered slightly under half of it to Nyla. She politely declined; the boy was far too skinny to have his food taken away from him. Besides, he told her that he'd gathered it from the bins beside Mr Jonas Fiddleworth's market, and as a general rule, anything that smelled worse than it appeared, Nyla daren't permit her mouth to suffer.

The sounds from above soon ceased, and all that remained was the munching and crunching between Coccin's lemon-yellow teeth. 'Look, I don't rightly mean to intrude,' he muffled, pushing the squished-up bread to his cheeks. 'But what exactly brings yer to these parts? A pretty girl like you is meant be in a castle or palace way up in the hills or summat, not down here with a wee peasant like me.'

'You are no peasant, Co, just as I am no princess. I live in a shabby cabin that I swear would fall apart,

if not for the thousands of rats holding it up. I'm just a girl. An unwanted *girl,' she corrected.*

'Whoa, wait one tickidy-tock minute; heard about you, I have. Yer that daughter of the McArthur fam ain't yer? Better off without them, I'd argue. Horrid peeps they be, especially that fat—' Co swiftly slapped his hands against his mouth to halt his words, but Nyla only sniggered. 'Scuse me, Ny. I shouldn't be speaking that way. I do run me mouth off on occasion, least that's what my own rents do tell.'

'Your parents? They're here with you?'

It was now Coccin's turn to do the laughing. 'Oh, Great One, no. They're locked up safe n' sound at home.'

'If your parents live at home, why would you be down here in the sewer?'

'Ah, sweet, sweet Ny. I could very well ask you the same thing.'

The sewer ground was rough, the air damp. The cold night winds were blocked mostly by the tunnel walls. Not that it mattered much; the poor girl was used to sleeping in the barn not so far from the cabin when kicked out and punished for Eliza's mistakes. Even though the hay spiked hard and the sheep shat soft, she always preferred the farm to her tiny room. At least there she had the space to practice those strange talents she had developed, especially since stealing that medallion.

Nyla spent the night in the sewer tunnel. Where else to start a new life but from the bottom?

The moonlight soon took its leave, leaving a black gift of darkness. Once Coccin had fallen asleep, it didn't take long for Nyla to start closing her eyes and for Eliza's darkened gaze to shine through.

***

As sounds from above again scratched at Nyla's ears, her eyes flickered like a broken lamppost. Broken most definitely, for when she at last woke from her troubled sleep, the sewer had somehow retained its darkness. Scratching. Scratching. Had the paugs returned?

'Nyla, wake up!' The boy was a blur. 'We have to leave right now!' His words were a muddle of terror.

It took a short moment for Nyla to recall where she was. No longer was she snuggled at the farm or in her bed. No more was she jabbed awake by Mrs McArthur's favourite nailed bat. No, this time the jabbing came from Coccin's lips. Only then did her ears recognise the sound above for what it was; screaming. If horror only had a voice. Without question, nor even a second thought, Nyla advanced towards the closed grid.

'No,' Coccin urged. 'Not that way. Yer'd soon be trampled.' He beckoned the dazed girl over from few yards down the tunnel and the distraught expression with it brought a chilling shiver to her spine.

'Co, what's going on? All that screaming—'

'Kulla,' he whispered, slowly turning his head. 'The whole town has turned red.'

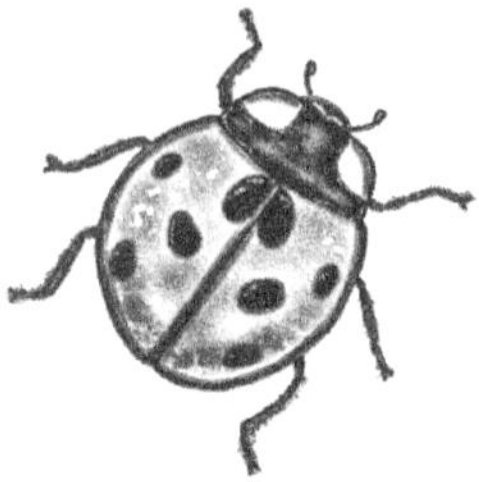

Chapter Eight
A Heartless Emperor

As Dragon Claw almost completed its entire turning, scraping autumn's pumpkin-coloured tilt, Lozari had returned to Kalan almost unharmed, Nuii had been gifted to Khosi Trajan and an unseen, unfortunate plague spread its wings over the Ramorian Empire. Some claimed it the Voice of Death, for it was written in the Aj'ayahic Testaments that, "When the day comes of morality's collapse, Death's whisper shall burn throughout the lands of the Claw."

Yet, no-one died. How could it have been the work of Death when no-one died? The city of Kertu had merely spread a light sickness throughout Ramoria, was all.

No-one di—

Pains suddenly centred primarily through his temples. Parra would think nothing of it, for Thaddeus was only nineteen years old. Nothing so severe could surely happen to a mere boy. But it did not take long for the fatigue to come, followed by vomiting, weight loss and finally, the red coughing. Thaddeus was dying and no healer could explain why. The boy worsened each day. For the sake of Ramoria, Parra kept the matter hidden. If news of the alleged Voice of Death at the Siren were to reach Danjin, Trajan would soon force an attack.

But a public figure hidden from the public? Ramorian cities were quick to turn against the silent Siren, (especially since folk had always suspected a peculiar abnormality in their leader.) Everyone believed the boy to be dead, which in turn birthed rumours, theories and conspiracies of what dark happenings could be taking place at the palace.

'Absurd!' Rapture roared. 'Torture they scream, filicide they shout. I may be a heartless man, but that does not make me cruel. If news of Thaddeus' death

*was to truly get out now, the Rapture name will forever be ruined. How could I be so ignorant? Surely, something can be done to revive my boy. I am a sorcerer, yes a sorcerer dammit! I can use my powers in secret to raise him from rest. '*Parra beckoned his buck-toothed servant boy to refill his glass of plunkberry wine. 'You agree, don't you Gross Gabriel?' he asked, mockingly. And although the boy wished to speak, Gabriel Syrus spoke no word. 'Ach, screw you and your wine, boy. Get out of my sight you ugly toad.'*

'Lord Parra, to use your powers so freely would be unwise,' Joje Sebastian pushed. 'Necromancy is the Devil's game, but that is not to say we lack hope.'

The emperor paused. 'I'm listening.'

'My men have heard tales of a sorceress within the Aj'ayah.' This was the first time Joje had ever lied to Parra. His men had heard no such tales.

'Do you trust them?'

'With my life,' he assured. The knight dared not to tell the emperor that this strange sorceress had actually spoken Thaddeus' name to him in his dreams.

No, his nightmares.

'Yes, a fool I may sound, but I trust them with my life. Never would I lie to you, brother. Forgive me, but in your absence tending to Thaddeus' funeral this morning, I took it upon myself to send three of my men and a servant boy to Green Sands in search for this sorceress.

Parra leant in intrigue.

'I received word back shortly after that in four days and four nights she is due to arrive at the Siren gates.'

***

And on the fourth night, come she did.

Like the White River of Ramoria, her thin, delicate strands of hair flowed majestically from her head and down to her shoulders. Parra had never been struck by such beauty. Many a time, he had experienced such pleasures in his company. 'Soft, little things,' he'd describe his mistresses. 'Seducers with mellifluous, luscious lips.'

Korine, of course he loved with most of his heart, alas, such mortal women soon grow tiresome for heartless men like Parra. He wanted more, longed for more, and there she stood right at his door.

'Allu Allu, unfamiliar woman,' Parra greeted atop the Orca. 'I heard only of your business four days ago. I have awaited your arrival with grand anticipation. First, do tell me your name.'

'It's Mia.' She gave it nonchalantly and plain, to which Empress Korine offered a considerable look.

'Mia, as in special?' Korine was referring to the ancient tongue.

'No,' Rapture grinned wide, capturing the pink in the woman's eyes. 'Mia, as in divine.'

The emperor explained everything to the beautiful woman, leaving nothing out, but Mia refused her tongue lest they two would speak in private. With no hesitation, the two walked alone into the palace gardens.

The light of the rising sun stroked softly as they entered through its ivy gates. Parra assumed the white atop each rose and tulip appeared from the reflection of Mia's lengthy locks, before raising his head to the purple skies and noticing winter had sneaked through with a malicious, icy grin.

'Pardon me, most curious woman, but I will speak clear and true. You are the sole definition of beauty itself, a magical taste has that word upon my lips. Now that you have me alone,' Parra grinned egocentrically, eyeing her from open blouse, right down to her skin-tight pants. 'Whatever will you have of me?' He took her tightly by the waist and pulled her close enough for their bodies to become perfectly aligned. The top three buttons of her blouse were purposely left undone, boasting a sweet, curved outline atop her breasts. (If examined diligently, Parra was certain he could hear the suffocating screams of the next few latches, begging to be opened.) Yet, strangely, for the first time in his forty-four years when staring at a woman's hearty chest, he looked not at her busty, beauteous bosom. Rather, it was the thick golden chain to steal his gaze, hanging to meet the medallion of a ladybird. How strange it seemed that he somehow felt lured in by this inanimate piece of jewellery.

'That necklace,' he began. 'How curious it appears.' He planted his lips, gently onto the side of her neck, slowly stroking up to the touch of her lips.

Initially, she allowed his light kisses. Boys will be boys after all. Girls, on the other hand... well girls can be whatever they desire. As long as they have the right man at their grasp. Abruptly, Mia pushed back from his hold, albeit slightly aroused seeing the redness rise in his cheeks.

'You refuse me?' bafflingly, he demanded, followed by an unhealthy chesty laugh. 'Must be you are unaware of whose company you share, witch!'

'Ah, but I know very well who you are, Emperor Parra Rapture, sorcerer beneath Ramoria's Sapphire moon.' she spoke much colder than any winter winds. 'Fact is, I know you better than you know yourself.' Then, it was with the mere touch of her finger to his forehead that a memory he had tried his best over the years to repress, soon returned. And once more, he stood in the cold rain of Fortunae Forest.

'Yes, the number is four,' the strange girl in the shadows spoke eerily into his mind and though young Parra only scarcely saw her, Yakub Sebastian saw her not at all. How could he? For when Prince Parra

turned to him in hope of comfort, he saw that his friend was frozen still.

'If our number is four,' Parra's courage grew, 'Then four questions I'll ask and four answers you shall give.'

She allowed.

'What if I choose only to have one child, else two? What then of your four?'

'You will bear four. For this, you have no choice.' Each time the strange girl spoke, she moved closer to the young prince.

'When will we two next meet?'

'At your first son's end.'

Parra ignored this, as he could not help but blurt out his next question. 'Four deaths I cause. Whose deaths?'

'Father, friend, brother and son.'

'You lie! Why ever would I cause death to those I love?'

'Because young Rapture you will become a heartless emperor.' Closer still, almost touching.

'Finally, how will I face my four deaths?'

'Four answers you required, four answers I have given. Our first meeting has finished. Until next

time.' It was with the mere touch of her finger to his forehead that Emperor Parra's consciousness returned to the Siren.

'It cannot be!' There and then he could dismiss and be done with this strange girl for good, but fascination grabbed his ego by the throat, ceasing the dismissal from ever reaching his tongue.

'For four days you awaited my arrival, because four days I required. Your firstborn son is dead and we two meet again. A great and noble sacrifice, but I can assure you that my reasoning for this visit is quite necromantic.' She raised her eyes to the winter clouds as the cold quickened pace, launching a thick white powder over the gardens. 'The Voice of Death the testaments say. A religious cleansing of all who have lost their way. I can promise you Parra, it was not Death's voice whispering into your son's ears, not unless you consider Kraal Syrus the Reaper.'

'Syrus? You mean? That son of a —'

'I'm sure it is no secret to you that Trajan holds the most power across Dragon Claw; Kraal Syrus joined alliance with Raylan Fallen and Khosi Trajan right under your nose.'

Astonished at the thoughts of betrayal, a barbarous combination of displeasure and distress hit Parra hard.

'Rapture - you were born with a magnificent strength, an energy so rare that most will never know its taste. For that, you will always be their enemy. Yes, for that you are an enemy of Dragon Claw. You're a damned fool if you believe Thaddeus died of a plague. Thaddeus's death was a mistake. A poison from a stupid servant boy; an attack meant for you.'

'If the poison was meant for me, how did Thaddeus come to drink it?'

To this, Mia released a laugh, deliberately to agitate the emperor even more. 'Why, because you gave it to him.'

The memory hit him once more. This time, even harder. "'Four deaths I cause. Whose deaths?'"

"'Father, friend, brother and son.'"

A single tear slowly grew in the corner of his eye. 'I killed my son?'

'The boy was thirsty, Parra. What else were you to do? Blame not yourself; it was not your poison after all.'

A darkness is coming, *Joje had once told Parra. 'Aye, it is,' he thought. 'I'm talking the darkness at this moment. 'Treacherous, traitorous bastard. I will tear out Kraal's jaw! And you… you speak as if you know their unit well. I demand you share all of their secrets. You can start with Nuii.' The emperor saw her flinch as if the word drove a sword through her mind. 'Trajan knows I'd have given Ry, the city of Silver Coins, else Tralar of Golden Chalices for Lozari's return, instead he asks for the swampland. Why?'*

'Tell me truly, Emperor Parra, how much do you actually know of the Aj'ayah?'

'Screw the Aj'ayah, I say!' he shouted. 'I care not for such supernatural, unsupervised folk. I am a man of rule, not of religion.'

'Then you have already lost this forthcoming war,' Mia divulged. 'Nuii may not mine gold, but it shares its touch with the Aj'ayah. If anything, Khosi Trajan is known for his strengths in bargaining. And mistake not, he has become quite friendly with these "supernatural, unsupervised folk" amongst the island. It has been written in the stars, seas and earth that his army shall thrive.' Mia stepped in, close

enough to lay her small arms upon Parra's broad shoulders. Her breath was warm on his, her crotch felt warm against his. 'If the prophecy holds, Khosi Trajan will take Dragon Claw wholly for a long time. No more Raylan Fallen nor Kraal Syrus, no more Parra Rapture. Don't you see?' slowly, she reached out her hand to stroke gently at his beard. 'The war of four lands has already begun.'

Parra trembled from fear and frost. 'And if your prophecy speaks true, how does this war end?'

'Oh Parra,' Mia raised her eyebrows. 'This war will never end.'

'Nonsense! I will stop Trajan— I must—'

'Hush now, sire. A prophecy may take rule, but such things are made to be broken.' Mia bit the inside of his lip so fiercely, she could feel the warmth of his blood dribbling through her gums. 'Parra, I would never deny you. Such fury, such fire!' Again she smiled through the pink of her eyes. 'I give my word that tonight I am yours.' Her grin soon took a grim turn and her eyes became restless. 'But for now—for now you are mine.' Swiftly, Mia drew a small blade from her thigh. She cut straight through Parra's

chest and effortlessly reached her hand to remove his still-beating heart.

Although withdrawal took only few seconds, in Parra's mind it was like reliving all his years. Pain, he could not feel, but shock and panic scratched out from his eyes like a sharpened claw.

'Worry not, Parra. It is my understanding that men can quite easily live their lives without their heart,' Mia half-laughed, staring darkly into the unsettling nothingness of the emperor's eyes.

'Y-You evil bitch!' he breathlessly screamed, and all he could hear in return were the vibrating chants of 'four days and four nights, four days and four nights, four days and...

... Four nights earlier, four men stood at the foot of Mia's door. She had no interest in awaiting Sir Walter Fitzgerald and his men's arrival, for she held already gathered the knowledge of their purpose long before Thaddeus was even sat at the big-boy's potty. "For four days and four nights your emperor will await my visit," she told them.

This part, she did not say: And on the fifth morn, winter shall rise a new and I shall be granted with the greatest gift of all. The gift of life.

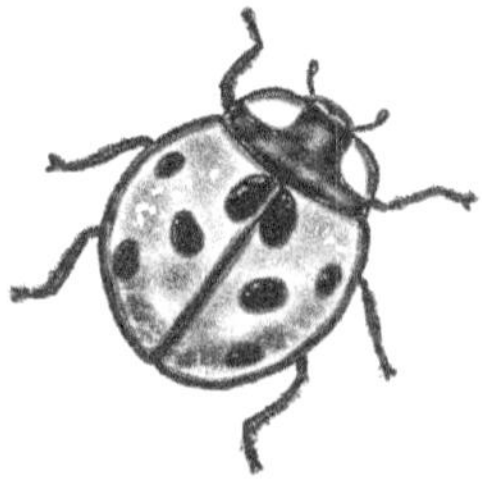

Chapter Nine
The Amethyst Cavern

Ella-Rose found that the words struggled more when falling from her lips, than flowed gracefully, as they usually did when Caesar Azerius tells the tale. Nevertheless, she had shared the Legend of Eliza as best she could with Finn, who now sat dazed and confused, gazing at the trees where Kulla Town Centre once stood. 'The Kulla had turned red. It was said that Eliza burned down Kulla, murdering everyone who was there,' Ella-Rose taught. 'The fire destroyed everything; it even reached the cabin where Nyla was brought up.'

Finn studied the sign once again. **Welcome to Kulla Town Centre**. This time, a cold shiver took to his skin. The wood of the sign was broken and charred. Kulla Town Centre had indeed been burnt down under strange circumstances long before the two were born, but that did not necessarily prove that Caesar's stories were real events. 'Is that why you've brought us here? To tell spooky made up stories. Besides, who even was Eliza? Just a made up person in someone's head, I gathered. And how does this really have anything to do with your dreams?'

'No, Eliza was a part of Nyla's consciousness, so whatever power Eliza must have owned, Nyla possessed too. She just hadn't the ability to control it. Not until—'

'She stole the medallion!' they finished in unison.

'Exactly!' Ella-Rose clicked her fingers.

'How do you know Eliza was actually real? Maybe it was just the medallion that held all the power.'

She ignored the question as she continued to try to figure it out for herself. 'See, Nyla had nothing to do with the burning of Kulla at all, it was all that demon, Eliza's doing! But after the town was ruined, Nyla tried to use sorcery to reverse Dragon Claw – to go back in time and save everyone.' She whispered that last part. 'But Nyla never actually was a sorceress; without the medallion, she was just a girl.'

'I don't understand.' Finn had heard the Legend of Eliza before from the furry lips of the professor himself, but while Ella-Rose had been fascinated by Caesar's mystifying words, Finn clearly must have dozed off.

'She tried to reverse Dragon Claw, but failed and instead ripped our world in two. I think Dragon Claw remained to all as it always had appeared, but everyone knew that something else was created that day. A spiritual, boundless creation,' she said as if repeating the words that the professor had once taught.

Finn rubbed his face with a handful of confusion. 'You mean like another dimension?'

'Sort of,' she squinted her nose. 'Well, actually no, not really.' Ella-Rose forced her way through tough vines and thick leaves, past the charred sign and into what once was Kulla Town Centre.

The town had been gone for years, replaced now by beautiful exotic flowers and a large memorial stone, carved with the names of all those who lost their lives in the incident. The charred sign, which now looked to Finn to say: **We come to Kill a town centre**, what with the burned off 'l' and half of the 'u' missing, was all that remained from the original town.

'There!' Ella-Rose pointed to a large set of emerald trees sitting atop a hill in the distance. 'There, do you see it?'

'There what?' Finn squinted as hard he could, but didn't share Ella-Rose's advantage of height. 'Is that? It can't be. It looks like a cabin, only broken and… crooked.'

'The exact place where the cabin in Caesar's "made up story" would have been, don't you agree? Something's happened to that cabin. Something terrible.'

'It looks pretty normal to me.'

'In our world, yes. But there's something powerful inside those broken walls.' *I can feel it.* Ella-Rose thought she had said this aloud, but was thankful she hadn't.

'What happened to Nyla and Eliza? What happened to the medallion?'

'When Dragon Claw ripped in two,' Ella-Rose began, taking a dramatic step back, preparing for the next words to fly from her mouth. 'Nyla accidentally divided the medallion in two. Imprisoning Eliza with one piece inside that *crooked world.*' Somehow, it felt right calling it that.

It was then that Ella-Rose noticed she was unintentionally scaring Finn a little. 'Don't worry. Only the strongest sorcerers could channel the power to open those spiritual gates leading to that world, and all the sorcerers are gone, Finn. There's nothing to worry about. All that we'd see up there is a pile of burned, broken wood. Trust me, we can't see the crooked world or Eliza.'

But the memory of her recurring nightmare returned into her mind and Ella-Rose soon realised that she had in fact seen someone inside that crooked cabin.

'And the other half?'

'What?' Ella-Rose came back to.

'You said, half is in the *crooked world*, where is the other piece?'

The answers you seek lie deep within Fortunae. Hurry. Please hurry!' This time, those words sounded as if they were spoken loudly and clearly from the forest trees. Although, from the none-the-wiser, waiting-for-an-answer face Finn was pulling, Ella-rose knew that the voice spoke only inside her crooked head.

'I think the other half is here, Finn,' a beaming smile lit up her face, brighter than the shining sun. 'Right here in our very own Fortunae Forest! Wouldn't it be wonderful if we found it and took it to Caesar?'

Still sceptical, Finn raised his eyebrows. 'Come on, you do realise all of Caesar's stories are fictional, right? This is all crazy. I think we should head back.'

'But what if all these tales were real? The medallion, the crooked world. Look, somehow I know they're real, I just know it!'

Ella-Rose explained all that she could remember of her recurring dreams, hating how crazy she actually sounded. 'I don't expect you to understand. Just please trust—' abruptly, her voice reached a halt. 'Wait. Do you see that? Goodness! Tell me you see that!'

Finn turned to see what Ella-Rose had spotted, expecting with the way she'd so nonchalantly grabbed his attention it would only be a luscious flower or a glistening waterfall, though what she had seen was something much, much more magnificent. The two children were miles from the path they would usually travel along, but never in a million years did they expect to see something so exquisite. Through Fortunae Forest's emerald leaves, Ella-Rose had spied a bright, violet-lit cavern, sparkling with amethyst gemstones.

'Oh Finn, come on, we must go inside!' she beamed, holding out her hand for the boy to take.

Intoxicated by its enchanting allure, they each took a step closer. Finn more hesitantly. The stone walls shined from wetness and the sunlight raced in and out of the cave's gaps.

'Who knew there could be something so glorious in this forest?'

'Do you think it's dangerous?' Finn asked unsteadily.

'Probably,' Ella-Rose giggled. 'But the fun things always are.'

'Can we not just go back to the village now? There are loads of fun things to do there. We could play Enchantments with Michael,' he suggested, before releasing a purposely-faked cough and pointing towards the cave. 'You know, dark creatures and all,' he whispered.

'Finn, we're both so far from the village, about to enter the most wonderful place we both have ever seen. Besides, if there were any "dark creatures" inside, wouldn't you suppose they'd think we were the actual dark creatures, hmm?'

'Um—'

'And we're not creatures are we, Finn?'

'I guess not.' His smile was innocent. Too innocent.

As soon as they set their feet inside the Amethyst Cavern, the smell of natural, fresh water hit them, before seeing the exotic purple stream flowing so majestically within. Songs of tropical birds blessed their ears with soft melodies overhead.

Without a single thought, Ella-Rose threw her summer coat to the ground and dove head-first into the pool of purple water, knowing she would soon dry off with Ramoria's vibrant sunshine. She swam as fast as her arms would allow to reach the other side, then turned back to Finn.

But Finn was nowhere to be seen.

A bird squawked above, sending frightful shivers down her spine. Not a tropical bird. They had been replaced by a single black raven. Ella-Rose called out for Finn, but received no reply. Her heart became paralysed. The cavern had somehow shrunk; the walls were closing in. The once beautiful brightness had turned into darkness. There was no change in the weather, only in her mind. The violet gemstones surrounding stared at her, never blinking.

The silence was both beautiful and dangerous.

'Finn!' she called again.

And, although the boy did not show, Ella-Rose knew that she was no longer alone. It was a strange feeling, but it was the same Ella-Rose thought she had felt earlier that morning when gazing out of her window. She was being watched. The cavern walls continued to suffocate her. The darkness clawed at her wet clothes, causing her whole body to freeze still. Thousands of questions raced through her mind, all to be returned with the words: *The answers you seek are deep within Fortunae.*

'Ella-Rose,' the cavern echoed. It was an unknown voice, yet strangely one she felt that she recognised.

She wished to speak, but her mouth had nothing to give. Suddenly, she felt something scorch into the palm of her hand. Something broken. Yet, still, she saw no-one through the darkness. And before Ella-Rose could even ask any questions, everything was gone.

No, not gone.

Everything was changed. No longer did Ella-Rose stand inside those mystifying cavern walls, but instead amid the path surrounded by emerald trees staring at the crooked cabin. Alone. She felt a harsh chill brush against her.

'Finn!' she called. Her voice merely echoed, coldly through the silence. 'Finnnnnnnnnnnnn…'

One step. That was all it took. That one step towards the crooked cabin with her hair waving softly behind her in the wind. That mere singular piece of footwork caused the chained door of the crooked cabin to croak slowly open and a long claw to reach out, searching for the very thing Ella-Rose held at her hand.

She heard a voice, shouting from the cabin. Strangely, the voice belonged to Finn. Calling her name. Calling her name. Calling her name. Never stopping. Raging through her mind.

‘Ella-Rose!’ the voice shouted. ‘Ella-Rose! Ella-Rose! Ella—

Rose!’ The sound of Finn’s real voice suddenly relieved her of the torment. ‘Do you hear that?’ he asked, only it was not the sound of the Amethyst Cavern, nor the monstrous sound of his own voice screeching from the crooked cabin to which he was referring, for strangely, Ella-Rose still stood beside the charred sign of Kulla Town Centre.

‘W-What’s going on?’ She questioned. It felt like another nightmare, but she didn’t recall falling asleep. Immediately, she looked at the palm of her hand where a broken medallion piece sat silently still. ‘F-Finn?’ Her heart tightened and a frightening, yet overwhelming rush of excitement spilled within.

‘Shh!’ Finn whispered urgently. The look on his face was enough to wipe the excitement from Ella-Rose’s. ‘Do you hear that?’ he asked once more.

A crack, a crunch and a rumble in the bushes. It was not loud, nor was it rough, but it was certainly enough to raise a shiver up their spines.

‘Finn—’

Firmly, the small boy thrust his small hand up to halt her mouth. ‘There! Get behind that tree now!’

‘Wha—’ Ella-Rose forced a halt to her own voice this time. She had started to hear the eerie noise too. The intense and increasing sound of large footsteps drawing closer.

Closer.

Closer.

Chapter Ten
Matra

Four nights prior to Mia's arrival at the Siren, Gabriel Syrus, a buck-toothed servant boy at seventeen years old pushed passed Walter Fitzgerald and the other two men that Joje Sebastian had sent, so that he could stand face to face with the most glamorous woman he had ever seen. 'I have to know,' he began, 'you must please tell,' a warm shiver tickled down his spine. 'These tales they share across lands, are they spoken true?'

With empowering embrace, Mia locked eyes with the frightened boy. 'Probably not,' she smiled. 'But you wouldn't leave a girl curious as to what they say now, would you?'

'Well I -'

'Halt child!' Walter forced. His eyes were drawn to the golden chain hanging around Mia's neck. 'Forget not your place, servant.'

'Foolish man!' Mia returned. 'Let the lad's tongue fly freely.' Her voice took the flavour of impatient lust. 'We are all but social slaves to the Claw after all.'

Gabriel saved her gaze, frozen and unyielding. Was it her unique beauty, unrestrictedly fixing his eyes, or could it have been sorcery? What was the difference? *His mind asked, then he trembled. 'T-They say witchcraft.'*

Mia giggled. 'Ooh, a lady's magic.'

'Necromancy.'

'Death's game.' Her eyes set alight.

'Surely ain't all what they've been sharing though, mistress.'

'Halt at once, boy!' The heavy shout from Walter's lips forced a quick shift in Gabriel's stare. 'We are here because of Thaddeus's death, nothing

more. By order of the Orca, I demand that you keep your tongue.'

Bowing both respectfully and frightened, the boy muttered, 'Sincere apologies, mistress.' No-one noticed his awkward mispronunciation of the word sincere. Else, no-one had cared enough to say. 'Might be that I've overstepped. I offer my apologies once more. Please allow my leave.'

In that moment, there was nothing in her face. No expression to be read, nor inclination of an emotion.

Walter's face contrarily held stern. 'Come now, Ga—' And it was amongst that strange moment, there came a pause; a long and unnatural halt in the lands of Dragon Claw.

'Sir?' waved Gabriel. 'Master Fitzgerald?' Not a word could raise Walter's mind, for all but the white-haired woman and the buck-toothed servant boy stood motionless.

The wind held its breath, awaiting the right moment to again blow.

'Come now, Gabriel,' Mia spoke melodically inside his head. 'Such a good heart, you keep. Vigorous and full of life. Tell me, what it is that they speak of me, Mia of the Aj'ayah?'

'T-They say you're a god, you know?'

'Oh?'

'See, reading is tough on me, so it is, though I do try. But believe me, them Testaments of Aj'ayah show nought of a lady god. Fact is, only woman of divinity in them books be the Matra herself.'

Translated into 'Mother' from the Aj'ayahic Tongue, the Matra is claimed to be the most powerful being in all of Dragon Claw. A being believed to one day birth a Demon, known to all as the Ladybird.

'What is it you claim, child?' Or, "Spit it out!" *as she had wished to say.*

'I claim you... Matra.'

'Why? Do not keep your tongue. Tell me what you believe this testament says.'

'It says,' Gabriel stuttered and a salty wetness formed around his crotch. 'It says the Matra is the most powerful sorceress. Not only that, but an infinite being. Possessor of bodies, manipulator of time, space and energy. It says the Matra is the stealer of light, and— and—'

'Yes?'

'Mother— of the Demon.' He dared not repeat the one line which stuck hard into my mind: "The

Ladybird will rise and the gates to a crooked world will soon be opened." 'If I speak true and you are Matra, I beg you, do not spawn this Demon.'

Mia stood perfectly still, as if she too was frozen. 'If *you speak true, you say? Then, you must first teach me what it is you mean by* truth. *All of which you have told me today, you have convinced yourself true; all I wish to know is what* truth *entails. Of course, to be able to understand the truth, one must also understand the false, don't you agree? I personally see no apparent distinction when regarding a matter's certainty, for when the entire world believes in a lie, it simply becomes a truth. What is true belongs to the majority. A fact is simply the survivor's word.' Mia released a cold, dark laugh. 'You petty mortals with your insignificant beliefs live your lives holding faith only in false Gods. These Testaments of Man, Monster and Magic; they are nothing! Stealing their ideas from the air we breathe and for what? Worship? Love? Order? Gods, emperors and peasants, they are all the same. Damn your Testaments and damn your Great One. Don't you see? Sorcery is the only thing that owns rule across Dragon Claw. Sorcery is the one, true omnipotent power.'*

Gabriel trembled unstoppably and defeated. He turned back to his frozen brothers for aid, but none could, nor would have looked back. 'Are they still alive? Tell it true that Master Walter and them are alive.'

'Huh? Ah, yes, yes, of course.' It felt as though a weight had been lifted in the room.

'And I? Am I in any danger?'

'Why, for you I have a gift. A sliver of guidance if you will. I hope that it will certainly help you change your ways,' she leaned to whisper into his ear. 'Dearest Gabriel Syrus.'

He flinched.

'You mustn't go around believing in all that you read and hear.'

The simple servant boy couldn't help but giggle as her voice tickled into his ear.

'Suppose you repeated this discussion with somebody else; it could cause us both quite a bit of bother.' Mia pinched Gabriel's cheeks with her claws and studied his face curiously. 'How could

anyone with a face as adorable as yours ever be in any danger, hmm?'

To this, Gabriel's face beamed pinker than her eyes. Though, the sardonic look he found in the reflection of the blade she had raised up to his face gave a most uneasy turn to his stomach.

'Such naïve idiocy.' Mia pulled the boy's face up by his greasy, blonde hair and forced his mouth open with the mere nod of her head. It was only when she held the blood-soaked tongue in her hand, directing his pain-ridden cries like a conductor of an orchestra that Gabriel Syrus knew he could no longer speak.

He released a muffled cry from the black hole of his mouth that sounded like: 'Why?''

'Well, because you talk too much.'

More cries and more muffles, this time Gabriel screamed as much as his mouth would allow: 'Y-You e-evil ...'

'...Bitch!' Emperor Parra Rapture screamed, losing consciousness at each breath.

Mia simply howled with laughter. 'Oh, how rich. People like you have no need for a heart,' she claimed. 'But don't worry, I would never break my word,' she looked to the pulsating heart sat at her palm, its thick purple juice dripped through her fingers, melting through the thickened white ground. 'I most certainly have you, Emperor Parra Rapture of Ramoria,' she ripped open the buttons of her blouse, biting dangerously at her lip. 'Now, you will have me!'

***

Gods, emperors and peasants, they are all the same. Whether it take them all day, whether it take just four seconds, all men finish the same. And as soon as Parra's cold, heartless body fell lifelessly to the floor; already, Mia could feel the extraordinary growth within her womb.

Four: the children your seed shall bear.

'As I said, my reasoning for such a visit is quite necromantic. I promise, you *will rise again. But I fear Death's work comes only with a price.' Mia sat down in the slush of the snow and placed Parra's shaking head on her wet lap. 'We two are but servants to the writings in the stars. Let us celebrate this night, for it is on this night that the Ladybird*

comes to be.' Then, gazing down to the golden medallion upon her chest, Mia listened as winter fell silently across the palace gardens.

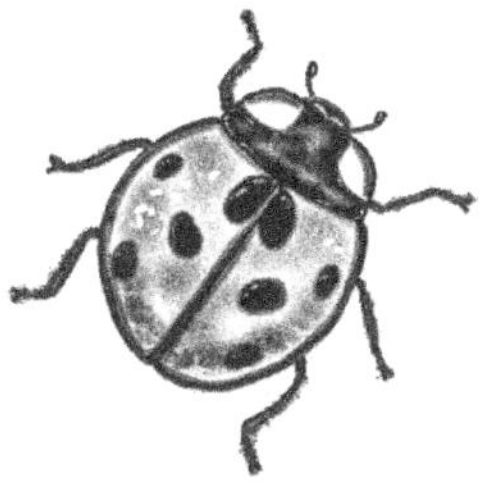

Chapter Eleven
Dark Creatures

A crack of broken twigs, a crunch of crusted leaves; the noise crept dangerously throughout their ears. It wasn't necessarily uncommon to hear such sounds in the forest, for stripped of its bewildering beauty, Fortunae was no different than any plain old woodland. But to hear footsteps so distant from the path was more than enough to raise caution. As time took a quickened turn, noon soon changed into evening. The bright sun sank and the sapphire moon began its ascent. Darkness soon fell across Fortunae Forest.

Manoeuvring behind the tree was no bother for Finn Alfred Reginald Hampson, even given he was only two-feet tall. He managed to climb high and hide, peering his eyes towards the rustling trees ahead. A professional *hide and seek* player. 'Come on, Ella-Rose,' he whispered, lowering his tiny hand.

For Ella-Five-Foot-Six-Inches-Rose, dodging past the surrounding nettles proved a much more challenging experience. She could hardly see a thing. The quicker she pushed, the harder the task became. By the time she managed to squeeze herself behind the tree, her arms and legs were covered completely and bitterly in small red and white bumps, begging for itches. Whenever she gave in to the trickster rash, the stings just screamed out in pain and anger. As she rested her foot gently on a lower branch, she caught slight glimpse of a grey, clawed foot scraping out from the bushes.

Crack, crunch, crack, crunch!

Dark creatures, they both thought, but said nothing.

The footsteps doubled. Tripled! Each clawed scrape across the earth was just a torturing delay towards inevitable horror. She spotted another foot, then another. There were at least three of them. As their monstrous paces slowed down, Ella-Rose's heartbeat sped up. When their beastly movements soon ceased, nightmarish voices were replaced, adding eerier torment.

'Someone's here, someone's near.'

'Yes, yes, I know it.'

'Ooh, I smell it!'

Only then had it occurred to Ella-Rose they would have been much safer had they attempted to sprint back to the path at the first sound of rustling, but her mind had literally been elsewhere. With a deep breath held tightly to her chest, she watched the six clawed, grey feet form a semi-circled around the front of the tree they were hiding behind. Pins and needles stabbed into her body. Her throbbing hand remained tightly to Finn's. Had it not been for this sealed bond, they both knew they would be shivering uncontrollably with fear.

'I spy, with my little eye,' a voice sang sinisterly, slithering like a snake. A prolonged stress upon the 's'.

'Ooh, let me play, let me play. Something beginning with…'

'*Meat*!' One of the creatures moved its slimed, grey body behind the tree with a dark smirk stuck to its face. It lifted Ella-Rose by the neck of her clothes from behind the tree without even noticing Finn hiding above. 'Well, look what we got here. I found me a little elf!'

Ella-Rose, adrenalin pumping, violently yelled out. 'I'm not an elf, you filthy creature!'

'Creature? It calls me creature?'

Such a name was an immensely harsh insult to the being's true species: *globbers*, as they were most commonly known. Famous throughout woodlands for their bothersome nature. Globbers were born to the race of Monsters. Not necessarily dangerous beings, nor clever for that matter; dauntingly hungry than all else. For the majority of the War of Four, it was said that they spent their time eating the flesh of fallen soldiers. Of course, when this became known, monster hunters known as the Bourgaleu soon tracked the species down. The Bourgaleu was made up of wealthy men and women from Empora who studied the globber's every movement. They learned how they acted, analysed how they thought. The hunting soon became a sport for the rich. Globbers started to die out; handed into the cold hands of extinction. Some, however, managed to survive, fleeing to Ramoria the first chance they got. Those who escaped death were thought as the unfortunate few, as they spent the remainder of their days living in tunnels and sewers across Ramoria. It hadn't taken long for the lack of sun and meat to take its toll. Evolution had not played nice, forcing that warm blood pumping through their veins to turn cold and fade to grey.

'What did it call us? Fil fee creet cha?'

'Well, that doesn't sound very nice, does it?'

The globbers licked at their lips almost in unison; their tongues long and black like an eel. Fact is, they all seemed very similar in appearance, what with their thick, grey skin, rat-like tails and devilish red eyes. They were not much larger than Ella-Rose herself, but they were definitely wider.

'So as to not be so rude,' the tallest of the globbers smiled. 'My name's Zebu.' She held out three loose fingers as if to be shaken, though Ella-Rose did not comply.

'Tonzil is my name,' the next one said, flapping his eel tongue side to side at each word. 'Down here is Rump. Or at least, I think his name's Rump. Either that or something else as stupid as his personality. Fact is, we never care to remember it.'

'Creet Cha!' Rump announced. 'My name's Creet Cha'

'Shut it you nitwit!' This reaction from Zebu showed that she was probably leader of the pack. 'Your name ain't Creature and Master Jra'bral would surely curse you for saying so.'

To this, Rump winced.

Ella-Rose remained silently still throughout their squabbling; her muscles refused to move even an inch, though her brain begged the idea of escape. She wished to look to Finn for comfort but would never allow herself to compromise his position.

'Now it's your turn. Tell us your name, elf.'

Ella-Rose opened her mouth, readying to speak, but the adrenalin had worn out. Her words were too frightened to flee. 'I— uh…'

'Best speak up, elf,' Zebu interrupted. 'My ears ain't too much what they used to be.'

'I'm not an elf,' Ella-Rose blurted having finally found her voice. 'I'm a girl.'

Zebu and Tonzil shared a puzzling look.

'What's a Not-An-Elf-Am-A-Gul?' Zebu mistakenly repeated. 'Strangest name for an elf I ever did hear.'

'Oh, can't we just eat it?' begged Tonzil, holding tightly onto his stomach. 'I'm starving!'

Ella-Rose backed away timidly and carefully. She had to make a run for it, there was no other way. Slightly turning her head to the tree she had once hid behind, she noticed Finn in the corner of her eye. He had accidentally fallen and was hanging upside down on a branch. His eyes glared at the three globbers with anger. Until, CRACK! The branch broke. THWACK! Finn crashed to the ground.

With a long, strong whiff, the three globbers stopped and turned to face this new character of their lunchtime show.

'Well, well, well,' Tonzil smiled once more. 'What have we here?'

'Mm dessert, I think! Quick, grab it before it runs!' Just as Zebu gave the order, she turned her gaze back to Ella-Rose and suddenly, the creature's face dropped with fear. The young girl had just remembered what she still held tightly in her hand.

Ella-Rose stretched out her arm as far as she could reach with the medallion piece at her grasp. Finn manoeuvred past the globbers and to her side, trying to appear as intimidating as he could.

'W-What have you got there, elf?' Zebu asked nervously.

'Looks, uh, sorcery-like to me. Don't you be knowing you shouldn't mess round with things like that?'

'Sorc'ry be dange'rus stuff,' Rump joined in.

Ella-Rose smiled down at the broken ladybird piece. Of course, she had no idea what it was actually capable of, but she knew that confidence was key. 'Move on, now!' she demanded. 'Else I'll, um—'

There was a sharp change in the wind and Zebu's fear slowly returned to a high-pitched, annoying laughter. 'The elf don't know how to use it,' the creature sneered.

'Probably fake anyway,' Tonzil sniggered.

The largest gobber took a slight, hesitant step closer towards Ella-Rose and the others were quick to follow.

'Stay back, I warn you!' Ella-Rose shouted, strengthening her grip. 'I'm— I'm not playing around.'

Zebu ignored her words and continued to advance.

'Run!' Finn shouted, snatching Ella-Rose by the forearm and pulling her through the darkness of the forest.

They were too far from the village to go back, not that it would be wise to invite three globbers into their home, nor clever making Sara Azerius aware of their defiance. Instead, they decided to head back to Kulla, towards the emerald trees leading to the crooked cabin.

'Well, what are yer waiting for?' Zebu roared. 'After them!'

The globbers followed close to their tails. Their eyes were much better at seeing in the dark from adapting to living in the sewers.

Running was never something that came natural to Ella-Rose. When she was just three years old, healers had told her she had a condition which caused inflammation in the tubes that carry air in and out of her lungs. She raced as quickly as she could behind

Finn, trying her best to catch up, but found that her heart could not keep up.

Her chest tightened.

Her lungs paused.

Suddenly, her breath was nowhere to be found. Unable go on, Ella-Rose fell unconscious and collapsed, tumbling rapidly down a large, bumpy hill.

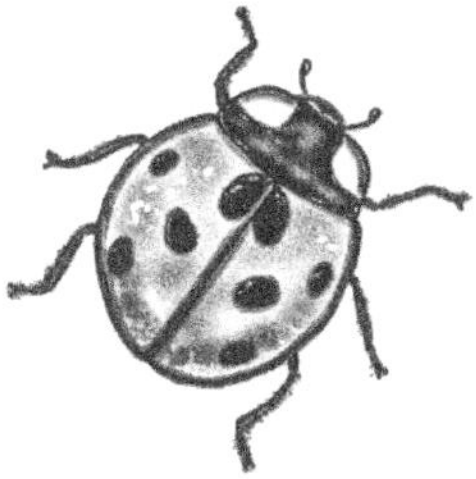

Chapter Twelve
Lozari Rapture's Rule

Caesar set the book down to check whether Michael was still listening. Neither of them had seemed to realise how quickly time had flown by. 'You see, not long after that, Parra Rapture was publicly exposed as a sorcerer and went into hiding,' he explained. 'The United Dragons declared war against Ramoria and with the heartless emperor gone, Lozari was sent back from Kalan to take charge at Siren.'

'Where did Parra go?' asked Michael.

'Where else could a heartless man go but to the slums of the cities, begging for the one thing he could no longer give.'

'Love,' said Michael.

'Of course. Lozari took the throne and he certainly had vengeful plans towards Raylan Fallen alone. He acted immediately by sending an army into Posre. The Fallen wizard fought hard, though he was soon captured and brought to Lozari for a delicate removal of his head.'

Michael winced a little, but tried his best not to show it.

'As sixteen long, tiring, bloody years passed,' Caesar went on. 'Lozari chose then to ignore the threat against Ramoria and deserted his post as ruler, leaving none other than Sir Joje Sebastian to sit atop the Orca.'

'No way! But he was just a knight.' Michael didn't even have the *Joje Sebastian* Enchantment card because he thought it was worthless.

Caesar smirked. 'Oh, he was much more than a knight, believe me. However, it just so happened that Joje Sebastian was fighting at the Battle of Quae at the time and wished to refuse the post, for he knew nothing about ruling a kingdom and his rightful place was in battle. But Lozari was nothing like his father and a refusal would not have been met well.'

'I just don't understand. Why would Lozari leave the War of Four? I mean, he was a sorcerer!' It did not seem like the Lozari Rapture Michael knew from his Enchantments game. He was a strong and powerful sorcerer, not a deserter.

'Because of the Matra!' Caesar roared out these words, causing his teeth to almost drop out of his mouth. 'For four nights, he heard the Matra speak to him in his nightmares, telling him of a door between worlds. Lozari walked all the way from the Siren to the north of Fortunae Forest in search for this strange, different world. When at last he found a path surrounded by emerald trees leading towards a door of a crooked cabin, something happened. Something even he could not explain. Lozari entered a broken world and became more powerful than he ever could have imagined.'

'Crooked cabin? Broken world?' Michael was lost with this tale now, but Caesar went on regardless.

'Lozari used the power he'd gained from that strange world and rose every fallen warrior of every race to fight once more, only this time… they all fought for the Raptures.'

'Then Benjamin Syrus, at only thirteen years old, managed to slay Lozari Rapture, bringing an end to his army of the undead and ending the sorcerer's race forever, right Caesar?'

Caesar neither confirmed nor denied and instead turned a few pages and began to read on:

The Emerald Desert, Quae turned into a battlefield long before its residents could have evacuated. Those caught within found themselves pleading for a ticket to Death's door. Where else could they go? Danjin was deemed the safest empire in Dragon Claw during the war, and yet Khosi Trajan had heightened all security over the land allowing only those with a desired skill to be granted entry.

A boy of thirteen-years, named Benjamin Syrus, strolled steadily past the hundreds of dead bodies, dragging the nine-inched sword he'd named Butterfly Wing in his left hand. Taught by Master Yro Kili to dance the dance of death using only his right hand, he learnt that only idiots kill with their left.

"Are you an idiot, Benjamin Syrus?" His master had asked. He couldn't help then but laugh at the memory. Walking so cavalierly past his fallen companions, and he couldn't help but laugh.

He passed Jimmy Buck, the boy of twelve who had told him he'd once spied a large-breasted lady on her knees doing some peculiar things with a fellow's thingy. Past Chase "Mac" McCullough, a boy of seventeen who once told him he'd stuffed firecrackers through Mrs Patterson's Bakery letterbox.

The laughter soon ceased when he reached his destination. Benjamin stopped at a struggling man with a scar above his left brow in the shape of a jackal and a spear buried deep through his chest. Kraal Syrus, he knew. Both Emperor of Empora and his father. The spear had hit just left of his heart, possibly even slightly scraping the slow beating organ.

'My son, is it you?'

'Aye it is,' Benjamin answered, he didn't mean to sigh, but it came nevertheless.

'Then, I beg that you heed my final words.'

'Father—'

'You must deny the Great One, son. Deny him because he teams only with what is right. There is no way the Great One would choose a side in a war as wrong as this.' Kraal's words fell without flow. 'This world runs only on opposites, my son.'

'Father—'

'Where there is bad, there must be good. Where there is war, there will one day be peace. Wrong for right. Dark for light.' An uncontrollable fit of red coughing burst from his lungs. 'When there is life, Benjamin... there must be death.'

'Father I don't—'

'Do not fear it, lad. Dragon Claw... it runs on opposites, for where there is death... again... there will be... life.' The boy watched his father's eyes close and head lean "idiotically" as his master would have said, to the left. 'Take care of your brother, son. Empora... belongs to you.' Kraal choked on a flood of his own blood. 'Don't let that son of a bitch Lozari take it from you!'

Before Benjamin's tears had a chance of falling, a panting voice pushed through from behind. 'My lord, what are our orders?' Benjamin turned to see

Kraal's brother, Farah Syrus, but instead of looking to Kraal, his eyes lay on the thirteen-year-old boy.

Farah was a broad man, pushing forty, perhaps even thirty had he a rough life.

Benjamin stood to face his uncle. His forehead reached only the man's blood-stained beard. Orders? He had to laugh again, as all that entered his mind in that moment was the memory of having once been threatened by Farah – threatened to live his days in a dungeon were he to interrupt his father's council meetings again. Now, this same man stands to asks for orders.

'We fall back,' Emperor Benjamin Syrus commanded. 'Go find Alexander Fallen and pull out my men.'

'But, my lord, Emperor Kraal signed a treaty with the United Dragons. If you pull out of this battle, Khosi Trajan will—'

'Kraal's reign has ended, Farah. And I assure you, I signed for nothing!' Not calling him uncle for the first time didn't feel the least bit strange. The fact that it didn't feel strange was *strange. 'Look, if our report is to be trusted, Parra Rapture's crazed son has taken the head of Raylan Fallen. My order is to*

retreat. This battle belongs to Lozari. For now, I'm afraid Empora belongs to Rapture.'

***

Folk never questioned the mysterious disappearance of Parra Rapture, for due to the vast accusations of his alleged involvement in Prince Thaddeus' death, the heartless emperor was thought to have simply abandoned his people. Alas, the War of Four had indeed begun and Ramoria was considered weak for a time. There was but one heir to the throne to again raise power across the land, regardless how dangerous he may in fact be. Lozari Rapture.

The two reports arrived at Siren almost simultaneously. A half smile cut thickly through Lozari's dark skin when hearing of Sir Joje Sebastian's victory at the Battle of Quae. How he dreamed of himself taking Kraals pitiful life to avenge the death of his brother. Of course, Lozari had indeed been busy assisting Raylan Fallen by... well, taking the weight off his shoulders. What else was Lozari to do? He was nineteen years of age with only spider legs for facial hair when that bastard hung him cold, wet and naked, upside-down in the Shabrathian Dungeons. Cell D1-3183. He would never forget.

The two High Knights, each with a single scroll held tightly at their grasp, marched smugly into Lozari's small council. Sir Francis Sebastian was a clean-shaven man with dark, grey eyes. Not like a clouded night, but more a dusty shelf. Sir Phillop Roman was a large man of beyond seven feet tall. As a child, Phillop had worked for Roman & Robinson Funeral Directors, taking the job title of Dismantler of the Dead. It was when Lozari's wife, Savanah Rapture passed while giving birth, the emperor met Phillop Roman. A mere boy of eight-years-old he was and already Phillop stood taller and thicker than Lozari did. Phillop Roman was able to raise Savanah's coffin onto his left shoulder with no assistance, carrying it three miles from Siren to the funeral home. Such strength in the child. Lozari immediately forced him into training. No more would Phillop Roman spend his days as Dismantler of Dead, but rather a creator of it.

The emperor gave a first nod to Francis Sebastian and the young man unravelled a scroll with the mark of a white serpent's skull. The mark of a monster, *Lozari knew. Interest hit.*

Dear Lozari Harlam Rapture,

Emperor of Ramoria,

Fear not the sender of this scroll. It is I, Joje Sebastian. I acquired it from a prisoner of mine so that I could write to you with both good fortune and ill. Kraal Syrus is dead. His first son Benjamin now rules the Syrus army.

The Fallen family are now only to be remembered through songs and poems thanks to you. I write these words with great honour and pride: Posre and Empora now belong to you, Rapture. However, the United Dragons are still strong; I do not doubt that Benjamin Syrus will fight for his throne at Empora.

I hold two warriors in chains, a vampire priest and a mage, both I believe fought for the United Dragons. I await only your order for their fates. Though, I doubt not that any survivors will continue to fight against us.

On a darker note, our trusted ally Sarajai Sharjal, sorcerer and leader of the Black Magic is dead. But I warn you, the death of Sarajai was no work of Khosi Trajan, for the sorcerer was last reported headed to Ramoria, with crazed chants of seeing a Matra in his nightmares. I fear this news terribly, sire. (*Your father and I once experienced this too,* Joje Sebastian had thought whilst writing, but chose not to include it.)

With your word, Sire, I will sail back to Ramoria at once.

Loyally,

Sir Joje Sebastian

Loyally: a redundant end.

With the death of his old friend Sarajai Sharjal, Joje Sebastian was perhaps the only person across Dragon Claw Lozari could wholly trust. His father had known the Sebastian family long before Lozari was born. Marrying into a family so large and wealthy had been an additional advantage, given that Parra had married Korine for love. At least, that was what Thaddeus and Lozari would tell themselves, for the boys did often catch their father playing a most unfaithful game with the maid, Dana or Deena (or perhaps both?) Blonde, small, curvy and mouthy in all the right ways.

Aside from Parra Rapture– who had successfully hidden his secret from his children for many years – Sarajai Sharjal and Yakub Sebastian were the only others Lozari had known to own a gift like his. Sorcery *they had called it: an uncontrollable use of a magic much more powerful and darker than any other.*

'Do you wish to reply, my lord?' Francis Sebastian asked.

He is nothing like his father, or even his father's father, Lozari thought. *'Yes, yes, but nothing written.*

I will have you sail to Quae at once with an army of five— no, make it ten thousand. Tell your father to retain his guard upon Empora and to execute all survivors. You'll take an extra ship for weaponry alone. Our end game with Trajan closes in. I can practically taste his blood at my lips.' He gave a second nod to Sir Phillop Roman, and without a single word the large man unravelled his unmarked scroll and with a deep, scraping voice read:

Emperor Lozari Rapture,
Sorcerer of Ramoria,

> Forget your Empire; forget yourself. While Kulla burns, the Ladybird has unlocked the gates to a crooked world! Enter the cabin. Enter the gates to a powerful world.

Lozari rose from the Orca in a state of urgency, snatching the scroll from Roman's large hands. 'What signature? Boy, who gave you this message?' But the emperor did not wait for a reply. He already knew the answer, for she had already spoken the same words to him in his nightmares.

***

That night, an intolerable sleep fell upon Lozari. He could see the Fallen chains once more attached, only this time it was not at his own wrists, but his father's. Lozari dared not to call out his name, for even in his unconscious mind he felt the shame he had that day he was kidnapped.

'As the flowers grow and the rivers run,' Raylan Fallen smiled a thin, dark grin. 'The sun will burn and burn will the son.' The long-haired, cloaked boy turned and looked directly into Lozari's eyes. 'The sun will burn and burn will the son. The sun will burn and burn will the son.' Only, now his face belonged not to Raylan, but to Khosi Trajan. The voice of the Matra soon pounded into his mind. 'Forget your Empire; forget yourself,*' she said.* 'Enter the gates to a powerful world.*'*

Khosi Trajan reached out to Parra Rapture's chest and removed his still-beating heart and Lozari woke with force, clutching at his own chest. He woke, finding himself alone amid Fortunae Forest.

And yet, it was not Lozari's nightmare, nor the peculiar place in which he awakened that were the most disturbing things to occur on that night, but the face of the strange girl...

'*...Staring curiously at him through the window of a crooked cabin,*' Caesar finished with a long and tired sigh. 'Indeed, Lozari abandoned the Ramorian Empire and following the footsteps of his father, should we say, disappeared into thin air for a time. After being declared missing, Lozari Rapture soon reappeared in Ramoria, but he was never the same. He had discovered a power beyond all imagination.'

Caesar checked the time and noticed the darkness looming through the window. 'Dear me, I think that'll do for now, time doth turns and I'm sure Sara will be wondering where you have gotten to.' The old professor smashed the book shut, forcing dust to burst out like confetti. 'Quite fascinating though, ay lad?'

'Huh?' Michael was lay awkwardly across the floor. The blood previously running through his veins had been replaced by discomfort, rapidly streaming within his muscles. 'Oh yes,' Michael yawned. 'Very interesting stuff indeed. I particularly enjoyed that last part about the uh—dragon?'

'Hmm.' Caesar enjoyed more than anything to spend time with the boy, but he knew when it was time to stop. Oh, how Michael once loved listening to the old professor's grand tales all night long. But of course, boys must be boys. 'Here,' he smiled, shoving the book to Michael's chest. 'Take this with you and take good care of it. Might be you'll learn something new. Something quite magical, perhaps.'

'Caesar, really I-'

'Not another word, no, no I won't have it. Make sure you run straight home now Michael. Oh, and do remember,' he winked. 'Books bake bigger brains, boy.'

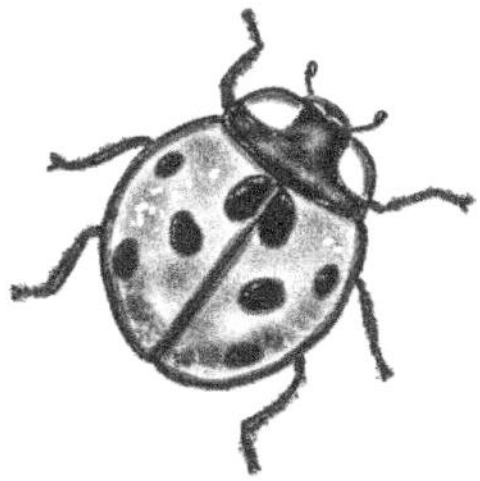

Chapter Thirteen

An Honest Liar

Caesar Azerius sat across from the window, waving at the boy who vanished from sight through the trees with the small, leather book tightly in his grip. The moon's bright beam dipped and dove through the forest, rendering a relentless blindness upon Caesar's vision. 'Hmm,' he smiled, directing his gaze towards the one corner of the room that the moonlight refused to hit. 'My, how long it has been.' He spoke firmly, as if to no-one. 'Course, Michael did not see you back there, heck I almost couldn't.' Awkwardly, the professor rose from his armchair and bowed loyally before a dark shadow which now stood erect and motionless in the corner. 'I wondered how long it might take for you to show, Zagan. Goodness, the last time I saw you, you were in your early twenties.' Caesar paused sadly. 'I take it that Ella-Rose now has Nyla's half of the medallion piece?'

The dark shadow entered the moonlight and transformed into an old man wearing rags at his body and an eye-patch attached to his left eye. 'Aye, she does. And now Michael holds the book.'

The professor let out a hearty laugh. 'Convinced the boy it was just another book of war, I did. I shared the harsh history of the Raptures.'

'Good,' said Zagan. 'I hope you understand there is no other way. I wish there was. To put these children in danger is the last thing I ever wanted.'

Caesar let out a long, exasperated huff. 'I do. Though, it surely was difficult to keep secrets from them for all those years.'

'You truly are the most honest liar I have ever met.'

To this, Caesar let out an old chuckle. 'The other piece of the medallion – is it still hidden?'

Zagan raised the eye patch, which so tightly clung to his face, and gave the area an itch. 'Aye, it still lies within the crooked world. None but Ella-Rose will ever find it, believe me.'

Caesar nodded, leaving his gaze at his feet. 'Pardon my asking Zagan, but how exactly did Nyla came to have the other medallion piece?'

The sorcerer pondered this for a moment. Of course, he wished to dismiss the question and say: *Why, because that was what the prophecy had foretold*, but he knew that just wouldn't cut it. 'She had it because of a mistake I made fifty years ago.' The old man pulled a chair that had been tucked at the table where the Daily Scoop lay. He glanced at the headline, but gave no heed to it. 'As you know, when the medallion split and the gates were opened, one piece fell inside, where still it hides to this day, while the other remained here on Dragon Claw.'

Caesar leaned in, the same way Michael had when listening to the professor's tales earlier that day.

'Fifty years ago, it was agreed that my brother and I would protect the two pieces. I would take care of the piece within the gates and he would protect the piece belonging to Dragon Claw. I made the mistake of trusting Thanisis to hide it from both Nyla and Eliza. How foolish of me! I always knew he was drawn towards destruction, yet still I trusted him.

He blamed only two people for the death of our father. Benjamin Syrus for slaying Lozari and Nyla for opening those gates.'

'And you? Do you blame Nyla?'

'The only one I blame for this chaos is myself. I should never have let this get so out of hand. Before giving the piece to Thanisis, there was a time I held the complete medallion in my own hands. I could have closed the gates there and then, but like Lozari before me, I felt drawn to its power.'

'You are nothing like your father! Zagan, you spent fifty years in that cabin to fulfil a prophecy that could have ultimately led to nothing. None of us knew that Ella-Rose and Michael would even be born, nor that you would reach Ella-Rose's mind through her dreams. All we could do was lay our trust in the prophecy. And thank the Great One we did, because everything has gone to plan. Don't you see? The children will soon close the gates to this crooked world and rid us of that demon forever. Dragon Claw will be free of war. The prophecy has not been wrong yet.'

Zagan brushed the sharp stubble at his chin and calmly closed his eye. 'You're right. Of course you're right.'

'Now, about the medallion – you said Thanisis had the other piece, how did it fall into Nyla's hands?'

Zagan took a deep breath. 'He wanted her to suffer for the death of our father. Suffer for the rest of her life. What better way to do that than to give her the one piece of her past that will serve as a constant reminder that she had lost everything?' Zagan rose from the chair, almost knocking it to the ground.

'He gave it to Nyla, knowing it could lead only to destruction.' 'Fortunately, the prophecy held strong and she came to me in search of the other piece. I never should have trusted him. I'm so sorry-'

'Sorry? My, you've nothing to be sorry about. It was never luck that brought her to you, just as it was never your fault that your brother was named protector of the other piece. Our hands are forced by our destiny. You have taken the piece from Nyla and now Ella-Rose has it in her possession. As I said, the prophecy has not been wrong yet.'

Zagan hobbled towards the professor's Good Arm and knelt before him. 'You really are a true and wonderful friend, Caesar Azerius.'

'Please,' the professor shot his voice as quickly as he could. 'Zagan, the least *you* could do is call me by my birth name.'

'Of course,' Zagan shared a half smile. 'Thank you, Sir Joje Sebastian.'

PART TWO
The Ladybird

'That's because there's no such place as here,' Coccin explained, wafting his tiny arms about the emptiness. He fluttered up to Ella-Rose's head and pointed a tiny arm at her temple. 'There's only here.'

'Then, why is it so dark? So cold and... lonely?'

'Because unfortunately dear girl, the mind can often be a dark, cold and lonely place.'

Chapter Fourteen
Creep

Michael's journey back to Shayam Village usually estimated just less than half an hour; he always did enjoy a long stroll through Fortunae at night. The trees watched caringly over him, all aligned at attention as he plodded along the path; the whistling breeze accompanied in sync with the songs of swaying leaves. Even the noisy flow of the White River beside him made no effort to disrupt the evening's tranquillity. Although the sun had long since fallen, the temperature still stood high and mighty. Michael soon became drenched in sweat. His clothes stuck annoyingly against his back at every step. He leaned in close to the white stream, watering himself down with hope of the wind's cool offering.

The forest was peaceful. The world was peaceful. Until Caesar's voice pushed briskly into the front of his mind. *Books bake bigger brains, boy.*

'No professor. More like bigger books bake boy's brains!' he laughed, eying the nameless book that weighed down his hand. He had indeed enjoyed listening to the tales of the War of Four, but how anyone wished to sit and stare at those things for hours every single day was beyond him. 'Man, what an old piece of—'

'Excuse me?'

Michael turned. The small, gruffly voice came from behind two bushes that appeared grey in the darkness.

'Excuse me,' the bush blurted once more. 'How rude it is to name one "old"!'

'Wh— but I wasn't talking to anyone in particular, I was saying that this book is—'

'Why, there is not another soul in sight,' the bush muffled and shuffled. 'In such case, I believe it is only myself with whom to speak, correct?'

'Not true,' Michael smirked. 'Could I not speak to myself?'

'Mm, indeed you might. Although folk around these parts might consider one who converses alone must surely lack sanity.'

Michael had to think about this for a moment. 'Why in the world would that be crazy? Some of the greatest things I hear come from my own mouth.' A sly grin formed at his cheeks as he peered ever so slowly behind the bushes. 'I mean, I enjoy my own company just as much as talking to a man as yourself—' abruptly, he stopped. Only now did Michael consider that talking to this forest stranger in the evening might not have been the best course of action.

'Ah, but you ought not to suppose that when addressing one who sounds like a man, it is in fact a man, for I am not.'

'What?' Michael moved quicker now for inspection and behind the bush there sat a peculiar-looking animal sharing similar attributes to that of a sphinx cat, only much less desirable. Its skin was wrinkled and grey, its eyes large and yellow. If Michael were to describe the thing in only one word, it would have to be *ugly*. He would use that word often when describing his twin sister. Thank the Great One they were not identical.

'What are you?'

'Why, I am a paug,' the thing told the boy.

'And does this particular paug have a name?'

The paug was confused at this. The stretching of its skin when it raised one eyebrow was a disturbing image. It reminded Michael of an elephant's wrinkly trunk. 'Nobody has ever asked a paug its name. A paug is nobody and nobody is a paug.'

'But you are a paug,' Michael rolled his eyes, not rudely, but curiously.

'I am nobody,' the paug continued to riddle.

Michael lay the nameless book atop a dry patch of grass to pull his deck of Enchantments from his pocket. 'In my entire life I have never heard of such a creature and I collect Enchantments, see!' He shuffled past sorcerers, dragons, elves and fairies, but there were indeed no paugs.

'Enchan-wha?' the paug sniffed. 'In the name of great Jra'bral, do you speak with an ill-tongue?' he cautioned.

'Who's Jrabble?'

'Who's Jra'bral?' the paug repeated with a high-pitched tone – a tone that essentially called Michael an idiot. 'You have got to be kidding me! Master Jra'bral? *The* Master Jra'bral? Really not ringing any bells?'

Michael stared blankly.

'Well, I suppose you are quite lucky.'

'Perhaps if I look through my Enchant—'

'Well, if you do not speak with an ill-tongue,' the paug said, blatantly ignoring Michael's words. 'Then I fear it must be this log that has so selfishly fallen atop my leg has somehow cut the blood flow to my brain.'

Michael clocked the small branch to which the creature referred, placed so delicately on the poor paug's leg. To say it was a log was a massive exaggeration.

'Boy, do remove this blasted log and I assure you may name me as you wish.'

'Oh gosh, yes, right away,' he spoke apologetically, raising the small piece of wood like he would a feather.

'Ah, I thank you, sir. I thank you indeed. Now, as proposed, why don't you name me as you please?'

Michael pondered his thoughts for a spell. The paug did not suit a name of a person like Tom or Dave, nor would he suit a pet name like Spot or Scratchy, (most certainly not Fluffy.) At last, he smirked and firmly said, '*Creep.* Yeah, reckon I'll call you Creep. Suits you well.'

'Creep?' announced the freed paug, standing on two legs. 'Yes, yes I quite like that. I like that very much. Thank you for that. We have only just met and already I am thanking you a second time.' Creep smiled deviously. 'And I will thank you a third for this!' The paug swiftly stole the small, leather book that rested so casually on the ground and bolted through the trees before Michael could even take his next breath.

'Hey, hey get back here! That doesn't belong to you,' Michael raged, as he pursued the creature through the dark forest. 'Stop, thief!'

Creep ignored his words and continued across the sticks and stones like a blur in the breeze, sniggering at his accomplishment. He was certainly quick and strategic, dodging each tree perfectly, as though he knew the area well and had perhaps done this before.

Michael could hardly match his speed. He could practically see the disappointment pushing through Caesar's grey bushy beard.

The book was gone.

All hope was lost.

Until…

WHACK!

Out of sheer luck, the boy watched as Creep unintentionally tripped and fell over himself, smashing straight into a pile of dead leaves. He caught the creature mere seconds later, pinning him forcefully to the ground and allowed an exhaustingly heavy breath of relief from his lungs. 'Yes, yes! Got you!'

Michael half expected to be glared at by the eyes of defeat and surrender. However, the horror and fear that the paug's eyes actually shared gave an unsettling turn to his stomach. Not because Michael gave the impression he was going to hurt the creature, but because Creep's gaze was not directed into Michael's panting face at all, but instead at the darkness that formed eerily behind the boy.

'*Yes*,' the Darkness whispered from behind. '*We have got you.*'

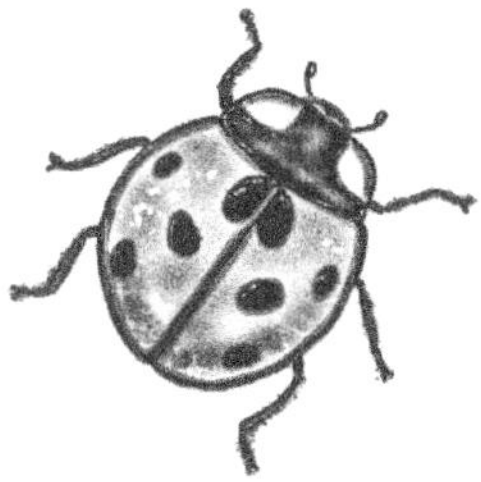

Chapter Fifteen
The Sewer

It hadn't taken long for Finn to notice that Ella-Rose had journeyed down a different path. The comforting sound of her following footsteps had long gone. Guilt soon injected itself through his veins; why hadn't he just grabbed her and ran before this all got out of hand? How would he ever forgive himself were anything to happen to her? He wished to turn back, but how could he, with three awful globbers chasing his tail? Before he could find and rescue Ella-Rose, he knew that he must first rid himself of the dark creatures. Though, that was a task easier said than done, for it seemed the more worn out Finn became, the more determined did the monsters. Luckily, the globbers had not clocked Ella-Rose's disappearance, else one would have surely pursued her.

Lucky for her, unlucky for me.

The ground quaked every time their rat-like tails would smash behind. Fairies and nymphs camouflaged in with the tree leaves. Not that they needed to; the darkness only turned the forest blacker and blacker at each second.

Finn put aside his concerns for Ella-Rose as he practised a grand jeté beside every tree. Dipping and dodging past sights he had never seen. Overgrown flowers stood over a metre tall, waterfalls painted purple by the light of the moon.

He knew that his fate belonged now to whichever route he chose to take. Right or left?

No.

If he ever wished to lose them, he knew he ought to not follow a path. His only chance would be through the trees, regardless how dangerous it might be.

'I can't keep up,' Tonzil spat. His lengthy blue tongue flapped all over his face as he slowed to catch a breath.

Finn could hear the frustration and anger that had risen in his voice. Thankfully, it was a voice that had fallen behind.

'Wicked elf,' Zebu shouted from afar.

They're giving up! Finn could tell. His heartbeats cheered for him. *Thank the Great One, they're giving up.*

Although he had slowed to a walk, Finn constantly checked behind his shoulder to make sure the monsters had not caught up. At last, he rewarded himself a victorious rest beneath what seemed an amateurly-built bridge. Below, where there once would have been a brook, was but a brownish slush full of waste and refuse.

Finn gazed at the warfare of stars in the sky. This was not the first time Ella-Rose and he had stayed late in Fortunae. In fact, the two often made a habit of staying late to watch the magnificent mysteries of the night sky. Finn was sure there would be no search parties yet - which was okay - but how he wished that they could just be sat in Shayam, each with a cup of hot chocolate, laughing about the craziness of their nightmarish adventure.

'Oh Ella-Rose,' he heard himself say. 'Where are you?'

He thought, then, of the broken medallion that he so clearly witnessed in her hand. *No*, he thought. *Surely she had just picked up a broken rock or something.* But even he couldn't deny that there was something quite alluring about the thing she had held so tightly in her grasp.

The atmosphere freshened the air with a warm stench of filth and the orange gleam in Finn's eyes turned ruby where the moonlight hit. He climbed to his feet when it seemed the coast was completely clear. Readying to take his leave, suddenly a large gust of wind thumped the small boy as if from nowhere, forcing him down to the ground.

'What the?' Frightened, he searched the area, but was given nothing in return. He did, however, manage to spot the crooked cabin from earlier, standing alone in the distance. He must have ran all the way around those emerald trees and now faced the back of it.

He coolly rose from the mud, overlooking his fall for a mere natural accident. He was only small and it was completely plausible for a strong gust of wind to knock him down, right?

But then it happened again.

And again.

This was no wind he had experienced before.

'Who's there?' Finn cried, climbing once more to his feet. Alas, before the boy could say another word, the powerful invisible force grabbed him by the feet and shoved him down a long, dark, muddy tunnel.

The tunnel consisted mostly of a sloshy, slushy sludge. After falling, for what felt like several minutes, (but was probably only ten seconds,) Finn had to wonder whether he would ever stop. Thankfully, with an enormously loud thud, he was soon back to his feet with bruised and battered elbows and scraped knees.

'Oh, what a day,' he said to himself, trying not to let the torments of the afternoon truly get to him. After all, Finn was always one who could turn the darkest things to light. 'I can't wait to just sit and laugh about this tomorrow.'

His clothes were ruined, covered completely in brown muck. His mother was sure to scold him when he returned.

If he returned. The dreadful thought struck fiercely at his nerves. He shook his head for a quick erase.

His sight was impaired by darkness. He reached out his hand and tickled his fingers across a smooth stone wall. Worry soon took him as his mind returned to the force that had pushed him down the slide. Surely nothing friendly would do such a thing.

Crawling, slowly through what he thought to be a sewer beneath Fortunae, he had to hold his breath to avoid the ghastly smells. Soon, he noticed a ginger, flickering flame opening his sight to what appeared to be a room at the far end of the tunnel. It was not exactly a big, beautiful palace, but at least it looked spacious enough to stand. The room looked to be filled with flowers and paintings, even the smell of jasmine and lavender blasted into his nostrils.

What a strange smell for a sewer.

Finn squinted his eyes, as if narrowing his sight would somehow help his vision. He crawled further through the tunnel, wary of his ways, when suddenly, he heard a faint, soft singing through the muck of his ears.

Hear me now, here I am,
I do all that I can.
I look for you, I search everywhere,
Oh, is anybody out there?

Hear you now, there you are,
We live in a world so bizarre.
All alone, in this lair,
Oh, is anybody out there?

Finn would not let himself be fooled by the sweetness of her voice. *Dark creatures lie beyond the paths,* his father had warned, and his father had been right. How he wished more than anything to crawl back through the tunnel and into his father's arms, but there was no back through which to crawl. There was no possible way he could climb back up that slippery mud slide that brought him to the tunnel. The only way out was through. What other choice did he have?

Though my flowers smile bright,
Among the still of the night.
It's my pleasure to share,
Oh, is anybody out there?

I had a sister once, I think,
She'd smile at me and laugh and wink.
Oh, what a pair they'd say we were,
Oh, is anybody out there?

He could wait her out. Wait until the one with the precious voice leaves or falls asleep, sneak right on through, escape the tunnel and head back home.

What about Ella-Rose? His mind queried. *Oh, she'll be so frightened if she hasn't found her way home. Wait, what am I thinking? Of course she has. Ella-Rose isn't lost.* He pictured everyone at Shayam Village together, hugging a returned Ella-Rose. *I'm lost.*

Now my thoughts turn dark,
I feel it in my beating heart.
I can't escape, I live the nightmare,
Oh, I know, there isn't anybody out there.

Dear, oh dear,
Of course, it's just me here.
Why in the world would anybody care?

'Oh,' her voice turned to a whisper. '*Who is that out there?'*

Finn stopped dead.

'Do not fear, I won't hurt you little one,' she called. 'Come on through.'

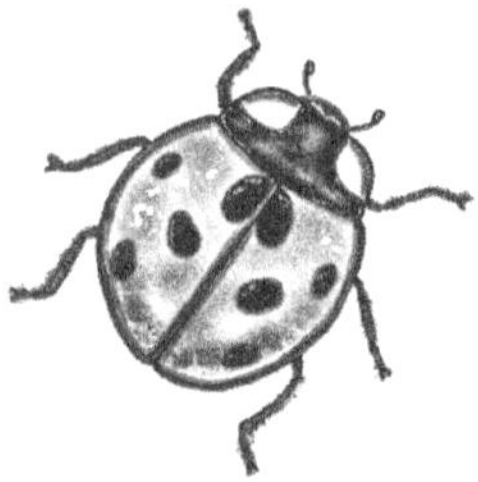

Chapter Sixteen
The Masked Clan

Michael had trouble remembering what happened over the next thirty minutes. He could remember being hauled through the forest in a large sack and he could remember capturing the ruby-red eyes of the masked faces that chained him up against a tree. What he couldn't recall was when Fortunae had turned pitch black. No White Rivers ran, nor emerald leaves fluttered where he stood, tied and powerless. The path was far from golden and the birds daren't offer a melody. Shadows lengthened, while ghostly whispers echoed from nowhere. Yet all Michael's ears could absorb were the slow daunting breaths, banging off the inside of the surrounding masks. He remained quiet and still, filled from head to toe with so much fear that he somehow appeared calm. Scarred, stolen and staring at Death in the eyes, and he felt calm. He used his first moments to his advantage, to uncover any dropped information from his captors. There were three—

No…

There were *at least* three of them. Clothed all in black, with the mark of a white serpent skull carved into the forehead of their masks; an appearance that drove terror through his every nerve. One pulled a long sword behind him, the words *MANKARASH* marked into its side.

Michael recalled the professor once telling tales of such a sword. After the aftermath of the destruction of Hjar, a renowned teacher called John. S. Smith wrote an Aj'ayahic-Luminous dictionary, in which the Aj'ayahic term *mankarash* translated into the words *torture and massacre.* It was written in the Testament of Man that, in this world, there will always be life and there will always be death, but mankar*ash* will stand between the two. Both a mercy and a pain, freedom and fate, love and hate. The sword itself was later created nearing the end of the War of Four, rumoured to be forged by the Matra using blood of angels and souls of demons. A gift meant only for the vampire priest, Jra'bral, in exchange for something he held quite precious to her.

The other two members of the masked clan stood with arrows against their backs, one with a jewelled quiver, the other, golden. Clearly, this group kept no true home; Michael had figured that from watching the ease with which they set up camp. It was as Mad Mandi used to say in those Chiller Killer Comics: *when you live nowhere, you live everywhere.* What Michael could not determine, however - the one thing that sent shivers up and down his spine – was not knowing what they were going to do with him. He simply stood silently and still, in limbo between life and death. *Mankarash.*

'Well, well, well, what do we have here?' Jewelled Quiver asked, pleasantly intimidating.

'Looks a pair o' trespassers,' said Golden Quiver with a harsher, colder voice.

Although the intimidation hit the boy hard, it failed to land on the paug tied to the tree beside him.

'I do beg your pardon,' Creep called out, addressing the one with the long sword directly. 'What ho! Yes, you there, the one in the mask,' he chuckled. 'I jest of course, I see you're all in masks.'

The paug blew a sharp-toothed whistle through the side of his mouth. 'Since you're simply standing back there in this pitiful darkness, observing these two fashion contest runner-up's – *ladies and gentlemen, introducing the new fashion trend... tacky white masks*! Am I right?'

Jewelled Quiver and Golden Quiver shared a look. If Michael could have seen through their masks, he would have sworn they offered the same scrunched up, bewildered facial expression as his.

'Ahem,' Creep continued. 'Well I'd bet my tiny pink bollocks you're the big-boy boss. Allow me to level with you, sir; I have had a god-awful day, just god-awful. First, this humongous log falls on me from the heavens, then this, this cretin-boy—'

The tall man holding Mankarash closed in to the small creature, nodding along to his sorry tale – sardonically, Michael guessed.

'—a cretin who, might I add, has bugger all to do with myself. If it suits you, as does me, Mr Mask, I'll be on my merry way, yes?'

Sniggering stirred from the other two masked members, while Mr Mask remained perfectly still; no muscle moved, nor sound was made. After a few seconds, however, which to Michael felt like a lifetime, Mr Mask leant in even closer to the paug and merely said, with a small croak of a voice: 'Suits you, does it?' It was only through his eyes that Michael saw the wide-toothed grin painted on his face. 'You're sure you wouldn't appreciate a glass of plunkberry wine before you head off? A slice of pie perhaps, Mr uh?'

'Oh, ah, uh, Creep,' was all that came to mind. 'Yes, Creep's the name and I do say, that sounds just delightful.' The small creature smiled toothlessly and reached out his roped arms as if to be rescued. 'Apologies, Mr Mask sir, but I don't think I quite caught your true name.'

'My name?' The man with the long sword stood back and he stood tall. His build was large, but disproportionate like a warrior untrained. During his youth, he might have taken on an entire army with his bare hands, though it was obvious he had weakened with age, (or perhaps something else.) 'I've held many a name in my time, but you two can know me as *Darkness*.' Each word landed so sharply. His breath cut right through the mask. 'Wish to know why?' And, with a rapid hit, swung as if from nowhere, he beat the creature's chin with a smack of the back of his hand. 'Because you'll never see me coming.'

Clicking and cracking his jaw, Creep listened to the musical ringing in his ears before passing out in a daze against the tree.

Michael clocked, in the corner of his eye, the other two masked figures searching through his belongings. Scrolling through the Enchantment Cards, Jewelled Quiver, whom he overheard was actually named Yolanda, threw every one of them into the mud. Down fell Parra and Lozari Rapture, Kraal and Benjamin Syrus. It was when she reached the last of his cards that Michael's stomach tightened, for she studied this card with such a harsh hesitation before whispering something to Golden Quiver, whose name Michael supposed was Spider, but had perhaps misheard. When at last she threw the final card down, Michael's focus followed the eyes of Agarov, the Great White Wolf as they staring up at him. Once the ground was completely covered in the multi-colour of Enchantments, Yolanda at last raised Caesar's nameless book and called out to Darkness, 'You're going to want to come see this, Kai-Sal.'

Kai-Sal? Michael didn't recognise the name.

His heart pounded fast and fierce. *Take good care of the book,* Caesar's voice strolled again, uninvitingly into his mind. This was the second time it had been stolen from him. He had to do something. Something… anything… 'H-Hey,' he called out, fearfully brave. 'Take my Enchantments, but p-please leave the book alone.' The words blurted out uncontrollably. His heart stopped.

Thoughtlessly, Yolanda launched the book to the ground and charged towards the boy, arm raised for an attack. She was so quick, had Michael blinked, he was sure he'd have missed her coming. Luckily, Darkness - or Kai-Sal - was quick to obstruct. Without a single word, he removed the mask from his face and directed his gaze onto Michael.

'Where did you get that book, lad?'

'I-I…'

Kai-Sal then gave Michael the look one would give to a well-behaved dog who had suddenly snapped and bit its owner. Perhaps, he felt a slight sympathetic towards the boy. But of course, a dog who bites must be disciplined.

Michael studied the face of Darkness, quickly as to avoid frustrating him any further. He was probably only thirty years old, but Michael was almost certain he looked to be in his fifties. Why he even wore the mask was a mystery, for the burned and scarred face beneath was far more terrifying. Had there once been a shred of beauty in this man, it left no trace.

You ought not to suppose that when addressing one who sounds like a man, it is in fact a man, Creep's voice travelled into his mind and Michael finally understood. Looking into the face of Darkness, he saw not a man, but a monster.

Chapter Seventeen
Cold Awakening

Moonlight often shone brighter than the sun over Fortunae Forest; the sapphire night skies would gleam with the luminescence of fairies; unlit bungalows and cottages sat silently in tranquillity watching the entire population of Ramoria lay to rest. Soothing winds offered their exotic blooms and pleasant tunes.

That was how she knew. She was no longer in Fortunae Forest.

The once beaming, orange skies had not turned sapphire, but instead a lifeless grey. The tree leaves had forgotten their famous glisten, holding nothing less now than a thick lining of…

Snow?

Like the drop of a white petal at the end of its bloom, the snowflake glided elegantly and dissolved into her palm. Ella-Rose awakened once again this day, attempting to attach what consciousness she had back to her physical body. Unfortunately, the only reply she received was the screaming concussion burning at the sides of her head. Peering down at her broken self, she noticed that her left leg had twisted unnaturally and most menacingly to the left. As she brushed the white fluff off her thigh, all signs of physical pain were yet to arrive; a visit to which she would not look forward.

As soon as she came to, her thoughts entered only the bleakest of places. Dark creatures picking at chunks of Finn meat between their teeth; rinsing their mouths with his blood—

'Stop!' she forced.

Not her legs, nor her arms gave out any discomfort. Only her head. Certainly not the physical ache that a lump would have given from a fall, no, this was a screeching, screaming and scraping throughout her mind. A squealing voice, rampaging through, sounding somewhat familiar. The more powerful the voice grew, the more she believed it belonged to Finn. Screams ran rampant in her brain. *'Ella-Rose... Ella-Rose,'* it yelled, worsening the migraine.

'I'm here,' she called out, 'I'm right here!'

But where exactly was *here*?

Perhaps it may have once been common across the cities of Danjin, but a summer snowfall in Ramoria was completely unheard of.

The last thing Ella-Rose remembered was falling— falling into what seemed a dark abyss of *nothingness*. But it wasn't nothingness, it was *white*. And something can't possibly be nothing, right? Was it at that moment she lost consciousness? At that moment she had lost her mind?

The soft petals became more determined to ferociously fall. She gave a moment to adjust with Dragon Claw's new motions.

Backwards. How else could she describe it? The world had gone insane.

Her brown hair turned white, her lips blue. Whether or not the numbness from the unendurably low temperature came as an advantage was still undecided. Beyond the confused, disorderly placed trees, she heard wolves perform their famed rendition of *Hunger*; a song with which she had now become ever so familiar; her stomach frequently played a similar tune.

Thrusting her arm from beneath its burial, she struggled in her numerous attempts to rise. Bruising ran monstrously across her thighs. Suddenly, a menacing heat emerged beneath her. The thick, ice desert upon where she lay was so cold it scorched.

She could feel it. Only for a moment.

That rules out death, she thought. *Or does it?*

Her thoughts of home soon warmed her, though the discomfort in her leg came viciously next. Fortunately, Ella-Rose managed to get to her feet. Hobbling alone amongst the icy mists, she searched the loathsome desolation for a soul. At last, she spotted a sign atop the snow.

A sign of life.

By the time Ella-Rose reached the wood, her breath was still trying to catch up. She collapsed onto it, holding her weight using the palms of her hands and read aloud to herself:

Labyrinth is Deadly

Yet, the only labyrinth she knew of, was the muddled maze within her mind. There was no labyrinth in sight. At least, not the type she was familiar with.

Finn and Ella-Rose had once created a maze out of old toys when they were five years old. She recalled tripping over Finn's old train set and grazing her knee. Of course, a grazed knee to a five-year-old is the same as being sliced open with a knife. The labyrinth was deadly.

It was then she realised that she actually recognised the sign. Not the words written upon it, but the wood itself appeared charred, as if once burned.

'How strange,' she said.

Then, a most peculiar thing happened. A small red and black-spotted ladybird glided elegantly along the whistling air and landed at the back of her hand. She watched it slowly crawl and tickle across to her arm. How peaceful it looked.

'Why can't my life be as simple as yours?' she asked the bug.

And much to her dismay, the ladybird coolly replied: 'Not so easy at all, I would say.'

'W-What?'

'Name's Coccin L. Idae,' the beetle smiled. *Actually smiled.* And though the ladybird's back appeared partly broken and misshapen and missing a couple of his legs, it did not stop his positive energy. 'Coccin to some. Though, friends say I'm Cocky. Co always seems to do the trick.'

For a brief second, Ella-Rose thought she somehow recognised that name, but she couldn't help but stare in absolute awe at the talking beetle.

'Just kidding,' he laughed. 'I don't have any friends.'

'Y-You spoke? But you're a… a…. oh, stop it Ella-Rose! You've had a nasty fall and now you're stuck in a bad dream is all. Another nightmare.' She shook her head, causing the pain to triple. 'I'm so sorry, Mr uh, Coccin. But you see, I have no time to lose my mind. I need to go back.' *Back to Finn.* 'I just—I just don't recognise anywhere around.'

Coccin threw a confused look Ella-Rose's way. 'Well, of course you don't recognise anywhere around here,' he laughed rather matter-of-factly. 'Yer *not* actually here.'

She tried to return an answer, but nothing came to mind.

'Then,' Coccin went on. 'What do yer expect in a world that don't exist?'

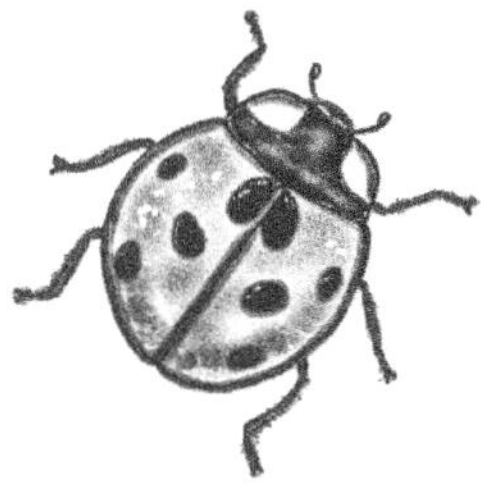

Chapter Eighteen
The Little White Mouse

As the shadowed outline of the girl closed in on him, Finn instantly realised that it wasn't actually a girl at all. It was a woman. An ancient woman in fact, probably not much younger than Professor Caesar. Though, through what must have been some peculiar enchantment, from certain angles, the woman in fact appeared a similar age to his.

He felt lured by her very being, but was quick to hug himself to the sewage wall. Camouflaged by the mud of his clothes, he was practically hidden in plain sight. The task was needless, because as he held his small body tightly against the brown splodge, (which he hoped was mud,) he soon realised that the unknown woman hadn't actually seen him, but something else entirely. Finn turned quickly to look behind, but he saw nothing in the darkness. Suddenly, something ran rapidly across his feet. He turned once more towards the girl's gaze, trying his best to blend into the darkness. It had not been Finn the woman had seen from the lit room, rather a little white mouse who had crawled through a tiny hole behind him.

'Come on in, little one,' the woman smiled loosely. The whites of her teeth shined brightly.

Finn's face beamed as he watched her raise the ball of fur so delicately and gently in both hands. She did not appear dangerous at all. Strange perhaps. After all, she is talking to a mouse inside a sewer, but there was no way she could have been behind his unnatural pull down into the tunnel.

'Oh, you too, little one,' the woman spoke once more. 'Yes, I see you. Do come on in when you're ready, Finn.'

A single drop of sweat ran from his temple and dropped down off his chin. His heart stopped and not a single muscle would offer a flinch. Only now did the tunnel's temperature become unbearable. It was as though he'd been shoved into a sewage oven, roasted, toasted and ready to be served to the worms.

No, how could she have seen me through this darkness? He must have heard her wrong. *Pin sounds like Finn. Yes, grin, chin, twin sounds like Finn. That's it,* a quiet sigh of relief released from his tiny body. *She has surely found a second mouse. A twin mouse, a-*

'Do come in,' the soft voice called, looking directly at the muddy child. 'You can't stay in that muddy tunnel all night, Finn.'

There was no mistaking it. *Finn sounds like Finn.*

The woman lowered the mouse gently and it scurried past the mud-covered boy and back into its hole. How he wished he could be that little white mouse, just for the moment.

A harsh, daunting silence took the tunnel where he stood for a day-long minute. What else could he do other than tuck his own tail between his legs and enter the room that oozed scents of jasmine and lavender? How different it was to find himself in such a well-decorated space through the unadorned tunnel of muck. A healthy, calm ambience breathed out from the variety of pictures hanging on the walls. Abstract acrylic apples; orange oiled owls; carved crooked cabins. The saturation of the painted sun brought light and warmth inside.

'Hello,' the woman smiled, beautifully. She could have looked seventeen, perhaps twenty from afar, but as Finn studied her face closely, he could see the many, many painful years she had lived.

'I've been waiting for you, Finn.' Her long, white hair flicked ostentatiously behind as she went to greet the boy. 'Dear me, you have had a disastrous day, haven't you, with those awful creatures at your tail. Just look how dirty your clothes have become,' she smiled, tickling her finger down his once-white t-shirt.

'Um—'

'Oh, and poor Ella-Rose, I do hope Coccin takes good care of her over there.' As she frowned, the calm freckles, surrounding her nose, showed in the light.

Finn found that he could not help but gaze into the lavender eyes that were fixed onto his own. As he searched her face, he noticed she had a small gap resting between her lips whenever she closed her mouth and thought it took the shape of a heart. The voice that swam so pleasantly from her lips must have been the prettiest sound he ever did hear. There was no denying the elegance of this woman. Which, of course, invited the question: what business would a woman like this have in a sewer? Living in a sewer?

He thought back to the Legend of Eliza. Remembered the sewer beneath Kulla where a young girl had hidden to escape the cruel McArthurs. And wasn't there a boy named Co—

'I'm so happy you're here. Do you understand what this means? Why, no I guess you won't.' Was she speaking to him or to herself? 'The prophecy – it's coming true,' she went on. 'I'm sorry, I'm so sorry, I'm getting far too ahead of myself, Finn.'

'H- How do you know my name?' he asked nervously.

She considered this a moment, almost bewildered by the question. 'Well, I've been watching you.' Now, her sweet voice immediately turned sinister.

Finn backed up slowly, hitting the sewer wall behind and nearly knocking the picture of the crooked cabin to the ground. 'W-What do you mean?' He moved quickly to head back to where he had fallen down, hoping, praying there was an escape, but he slipped on some mud and landed straight on his back as he tried.

What did it matter? Of course there was nowhere he could go.

'Oh no,' the woman stood over Finn in less than a second. How she managed to move so quickly he did not know. 'Please don't be afraid.'

'N-No, no it's not you. I'm sorry, I just have to go back for my friend, you see,' Finn insisted, struggling back to his feet. 'Th-Thanks for everything though, it really was nice of you to invite me, Miss um—'

The little white mouse scurried back over to the woman and she picked it up once more, gleefully. 'Eliza,' she finished with a beautiful smile. 'My name is Eliza.'

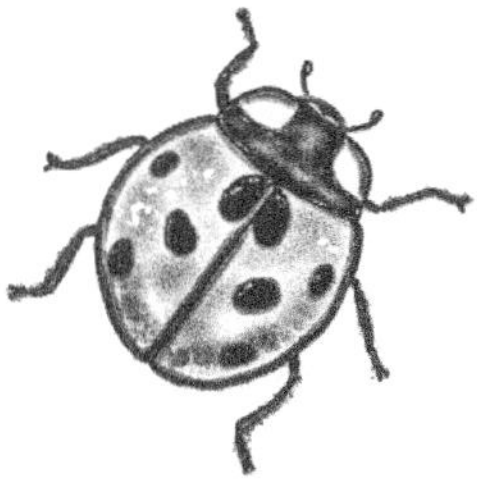

Chapter Nineteen
The Beast

It was noticeable in the force with which the knots had been tightened that this was not the first time the masked group had tied someone against a tree and it would probably not be the last. Michael's arms grew tired as the vines burned at his wrists. He tried to free himself, but it was without hope. Both Michael and his fate were well and truly stuck. Not to mention Creep, who still stood unconscious at the tree beside him. Although he knew the paug was the cause of all his problems, he couldn't help but feel sorry for him. He didn't deserve this – no-one did.

Dark skies faded in; darker noises shortly followed. Spider raised the book carelessly from the ground and examined it with fear painted over his face. 'This is it, right Kai-Sal? I mean, it must be.'

'How could it possibly be?' Yolanda argued. 'Why on earth would the boy have it? Last we heard, Zagan had recently given it to the Sebastian man.'

'Might be he stole it,' Spider shrugged.

'From Joje Sebastian?' Kai-Sal pitched in. The name obviously caused a pain from his past. 'Impossible.'

Joje Sebastian? Michael thought. *Wasn't that a name Caesar had mentioned from that very book?*

'Aye, very doubtful,' Yolanda scoffed, rolling her eyes. 'The only way someone else could have it would be if Joje handed it to them himself. Go ahead Spider, open it.'

'I ain't opening it! If that really is what I think it is, there's no way I'm touching it— damn sorcery.' His entire body shivered.

'Oh, don't be such a wimp! Joje isn't a sorcerer.'

'Aye, but Zagan is. He'll have put his voodoo all over the thing for Sebastian to have it. You do it!'

'Oh, you really are a—'

'Bring it to me.' Kai-Sal forced his hand, gesturing for the small book. When Spider anxiously placed it in his hand, he studied the leather casing, stroking over the silver-shining symbols in approval. Fearlessly, he opened it to a random page near the middle of the book, then turned to another. Then, another and another and another until, violently he launched the book into the tree just behind Michael's. 'Is this a jest, boy?' he raged. 'Those writings at its cover— those symbols, they feel so real. Argh!' He punched the trunk above where Creep stood, letting loose an angry and frustrated cry. 'Are you a sorcerer in disguise? Is that it? No, I don't believe that, else you'd have had done with us at our first encounter. But this is *the* book. I know it is, so you'd better start talking. Speak the truth now or die a slow and painful death! My friends and I have built up quite a thirst and believe me boy, the blood of a child is always the ripest.'

Blood? There's only one type of monster Michael knew that thirsts on blood. 'Y-You're a— a—'

But before Michael could finish his sentence, not that his tongue ever intended in doing so, Kai-Sal raged once more, this time showing the sharp crystal-white daggers in his mouth. 'Tell me! Why are all those pages blank?'

Blank? Michael couldn't believe it. Wouldn't believe it. How could Caesar have possibly read the very book to him hours ago if the pages were blank? It was impossible. Besides, why did it even matter? What is a book anyway if not a piece of wood without purpose?

No, even Michael no longer believed that. There was something more to this book and the monster certainly knew it.

'Right,' Kai-Sal started, then turned his back to the boy. 'Well then, what are you waiting for?' Only, these words were not addressed to Michael. They instead hit the ears of the two masked monsters in front. 'Bring out the beast!'

***

The last words to escape the lips of Darkness passed so savagely amongst the trees. Michael watched Yolanda march with such intent purpose into the trees and out of sight, muttering few words he could scarcely make out as she left.

'Tell me how you got your hands on this book,' Kai-Sal pushed through gritted teeth, diverting the boy's gaze back to his. Mankarash danced dextrously between both hands. 'Did somebody give it to you?' After a deep inhalation, the unmasked warrior struck the vines holding Michael to the tree, then he sliced at Creep's. They both hit the ground with a thump. The force of their impact forced surrounding leaves to gasp and scatter.

'I—uh,' Michael stuttered, noticing a small message engraved across the blade of his sword beneath the word MANKARASH. "*May they be deserving*."

Had he told the monster it was Caesar who gave him the book, who knows what they would do to the poor old man? 'It's— It's just an old history book is all. T-The War of Four—'

Creep, whose consciousness returned at the ground's impact, without second thought, made a run for the dark forest. Spider was quick to charge and seize the paug by taking hold of his little head in one hand and raising the creature to embarrassingly dangle in the air.

'Off me, you filthy cretin!' he demanded, kicking his legs rapidly in an attempted attack. 'Off me, at once. Master Jra'bral will hear of this, I assure you!'

'For goodness sake, let the creature flee,' Kai-Sal ordered, having again lost patience for the paug's exasperating nature. 'I've no use for the scavenger.'

No use for him, but you have for me? Michael's brain tortured.

Spider dropped the paug and as soon as Creep landed on his feet, he bolted once more to the edge of the forest. 'Well, well, I suppose I ought to thank you all for your generous hospitality.' Creep announced. 'I am of course upset that I never received word it was a fancy-dress gathering,' he motioned a raised eyebrow towards Spider's mask. 'Alas, it is absolutely time for me to be on my way. I daren't say I'll be writing, so farewell forever Mr Darkness and goodbye Mr I-Never-Quite-Caught-Your-Name. Au revoir, yes, au revoir mon ami.' Then, after a few air-blown kisses, Creep was gone.

The thought of escape tormented Michael's mind too. His legs flinched as if in agreement. Only, it was too late, for mere seconds later Yolanda returned with a tugging struggle. Spider hurried to assist.

Suddenly, it was not only the wind that forced the trees to sway back and forth, instead it was a ferocious, agonising roaring, followed by the grumbling and rumbling of the earth. The sound was mightier than thunder. Michael could hardly believe his eyes.

Fur as white as snow; teeth as sharp as swords; eyes as bright as the sun. The large beast, hauled in chains before him, was none other than Agarov of the Aj'ayah, the Great White Wolf.

Chapter Twenty
The Ladybird

Not only did the cold begin to torment Ella-Rose, but Mr Coccin L. Idae too.

I'm in a world that does not exist? How could that even be possible? This world is white and something cannot be nothing, she remembered.

'I've warned you Coccin, I've no time for this—this craziness. Go away if you're to be no help.' Stronger than she had meant, Ella-Rose brushed the back of her hand forcing the ladybird to fly unsteadily away.

The aligning stars helped guide Ella-Rose from their bed above. Of course, she had no idea where she was heading, nor still where she actually was. What difference did it make anyway when every direction was covered completely in a thick white blanket?

What difference would it make if this place really didn't exist?

One hour passed. Then two. Then a million perhaps. She found a hard, sturdy branch behind some trees to use as a substitute for the weight of her twisted leg. As she staggered through the new forest, she found herself accompanied still by Finn's screams in her mind. The cries banged inside her head. Ella-Rose leant onto the nearest tree, steadying herself as the world began to spin in circles around her. Whirling on a carousel, she wanted nothing more than to escape its spinning torture.

You have to jump off, she told herself. *The only way to stop the spinning is to jump off. But, how do you jump off a carousel inside your head?*

'My oh my, yer really have lost yer mind, haven't yer?'

She looked again at the back of her hand to see the ladybird had once again returned to the same spot as earlier. Her screaming mind soon surrendered, but that was the least of her worries. Her mouth had dried from dehydration. Not even the cool, passing air could soothe her now.

'Listen, Coccin, I have to leave. Please tell me where I am. Where must I go to leave? This place might not exist, but Finn very much does.'

Her words were met with silence.

Can this ladybird even talk, or have I completely lost my mind? 'Well, if you won't tell me where I am, at least tell me where you are!' she demanded, her patience had completely gone.

'I *am* where you are not. And you are not here, so I guess that means… I am right here.'

'But you still haven't told me where *here* is!'

'That's because there's no such place as here,' Coccin explained, wafting his tiny arms about the emptiness. He fluttered up to Ella-Rose's head and pointed a tiny arm at her temple. 'There's only *here*.'

'Then, why is it so dark? So cold and… lonely?'

'Because unfortunately dear girl, the mind can often be a dark, cold and lonely place.'

Her thoughts flew back to Finn's voice, calling dauntingly in her mind. Finn was there. *He's always there.*

'Am I dreaming? I am, aren't I? Another nightmare. Look at me, I'm talking to a ladybird!'

'I'm not a ladybird,' Coccin plainly admitted. 'I am a boy.'

'What?' It was at that moment Ella-Rose remembered where she had heard that name before. 'Legend of Eliza,' she said aloud.

'Kulla,' Coccin said to her, pushing his mind back into a dark, cold and lonely place…

… 'The whole town has turned red,' Coccin whispered solemnly. His words echoed, bouncing off the sewer walls and landing in Nyla's ears.

'Coccin I don't— I can't hear you,' Nyla shouted. 'All that… screaming.'

'Kulla is on fire!' The distraught expression the scruffy boy gave soon brought a chilling shiver to Nyla's spine.

Regardless her fear of being trampled to death by the stampede of screaming people above, Nyla forced the grid of the sewer up and quickly pulled herself up. 'I— I don't understand,' she began, but when she turned to face the McArthur's cabin, she witnessed it for herself. Kulla had indeed turned red with fire and blood. 'God damn you Eliza,' she whimpered.

Nyla ran as quickly as she could through the emerald trees leading up to the burning cabin, hoping and praying that her parents would still be alive. Coccin followed anxiously, begging her to stop. As she reached the top of the hill, she witnessed the cabin collapse on one side. The doors and windows were broken. The whole place had turned crooked.

Captured by the scrutiny of the two black pebbles staring from below, Nyla accepted the haunting glimpse of reflection gifted within the raven's eyes. However, the illusionary imitation of Nyla's white curls had been changed by the darkness of its glare. The Initial beauty in the brightness of her chestnut gaze had been stolen entirely. She lowered her body to study the raven's beak that was buried deep into the cold new scars of her parents' burns. The tips of the raven's horned jaws were covered lightly in golden flakes of sand and the rest of its beak was scratched white. Everyone must be fighting their own battles these days, *Nyla thought. Inside the raven's mouth sat the cold left eye of Penny*

McArthur. As its beak gently crunched down, the eye squelched and splattered, releasing juice like a cherry tomato. Looking down at the remains of her parents, Nyla realised she felt nothing for the two decaying fools. All that took her mind in that moment was a deranged admiration she imposed onto the nature of the innocent pebble-eyed raven.

The strange, emotional sensations affecting her both physically and psychically, Nyla didn't understand what she felt. Since she could remember, she had always associated her feelings with colour. To be calm was to see blue, like the bright afternoon skies reflecting onto the stillness of the ocean. To be afraid was to see green, like the monsters Penny McArthur threatened would devour her had she continued to awaken the house with her nightmares. To be loved was to see black. Strangely, yes. Not red, as she had once argued with Daisy Baker, whose uncle, she remembered, owned the Rott'n Teef sweet shop on the corner of Whittaker Street. Used to own it, *she thought, gazing down once more at the remains of Kulla.*

Apparently, Rott'n Teef was the only place In Ramoria ever to sell Dragon Breathers. Nyla recalled once seeing an empty box outside the shop, large red words on the wrapper roaring out of the dragon's jaws:

WARNING: THIS PRODUCT MAY CAUSE DROWSINESS, DIZZINESS, HEADACHE AND/OR MEMORY LOSS. **DO NOT** CONSUME WHEN DRINKING ALCOHOL FOR RISK OF SHORT-TERM INSANITY. **DO NOT** CONSUME WHEN PREGNANT FOR RISK OF BIRTH DEFECTS.

She imagined that same box now burnt to nothing but ash.

Yes, love was black for sure. Red was the colour of blood. Red was the aggressive terror in the flames Eliza had formed using Nyla's own palms. Burning, burning, turning the town to ashes. And for what?

'It is all your fault,' she said, staring at the crooked cabin. 'It is all your fault.'

At first, Coccin thought she was talking to him, but she wasn't. She was talking to herself. He watched a fiery rage take over her entire body. Watched as she started to tear out her hair and scratch at her skin, so deep that it bled.

'Ny? Nyla!'

It was at that moment that she pulled off the medallion from around her neck and forced an immense power throughout Dragon Claw. It was enough to drive anyone to insanity. Surpassing all nuclear, electromagnetic and magical forces, only the strongest sorcerer could have summoned it.

Coccin went to her – to save her, but the force was too strong.

Unbearable.

It was like an explosion, only worse, bursting out from inside herself.

When at last Nyla came to, she opened the eyes of her mind and stared into what she could only describe as the gates to a dark and broken world.

'C-Coccin? Coccin?'

The boy was nowhere to be seen. And for the first time in her life, Nyla felt alone. She lowered her gaze to witness only half of the medallion hanging between her fingers and showed no confusion. For she knew. Knew that the other piece of the medallion lay inside the gates. She knew that the other half of the medallion…

'… was me,' finished Coccin.

'You're the other piece of the medallion?'

'I sure am. Now, I know this is a lot to take in, but I've a job to do. Dragon Claw's in great danger Ella-Rose. Zagan Rapture himself has called for you to close the gate.'

'Zagan?' she recalled this name from her nightmares. 'Zagan is a sorcerer, isn't he? The tales Caesar used to tell said that Lozari was the last of the sorcerers, but Zagan— he speaks to me in my mind. Why would he want me? I'm just a girl.' Ella-Rose took a long, deep breath trying to keep her thoughts in one place. 'So, wait a minute, the tales are all true? Eliza does exist and she truly is the Matra's Ladybird, a demon trapped here inside this nothingness.'

Ella-Rose knew little of the Matra. Caesar had once read parts of the Aj'ayahic Testament of Magic to her in which the Matra was described as the most powerful being in the world with the ability to take many forms. She knew that the Matra will one day birth the Ladybird, a powerful demon and sorceress.

'A demon locked up. Well, if Eliza is trapped here in a world that doesn't exist, I don't see how Dragon Claw could be in any danger at all,' she said. 'And I don't see how I would have any ability to rid this strange, crooked world.'

'Ella-Rose, the day you started having these nightmares was the day, we knew, the prophecy came to be.'

'Prophecy? Wha— I don't understand.'

'Things may not always appear as they seem.' When Coccin flew atop the charred sign, that in the real world belonged to Kulla and in the crooked world had read:

Labyrinth is Deadly

Ella-Rose inexplicably witnessed the letters start to rearrange themselves. No longer was this labyrinth deadly, for the words instead changed to say:

Nyla is the Ladybird

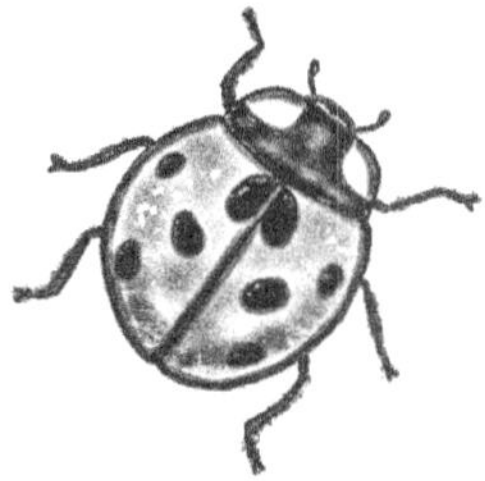

Chapter Twenty-One
A Lifeless World

Although the incense had burned out, the essence of amber and apricot oozing from heated lamps above orchids retained a dimmed everlasting light. Thin lines of smoke faded gently into the sewer's roof allowing bursts of tropical scents throughout the tunnel. The paintings began to sweat. Either that or the acrylics had the desire to run before they had dried.

Finn stood hesitantly across from the woman who now claimed to be Eliza. Could it be? Could this sweet woman, who so carefully and gently cupped the little white mouse in her hands, be a demon? Finn couldn't believe it. A demon is supposed to be a terrifying, hideous beast, not a beautiful elegant woman. Right? He struggled to stop himself blurting out the only thing he could. 'Eliza? You—you're Eliza? As in E-L-I-Z-A, Legend of Eliza, Eliza?' He scratched at the fluff of hair atop his head, still frightened, yet finding that he still could not help but get lost in her vibrant gaze.

The woman sat at a vintage dressing table, braiding the many layers of her bright, white hair. The fine-pencilled black line she had so gracefully drawn around each eye somehow gave the illusion that they appeared much wider.

'Are you thirsty Finn? Oh, what am I saying? Of course you are.'

Eliza stood from her dressing table and opened a cupboard below her to pull out a turquoise, translucent plastic cup. She took a large jug of liquid from the same cupboard and casually poured it inside, splashing little drops on the rug below. Finn stood and watched her, realising soon after how thirsty he actually was. He blamed his height for this. Oh yes, being only two-foot was not exactly advantageous to his eating and drinking habits. You would think the boy only needed to eat an apple to fill up his stomach, but no, Finn could eat a whole leg of lamb and still be hungry within the hour. *Passes through quicker,* he would say. Having no food or drink in hours, as well as being chased by those three, dreadful globbers, had definitely taken its toll.

The woman offered a cup, filled to the brim with a mystifying, thick, orange liquid, he didn't need to think twice before taking it. He knew there was a possibility – a large possibility - that it could have been poisoned by the spit of a demon and that his very first sip could have him lay curled on the floor, spilling white froth from his mouth, but he was too thirsty. The adherence of honey favoured his lips as it softly swam down to his stomach. How strange the mixture of peach and blueberry did taste when shared with the golden fluid, yet rather spectacularly warm when it caressed his uvula. The boy set the cup atop a small round table after gulping the last of it down.

'Feel better?'

He ignored the question with an uncomfortable silence, to which the woman soon broke.

'Yes Finn. I am Eliza.' Her voice was so calm that Finn could not help but feel safe in her company.

'But believe me when I tell you, these legends you hear, shared across Dragon Claw, they're not as true as you may think. Legend of Eliza portrays me to be a demon. I'm not a demon Finn.' Her voice raised a little, but she still smiled, combing her fingers through her immaculately straight hair.

Finn stared with a blank canvas of a face. His thoughts fell back to Ella-Rose. Only this time, his thoughts weren't kind to him. His mind had turned dark, cold and lonely.

'Very well,' Eliza said. 'How about I tell you what really happened all those years ago? The true Legend of Eliza. I guess I'll start where most stories do – right at the beginning…

I never knew my real parents. It was only later I learned of their true existence. I knew my brother though. My half-brother, I mean. His name was Lozari Rapture. My father was a sorcerer, my mother— my mother—'

She drifted off.

'My mother was a devil, or Matra as religion would claim. She told my father he would have four children and four children he did. Thaddeus was his first born; died at the age of nineteen. I never met him, but heard he would have grown to be a man with the kindest of hearts. Lozari was his second child; he died when I was only a teenager. My father vowed to his wife, Korine, that he would never allow her another child. But Parra's prophecy had already been written. He was to have four children and four children he did. When Nyla and I were born, we were born as one. Two pieces of consciousness, each of equal worth inside the same body, although I always felt like an intruder. My true mother took us to a cabin just beyond Kulla the day we were born to be raised by two loving people.'

Loving, yes.

'Straight away, the McArthurs noticed a peculiarity in the helpless babe they cared for with all their hearts. Straight away they knew it wasn't one child they had found, but two. Our cries were different, our laughter was different, the love they felt for each of us was different.'

'As the two of us grew within that same body, Nyla started to change. She developed a power. Well, I say developed, but I guess I knew it was always there. I suppose I should say that she developed the knowledge to use her power instead. Sorcery. But it wasn't any sorcery you would have ever heard of or read about in a book. This was a genetic power forced down from sorcerer and Matra.'

'The more Nyla used her powers, the stronger they seemed to grow. Years later, I gained a sliver of her powers. You understand, I had no access to Nyla's full sorcery, just as everybody else has no access to someone else's consciousness. It wasn't the body that held the power, it was Nyla's mind. Somehow, our minds were connected in a way I could never even begin to explain and a fraction of her power transferred to me. I don't think it was ever meant to, but it did and she blamed and hated me for it.'

'That was around time she forced us to call her Ladybird. That was when she told us that— that one day she was going to open the gates to a crooked world upon our parent's ashes. It was no surprise Penny and Wallim McArthur loved me more. Nyla was— she was... *evil.*'

Eliza took a breath and a dimpled grin shone out brightly from cheek to cheek. 'I'm sorry Finn, but I feel it only best if I *show you* the truth.'

Flummoxed by her words, the nervous boy went to ask what she had meant, but rendering him speechless, her fingers were already rested firmly at his temples. Eliza closed her eyes, showing only her decorated lashes. She commenced by chattering few words from a language Finn had never heard. The beauty in her voice was magical.

Warily, Finn opened an eye, albeit uncertain as to whether he was permitted to do so at such a show.

How absurd.

He was standing in the exact same place he had before closing his eyes, but everything appeared different. How strange the thought that before, the mud-filled sewer was somewhat actually beautiful compared to the damnable place his vision now so cruelly showed. The brown muck, which had heroically held the sewage room together, became an adversarial, cold grey, sinking bitterly amongst dead flowers and ripped paintings. The tunnel grid above them was open, giving sight to a cold and dark winter in a world that seemed lifeless. A crooked world.

His thoughts went straight to Ella-Rose.

PART THREE
Man, Monster and Magic

Down a most hostile path, the decaying man approached the bench painfully. Hauled like a raw piece of meat, ready to dance between Jra'bral's golden jaws. It was not surprising that the musky aroma of resurrected death did not faze Michael even once, for far too much had the boy seen this day to not be believing in ghosts.

Chapter Twenty-Two
The Secret Diary

Moments from death, Michael found that his thoughts turned straight to home. Shayam Village; a magical place. One that now seemingly belonged to a different world entirely. This dark, bleak forest, where he now stood mere meters from a ferocious beast, was not owned by the world he thought he knew.

Moments from death, his thoughts travelled to his sister. Could Ella-Rose's day have been as mad as his? Of course not. He knew that morning she had planned to go to the brighter side of Fortunae with Finn Hampson; a boy, who, though small in size,

Michael supposed had a lot of fight in him. Undoubtedly, the two of them would have been back at the village hours ago. Tucked up in their beds.

Ella-Rose was always first to bed and the last to rise of a morning. Always with those same nightmares torturing through her skull. Michael hadn't even seen her before leaving for Caesar's.

That was his first regret.

As twins, he always thought they shared a strange and powerful bond. Possibly due to the fact they looked after each other since they never knew their true mother and father. Though, nor did they ever wish to. They had each other and that was enough. She loved him and he loved her.

He always found it difficult to tell her he loved her, but the regret of not saying those words that morning scratched deeply at his mind. The paining belief that he would never have the chance to say those words again, burned a hole inside his chest.

Yolanda hauled the agitated beast through with a thick, heavy chain tied tightly around its fur. Agonising growls were triggered, loud enough to wake even the folk of Shayam village though miles away.

'Kai-Sal, you bastard! Release me of these shackles, else I'll make you pay,' Agarov warned, to which not even a single glance from the monster was offered. 'Listen to me, I gave you an order—'

'Aye and your orders mean nothing here. You must surely know that by now.' The unmasked monster turned to face his previous prisoner and after a tantalising grimace, he threw the small, leather book at Agarov's paw. 'Look familiar to you? I'm sure it does. Just as I'm sure you understand how foolish it would be to lie to me.'

The White Wolf stroked his furry paw against the golden ladybird atop the cover. 'Y-You've found it?' he stammered. 'H-How? I-It's not possible. The prophecy would never allow—' he stopped himself.

'It appears, a little Fortunae fortune has been brought upon us. As unbelievable as it sounds, this random child here had the book in his possession,' he smirked. 'But aye, the very book the United Dragons have searched for since the death of Lozari Rapture has fallen straight into my hands,' the insane laughter which then let loose from the Darkness was frightening. 'I needn't your lies of its true nature,' he continued. 'What I do need, is for you to read it. As anticipated, Zagan's sorcery has been cast upon it. I cannot read the pages, but I suppose you can.'

'Are you illiterate, Kai-Sal?' the wolf mocked. 'How can you know this book is the one you have searched for when you lack the ability to read it? Even if it were, do you really think Zagan would risk letting anyone without Rapture blood read it?'

'Joje Sebastian could read it,' Yolanda broke in. 'Isn't that right, Kai-Sal? Joje—'

'Don't be so stupid woman! It was Sebastian's role to protect the words that had been written. The wolf is right; Zagan would never allow for anyone but a Rapture to read it.' His eyes then fell on top of Michael.

'The boy might be able to read it,' Spider interruptedly pointed out, forcing Michael away from his mind. 'I mean, a book's purpose is to be read, right? Why would he have it if he can't read it?'

Michael realised he hadn't even looked through the pages; he had simply heard the words pass through Caesar's lips. The old professor could read it, right? Or could it be, he had told those stories from his own mind?

The wolf studied Michael with great consideration. ‘Come to me, child.’

‘Agarov, you are my prisoner. You are in no place to give instructions.’

‘True. But the way I see it, for two years I have stood as your prisoner and still I stand, why? Because you need me, of course. You’d have killed me in an instant, worse, drank my blood were it not that I’m held at a high price. So yes, I demand this boy come forth. Should you stand in his way, I’ll strangle myself with these chains and you will receive no reward. Don’t think I won’t.’ Uninterruptedly this time, the wolf called for Michael once more, who frighteningly hobbled over. It was only when standing inches from the beast that he recognised the colossal size of Agarov the Great White Wolf. ‘Tell me your name, child.’

‘M-Michael.’

‘Do you know what this is, Michael?’ He pushed the book with his paw.

He pondered the question a moment. *A dead tree?* Only few hours ago, the professor asked that very same question. He searched the folders of his brain, seeking answers that may not have been correctly filed. 'I-I haven't read it. I only know what I've been told. I-It tells the tales of the War of Four,' he uttered. 'S-Stories of battles?'

'Indeed, it does,' Agarov contemplated the boy's words. 'Though, I fear that what you have been told of this book is not all too genuine, Michael. For, this book is in fact so much more.'

Not genuine? How could it be? Caesar would never lie. Would he?

'The damned book is cursed,' forced Yolanda. 'It's— it's evil!'

'Camouflaged against folk like us,' added Spider.

The wolf's toothy growl forced the interrupter's silence. 'It is not evil! Far from it! This book is written by the hand of a great and powerful sorcerer.'

'It is the secret diary of Zagan Rapture.' Kai-Sal raised his head to the clouds. 'The only thing that holds the knowledge of how to close the gates to the crooked world.'

Chapter Twenty-Three
Dark Discoveries

Ella-Rose couldn't stop herself from staring at the sign that had magically rearranged its letters. Once, twice, one-hundred times she read it and still could not completely comprehend what had happened.

Wait. Had it finally happened? Had she completely lost her mind within the cold abyss?

No, not lost her mind, she had just misplaced it. It's like losing your keys or your purse - it always rocks up in the same place you left it.

Then, her mind was back in Fortunae right? *The real Fortunae*, Ella-Rose reminded herself. She walked towards the wood and passed her hand delicately over the words. *Nyla is the Ladybird*

Legend of Eliza, was it all a lie? She had gone from believing these tales to be fictional to believing they were true and now discovering they were all lies. Eliza was never a demon.

Nyla is the Ladybird. Nyla is the demon.

Ella-Rose thought back to the recurring nightmare showing Nyla's confrontation with Zagan. She had the piece of medallion, the same piece Ella-Rose holds today, but Zagan refused to tell her where the other piece was hidden. The other piece being Mr Coccin L. Idae himself.

Had Zagan known of Nyla's true nature?

Ella-Rose thought harder. Yes. Of course he did. She vaguely recalled the last words he had spoken to the demon before disappearing from this world. *You didn't honestly believe I wouldn't know who you truly are, did you?*

So many questions ran rapidly through her mind in that moment and she knew the answers she sought lay deep within Fortunae. *Well, here I am, old man! You can't get much deeper than this... can you?*

Ella-Rose took a deep breath, her eyes still refused to move from the sign. 'This crooked world inside my mind, Coccin, what is it?'

Coccin fluttered his wings until they were face-to-face again. With half of his back broken, the exercise must have been tougher than he made it look. 'This might very well go against everything yer've ever been told, but the gates to this world were never opened as a prison. Inside, there's this powerful energy, meant only for one thing,' his words came out far too seriously for her liking. '*Destruction.*'

Ella-Rose winced. That was the word you used when playing make believe. The word you used in games when flying your dragon to Danjin to destroy the goblins and ogres. It wasn't a word to be used in real life. 'You mean, Nyla wishes to destroy Dragon Claw?'

'Not only destroy it, but to absolutely annihilate everything and everyone in it!'

'But why? I don't understand.' Ella-Rose couldn't help then but make a typical fifteen-year-old girl humph! 'Why can't everyone just live in peace? Wouldn't that solve all problems of war and destruction?'

Coccin contemplated this for a spell and smiled at her through fractured teeth. 'In the many years I've lived in this crooked world—'

Lived? Are you sure you don't mean endured? Coccin's mind spoke so loud, Ella-Rose could hear it.

'—I've learned a lot from Mr Zagan. Peace is quite a strange concept, my dear. Everyone believed Dragon Claw found peace when Lozari Rapture died. Now they seem to think peace comes after the death of Khosi Trajan. Truth is, Dragon Claw won't know peace while these gates between worlds remain open.' Coccin lowered his tiny head, staring at the white fluff that had practically buried Ella-Rose's shoes. 'Inside this world lives a demon, aye. Spawn of the Matra herself. Peace is a difficult thing to come by when folk around the world have faith in different things. While your existence, Ella-Rose, is to bring joy and love to the world, unfortunately Nyla's is to bring an end to it. Luckily for us, to do such a thing, she would first need to leave this prison. But see, Nyla hasn't got enough power to leave this world on her own accord. Not without the complete medallion. That's where you come in, my dear.'

She tried her hardest to not laugh. 'Me?' she scoffed. 'What I am I supposed to do? You can't expect me to fight off a demon. How can I control who goes in and out of here when *I* myself don't even know how to leave?'

'Oh Ella-Rose.' Coccin flew once more to the back of her hand, dodging the frosty winds that fought against him. 'You will leave in time, but first you must listen to me. Nyla's powers may be strong, but without her connection with Eliza, they ain't strong enough. The demon won't be able to leave this world. Not without—'

'Yes, I know, the medallion,' Ella-Rose finished. 'So that's why she went to Zagan with the other piece? I saw it, in my dreams.'

Nightmares, her brain reminded her.

'She wanted the medallion to be complete so that she could leave this crooked world and use its power to destroy Dragon Claw, right?'

'It should have only ever been the demon to control the power within these gates, but because the medallion broke, there was an error in whatever spell formed this rip in space.'

'What are you saying, Coccin? That no-one other than Nyla was supposed to have access to this crooked world? But what about Zagan… what about us?'

'That's just it. The mistake that forced Nyla to be trapped inside, must have also somehow changed the entrance and exit. The gates allowed access for the most powerful sorcerers to enter through their dreams.'

Nightmares, Ella-Rose's brain shared.

'Sorcerers had access to this crooked world,' Coccin continued. 'But they would never hold enough power to destroy Dragon Claw. They did, however, have the capability of finding both medallion pieces and releasing Nyla. Which is where Lozari Rapture came in.'

Ella-Rose trembled. The thought that the demon could in fact arrive at any given moment cruelly entered her mind.

'The Matra decided to use sorcerers as an advantage. See, with Nyla trapped within this boundless creation, the Matra needed another to enter the gates to release her.'

Ella-Rose raised her eyebrows.

'And who better than Nyla's own half-brother, one of the most powerful sorcerers the world had ever known? Lozari Rapture, so named "last of the sorcerer's race."'

'Hold up. Lozari can't have been the last of the sorcerer's race, because Zagan is a sorcerer, right? I know he is, I saw it in my dre— my *nightmares*.'

'Right,' said Coccin, snapping his tiny fingers. 'Very clever.'

'Then, why would he need me at all? He's the sorcerer – can't he just close the gates with his magical voodoo? Or is it that he needs the medallion? Here, he can take it!' she cried, holding the medallion piece up to the malformed stars in the sky. 'I don't want this!'

Coccin shook his head to refrain himself from saying, *dear, oh dear*. 'I wish it was that simple. I'm afraid it's not just a dazzle of sorcery mixed with the medallion that can rid this crooked world, Ella-Rose, but something else even powerful sorcerers lack. *Willpower*. On many occasions Zagan had tired, but just like Lozari, Zagan hadn't the strength to refrain himself from the lure of the crooked cabin. Its energy is tremendous. Remarkable even.'

Ella-Rose rearranged the branch with which she had been resting her weight on. 'If what you say is true,' she frowned. 'Is there not another sorcerer? Perhaps Zagan had a brother or a sister? There must be someone!'

Coccin crawled across her hand, tickling her calm hairs as he went. 'Aye, he has a brother,' the bug said. 'Though I'm afraid the intentions of Thanisis are never all too clear.'

Ella-Rose let out another teenaged girl humph! 'Well, children maybe? Grandchildren? Not to sound rude at all, but surely a man of his age has children.' Her mind then went to Caesar. He was the oldest person she ever knew. Didn't he say he once had a child who fought in the war? She shook the thought when Coccin shook his head.

'Zagan was never fortunate enough to have children of his own.'

The young girl now lowered her head. *Hopeless*. It was all hopeless. There she stood, in a crooked world, with a ladybird telling her that she is the only hope for saving Dragon Claw from a demon.

What a load of—

'Thanisis had children,' said Coccin, interrupting the girl's thoughts.

'Brilliant!' Ella-Rose screamed. 'They must be sorcerers right? Let's call on them.'

'One of them is, aye,' Coccin smiled dimly, lowering his own head, as if afraid to look her in the eye. 'Unfortunately for you, she has already been called upon.'

Chapter Twenty-Four
Thanisis Rapture

Agarov opened the small, leather book gently with his claws. 'Can you see the words boy?' The slight, discreet shake of his furred head paired with the hopeful look the wolf gave Michael desired one type of answer from him; a lie.

'N-No,' Michael admitted, immediately shaking his head.

The White Wolf smiled. 'Right, that's that then. You might as well let the boy go—'

'He is lying!' Kai-Sal roared, pulling Mankarash from its resting place and quickly forcing it against

Michael's neck. 'Look at me, LOOK AT ME! Can you read this book?'

'Y-Yes, I can read it!' Michael cried. Tears started to pour relentlessly down his face. 'I-I'm sorry.'

'Then do it!' The vampire removed the sword from the boy's neck and shoved it straight back into the dirt.

Nervously shaking uncontrollably, Michael picked up the book from the dirt and began to read.

Diary Entry #1

At what point do we recognise an action to be considered good or bad? I could lie, I could steal, I could even kill and show no remorse for my crime. Yet, what would you question? My action? My intention? My sanity?

Our world is full of cruel people, that much I know. Though, what terrifies me is not that they believe their wrongdoings to be right, but that there is no way to universally deny it. Who am I to say my brother was evil?

My name is Zagan, second son of... Emperor Benjamin Syrus... at least that was what the world had me believe. I have now reached an age where I am able to write my story of enlightenment; the tale of a child in his discovery through right and wrong, good and evil.

I believed that dreams were once thoughts with no true meaning; cabins were warm and homely places and a ladybird— well, a ladybird was just a red beetle, wasn't it? I was six-years-old the day I truly saw the world for what it was. Only now am I able to comprehend those trivial details of my past life for what they actually were.

Empora's Castle Snow stood strong at the outskirts of Gyra, protected by the United Dragons' Treaty of Kashmir. I was only a child when sorcery became extinct. Everybody told me that sorcery was a sin punishable by death. So, when the War of Four was said to be won, triumphant by the hands of "my father" slaying Lozari Rapture and his unnatural army of the undead, I was happy.

Actually happy.

Benjamin told me that Dragon Claw again knew peace, for the first time since before the eruption of Mount Hjar.

But evil always did leave scars.

Diary Entry #2

A couple of days after I'd turned seven, Emperor Benjamin Syrus returned home after an entire summer's absence sorting dealings with the United Dragons. It was my brother, Thanisis who cared for me those days.

'We have no need for parents,' he assured me. 'We have each other and we have our secret. We oughtn't to burden anyone with the knowledge of our powers. They just wouldn't understand.'

'But what if it is a bad secret?' I asked. 'What if it's true that these powers are the disease of sorcery and we need to rid them? I don't want to sin, brother.'

It was always my belief that Thanisis wouldn't lie to me. Though, I always lied to him. Is to keep a secret a lie? I think so. If something you do burns at your heart and soul, then can it be the right thing to do? I never told him of the strange nightmares I was having, even after he told me of his.

Diary Entry #3

The night I crept into the meeting of my father's counsel, I remember my feet froze at each step. Unsure as to what it was I listening to, curiosity couldn't wait to take its hold. Benjamin Syrus, I saw only by candle-light. He sat with a company of nine, all of which I recognised immediately. Benjamin's trusted advisor, Alexander Ezra Fallen, brother of Raylan Fallen; Wyrell Syrus, Benjamin's younger brother; Yogi, a Healer; Lord's Xenon Ullman and Pele Jonas, Wisdoms of Westland; Roman and Ragas Raghar, Knights of the Red Castle's guard; Scorpio, a mute known across lands as Secret Keeper, and finally Yara Trajan, the Danjin Prince.

'The boys must be killed! Benjamin, open your eyes.' The anger flew from the lips of Alexander Fallen as he beat down the chair before him. He carried himself at six foot, four inches, his arms were thicker than my head and his face battered and bruised; each scar telling its own story. I can remember once having dancing swords together and him telling me tales of Kraal Syrus, right up to his untimely death at the Battle of Quae.

Alexander told me how the war had changed him; how it changed everyone.

'They are sorcerers, I warn you. They possess a power that cannot be trusted, nor can it be controlled. Thanisis, he told me he entered through the gates of darkness. Looked me in the eyes and told me he had spoken with a demon. Sorcery was destroyed, god dammit. Hail United Dragons, for aye, the war was over. Benjamin, heed my words. Only sorcery could summon the gates to that other world and you know it. These boys are our enemy!' Alexander Fallen shouted. 'Traitors who would kill us all, given the chance.'

'They are my sons!' Benjamin Syrus raged. 'Children. They're children. Stop with this outrageous babble. Lozari Rapture was last of the sorcerers and is dead by my own hands. Sorcery is a dead race—'

'Your judgement is black, Benjamin. These lads will destroy every one of us and you'll do nothing? Tell it now and tell it true; they are no children of yours. Are they? ARE THEY?'

The emperor smashed his fists upon the table, frightening me for the first time in my life. 'You are not a God, Alexander! You speak like a God, yet I see no divinity,' he spat, wiping the sweat from his reddened forehead. 'You force me to speak truly and yet you hold onto a dark secret yourself. Isn't that right, mage? *You are the brother of Raylan Fallen, yet I see nothing of him in you anymore.' Benjamin took a breath. 'The children—my children, they are just boys. Boys, damn you.'*

'No! Thanisis told me—'

'You lie!'

'I speak the truth and you're either too blind or too stupid to see it.'

A painful silence took the room, forcing my leave. I chose then to wake Thanisis from his nightmares and tell him all I had heard.

He simply kissed my head and said, 'Worry not, brother.' Those were the last words my brother ever spoke to me. Everything after that came from a dark place.

Diary Entry #4

I repressed most of what happened that night after I woke Thanisis.

I'll never deny that it was my own fault.

To me, morality was always a game. Good and evil were just words that played a part, but I never understood their meanings.

Though, they weren't just words, were they? For it is not a word that turns your heart darker than the black of the night. No, it is the meaning we assign to it. I thought I was good once. My brother too.

Worry not, brother.

Can words have more than one meaning? By that, I mean, can a word have two opposing meanings? My brother was good, yes, I believed that. However, we both saw the world in different lights.

No, I saw the light, whereas he looked only through darkness.

Worry not, brother.

If my brother was good, then what am I? I woke him that night and shared the counsel's voice with him. Then I watched as he murdered Benjamin Syrus where he slept. I didn't stop him. Should I have?

My mind became a labyrinth, and that labyrinth was deadly.

Thanisis was good! I always had those words imprinted into my mind. He looked after me, but did that make it true? Was Thanisis good?

Benjamin Syrus had fallen. Castle Snow had fallen.

When I confronted my brother, I knew he could see that I was *worried. Thanisis forced a blade on me to steal my eyes from their sockets. He promised that I would never have to gaze upon the true evils of the world. But when he dug the knife inside, the pain was so unbelievably unbearable, I had to defend myself.*

It was the first time I ever used sorcery.

Only when I lost my left eye, was I truly able to see my brother for what he was.

Thoughts that were pure evil by nature grew inside my head. There was no point in apologising for them, for how could I ever forgive myself when all I wanted was Thanisis dead? What's worse, I wanted to be the one to kill him.

I had no other choice but to run. Away from Snow, away from Empora and away from Thanisis.

Why?

Because I had become evil and there was no way to universally deny it.

Chapter Twenty-Five

The Prophecy

Cold winds sliced across the air as Coccin informed Ella-Rose of her father and how Michael and she had come to live with Sara Azerius under the protection of Caesar. She was hardly listening. Instead, Ella-Rose stared at the flakes of snow, dancing their way to the ground with a mix of wonder and fear. The broken jigsaw within her head had started to piece together. It all made sense to her now. The answers she sought, never before had she really thought about asking of her true parents, but subconsciously, she always held the desire to know.

Ella-Rose's father was Thanisis Rapture, that part she heard Coccin say. Her mother was a farmer's daughter named Isabella Arquette from Porque.

'Poor thing died at the depressing age of twenty-eight not long after you were born,' said Coccin. Seemingly, her final breath before her journey to the afterlife spoke the names, Ella-Rose and Michael.

'… and of course the prophecy stated that—'

'Huh?' Ella-Rose finally came to, staring at the ladybird with tired, worn eyes. 'Yes. The prophecy, what prophecy?' Her voice now monotonous and dry.

'Why, your prophecy of course! You've heard the tale of the Messenger Boy, right? I myself don't care too much for religion – all these Aj'ayahic Testaments were never to my liking, but I thought everyone knew the famous story of the Messenger Boy. The very tale that shares your destiny.'

Ella-Rose returned nothing but a blank stare. There was no way that a story in old scripture could have anything at all to do with her.

'My oh my, long before you were born, it was written in the Testament of Magic – Chapter Four – if I'm not mistaken. It was said that the Matra sent a boy from Old Wood, named Matthias Shallows from the Aj'ayah to climb to the top of Mount Hjar with the task of burying a stone tablet deep into its heated earth. The tablet wasn't like any old piece of rock, see, it contained writings concerning the fate of the crooked world. Now, I ain't gonna give you the whole jargon, but I'll paraphrase as best I can. The writings shared a warning to the folk of Dragon Claw – it held that the Matra will birth a demon to destroy Dragon Claw. The demon will summon a power, stronger than anything Dragon Claw had ever known and thrust it upon—'

Ella-Rose rolled her eyes slothfully.

'Right, sorry – you already know that part. Anyway, according to this tablet, a dark and powerful sorcerer – let's call him Thanisis – was destined to have twins. One boy and one girl – let's call them Michael and Ella-Rose. It was decided by the Matra that the boy would discover instructions of how to close the crooked world and the girl the object to control its power within.'

Ella-Rose studied the broken medallion piece at her hand once more, this time seeing it in a different light. No longer did it appear beautiful and mystifying, but terrifying. She seemed to witness all of the pain it had caused since its existence.

I suppose beauty is the most powerful magic.

Coccin shuffled his cold bottom, then set off to fly once more. Although they had moved away from the sign, the deadly labyrinth still appeared, only now as an empty white path leading nowhere. Ella-Rose hobbled across the snow, still using the branch to substitute her weight and Coccin flew steadily alongside. She averted her eyes only to the colourful clouds at each step. Her mind was so far gone at this point, she hadn't even noticed she was moving.

'Do you understand now, Ella-Rose? It's as if Michael knows the door to this crooked world and you hold the key. Together you will close the gates and restore peace throughout Dragon Claw.' He paused and they both reached a natural stop. 'Oh dear, girl, you're starting to shiver.'

She hadn't realised, but the more her mind seemed to escape her body, the more the cold tormented. 'I-I never properly f-felt it till n-now.'

The frost had hit her not long after her first arrival through the gates. While her heart reached out for Fortunae Forest, the *real* Fortunae Forest, she had managed to subdue the cold's torment. Now, she couldn't help but let the snow consume her. Her mind had lost all control.

'Come on, let us go inside before you freeze to death.'

'In-Inside? C-Coccin what are y-you talking—' Ella-Rose soon stopped herself when noticing that she stood at the foot of a crooked cabin. She could have sworn it hadn't been there before. It seemed so out of place, so… unnatural.

Near the black mountains, deep within a thick mound of snow, the crooked cabin sat peacefully, held together by burnt dead wood and ice. Whoever foolishly thought to have chained its door so powerfully must have taken ill to the mind; for where there ought to have been windows, were only welcoming entrances for the cold. No trees surrounded it, no honeysuckle nor daisies. Only a wooden sign on the front, scarred and covered mostly in snow, that read:

Only
by the hands of
Eliza
can peace
forever be restored
throughout
the lands
of Dragon Claw

'E-Eliza?' she questioned. 'O-Only by t-the—'

'Go on inside, dearie,' he said, flying again to the back of her hand for a calming touch. 'Everyone has their own destiny. That prophecy does not necessarily belong to you.'

The door - if the battered thing could even have such a claim - opened wide with chains dangling at either side. As soon as Ella-Rose took a step, she heard a voice calling from inside: '*Ella-Rose, Ella-Rose! I'm here!*'

No, not inside the cabin; it was the voice of Finn still imprinted within her head. Ella-Rose hobbled through until she stood directly amidst the very room Zagan had spent fifty years of his life, placing all thoughts calmly into her back pocket.

'I've been here before.'

She gazed down at a perfectly drawn chalked circle and four unlit candles placed carefully surrounding. 'What is this place?'

However, before she received Coccin's word, the question answered itself. Nothingness. The place was the very definition of nothing, yet when inside she thought she could feel everything. There was no way to explain it, but the blood that once ran warmly through her veins had turned cold and thin. As she walked further inside, her heart pumped faster and faster, seemingly until it would explode. She felt the sun and moon. But mostly, she felt the eyes of Finn watching from within.

Yet, the cabin stood with its nothingness.

Suddenly, an eerie creak screeched at the crooked door. Slowly and ever so frightfully, Ella-Rose peered over her right shoulder, meeting the cold, grey eyes of a woman.

Only, it wasn't a woman… it was a demon. Eyes of the Ladybird.

Her nightmares had lied, for in that moment, Nyla hardly resembled a woman at all. Her entire being appeared much darker. The creature did not stand. Instead, it floated, wafting a pair of gigantic wings to remain in flight. Its teeth were daggers and its nose flat like that of a bulldog's. It was not only the appearance of the demon that caused the terrified freeze in Ella-Rose's every muscle, but the black energy that radiated from its body. She could practically hear the folk of Kulla screaming out from it. There was blood and death about its being.

Ella-Rose opened her mouth, wishing to scream, but found that her lungs refused to sing. She had forgotten how to use her voice.

The demon smiled, like an uninvited clown at a children's tea party, and twisted its neck to one side.

'Good, Coccin,' it said. Though it spoke only two words, each came out as a deep and malicious clicking that haunted the ear.

Coccin could feel Ella-Rose shivering uncontrollably. When she looked down to him, reaching for comfort, the beetle simply sighed. 'I'm sorry, Ella-Rose, but I did what I had to. Goodbye forever.'

That was the last time she ever saw Mr Coccin L. Idae. At least, in that form. For when she looked down at the medallion, it no longer appeared broken. The piece that had once been Coccin connected with the piece at her palm. The medallion was whole, but no longer did it lie at her cold, cyan grasp. It was floating straight into the hands of the demon and there was nothing anybody could have done to stop it.

Ella-Rose tried straight for the door, but a sudden thrust of wind, forced by the wings of the demon forced it shut. The chains somehow attached themselves robustly against it. She turned rapidly back to the demon, who, instead of staring back, seemed only to be gazing upon something Ella-Rose could not see.

Sluggishly and calmly, the demon raised a long claw, not directed at Ella-Rose, but to the left of her, where it appeared nothing stood.

A harsh wind soon took Ella-Rose's shoulders and she turned frightfully to see what could possibly be standing beside her, but there was nothing. Nothing within the nothingness. At least, not that she could see. She turned back to Nyla, but even the demon had disappeared.

The crooked cabin had disappeared.

Coccin had disappeared.

Nothing remained but Finn's raging voice, pounding inside her mind. *'Ella-Rose!'* it raged. *'Ella-Rose!'*

'Please… please stop.'

'Ella-'

'STOP!'

There was nothing Ella-Rose could do but sit with her hands over her ears.

When at last Finn's raging words halted, the voice of Coccin L. Idae crept maddeningly into her head.

Goodbye forever.

He had betrayed her. He had betrayed Zagan and the prophecy and everyone else who had ever trusted him. And for what?

Love, her mind told her. Of course, he loved Nyla. At least, he loved the idea of Nyla.

Strangely, as Ella-Rose struggled through her cold, dark mind, unaware of what ill-fate was next to come, she couldn't help but long for his company.

Goodbye forever, he had said.

What she had failed to understand was whether it was goodbye *from* him, or goodbye *for* her.

Chapter Twenty-Six
Falling Snow

Diary Entry #5

For four direful, tiresome nights I made my way across Empora's frozen palm. Off the west coast, a foul and loathsome city named Gyra cunningly hid. Winter's frosted kiss alone dropped far too low for invitation, let alone the dark inhabitants that would roam within. Largest infestation being the black-scaled mountain cats; as tall as nine-feet and long as ten. Yet, they were not even close to owning the claim "dangerous" when compared to the unseen*; so named because any who* *dared to lay their eyes on such a creature, never lived to share a description. Were it not for the savage cries echoing from the mountain peaks, their existence would have been wholly unknown.*

Gyra was not always the ghost it had quite recently become; famous for its statues of Dragon Claw's influential, political figures, names such as Savanah Fallen, Parra Rapture and Kraal Syrus used to stand as high as three-hundred feet amid its centre. Now—

Now shadows lurk every corner and cobwebs every street. Ahead, I saw the cut marble head of Benjamin Syrus. Once beloved and noble leader, now just a scrap of litter with the word SCUM painted across his face. Gyra was never the largest of cities, but always the most populated. Though once a smooth blend of diverse cultures, Gyra now lies as dead as Benjamin Syrus himself.

The day the Emperor of Empora died was forever known as the Reckoning. Describing those horrific events which took place at the Fall of Snow. The riots at Castle Snow came only hours after the emperor's death, avenging for their lives of poverty and their hatred for Benjamin. People from all over Empora travelled to join in with the demolition of the castle. They say it took over two weeks for Snow to completely fall, but I always knew the true reckoning belonged to the night that my brother sliced Benjamin's neck.

Khosi Trajan, who had claimed Wyrell Syrus and himself as the two last living monarchs of the United Dragons, simply overlooked the events at Snow as a price of war. It was only those in Syrus' close council who would recognise that it was nothing other than a personal slaughtering.

Sixty-seven people were injured that night, over half were fatal. Forty-six confirmed deaths, including Benjamin's trusted advisor and Raylan Fallen's only brother, Prince Alexander Ezra Fallen. Murdered, as the songs would sing; innocent lives stolen by the hands of my brother. Thanisis Rapture.

Castle Snow had fallen, and it was said that Lozari Rapture had sent a trusted friend to raid and destroy Fallen's Silverstem Castle in Posre. The Bear Throne was the first to be shattered. I wouldn't be surprised if Lozari had pissed on it beforehand. I never did meet him, but like everyone else, I heard the stories.

The Elephant Throne was destroyed at Snow and I had heard rumours that the Devil Throne at the Red Castle had been burned to nothing by the deranged Khosi Trajan himself.

Why? Because Trajan had no further need for the Red Castle. With Parra, Thaddeus and Lozari gone, there were no leaders left at the Siren to take the Orca. Raylan Fallen had been murdered and his brother, Alexander died just six days past. Wyrell won't survive for long, I thought. Surely war will take him too. Which meant Rapture, Fallen and Syrus were all names of the past. Trajan wins.

Fighting for Wyrell Syrus was never something I intended to do. The thought to do so never even surfaced at the time. Thanisis and I had always known that Benjamin was never our true father.

Diary Entry #6

Mr Farash was a rude man. Always talking about the height of prices they'd charge for laying with the "ugly bitches". According to Farash, in the ol' days, you would only be expected to pay half price if the broads had a hairy mole in the middle of their face and teeth like a broken fence panel. Apparently, those days were long gone. It cost twice as much now for the ugly bitches and only a rich man could afford a pretty one.

Nevertheless, Mr Farash was also a kind man to allow me safe passage across the Stolen Sea, since his planned stop was hours before at Filldrop Central. Probably to waste the millions of refuse piled atop the small boat he sailed. After all, Filldrop was always known to have the BEST GARBAGE DISPOSAL SYSTEM IN ALL OF DRAGON CLAW. WHY NOT (FILL)-DROP BY? As the banners would always read.

But, what in the world was garbage? *I assumed it meant waste.*

'What takes yer to Ramoria then? Hear they got a nice, big ol' forest there. Not much else mind. Few villages mayhap. S'pose they be quite close to them black mountains, ain't they? Only across the sea in Posre. Mount Hjar being one of them. You ever hear 'bout that eruption all them years ago? Nah, Ramoria ain't the place for me. You ought to try Danjin really. They got bars n' clubs n' damn are them bitches sexy!'

I ignored his questions. After all, I didn't even know what exactly had led me to Ramoria. Nevertheless, my fate had spoken and what better way to rid the memories of my past life than sail as far as I could?

My past-self had perished – seven years I had given to this world and I feared I was already finished. Thoughts of family and friends distanced at every step I took when arriving at Ramoria.

Only later did I discover the true reason my mind has led me there. I was led by my nightmares.

Led towards the crooked cabin.

Diary Entry *#7*

Throughout my time in Ramoria, I felt nothing.

Ghosts. That was all my memories became. Gone they were and gone was I. No pain had ever surfaced since the night Thanisis stole my eye. A bulging hole packed with blood, pus and disease, yet, I felt nothing.

Winter slaughtered all the light across the black mountains; a wonderful season, spreading darkness quicker than Death's whisper. I scoped a dead town not far from one of Fortunae's many entrances. Its haunting nature reminded me of Gyra. Behind me, Mount Hjar watched my every move.

***

The cold eyes of a dead boy ten feet ahead of me followed me as I pursued my prey silently through the dead town. According to the charred sign behind me, I stood where once had been Kulla Town Centre. Since saying my goodbyes to Mr Farash, I had eaten nothing but twigs and vines from the luxurious five-star restaurant of Fortunae; I had to wonder whether the fawn I had tracked these past few hours was even there at all. The purple plunkberries I discovered near the Siren gardens days ago served well to cancel out the taste of stick. Even so, every slow minute, I heard my stomach screaming for mercy, like a prisoner of Death's Door. I knew if I didn't taste meat between my lips over the next few days, I would surely end up as dead as the boy staring at me from below.

The fawn's snout sunk deeply into his ripped stomach.

Where was the fawn's mother?

Where was the boy's mother, for that matter? He had clearly been dead for days; that much was clear from the horrid odour bursting from his open carcass.

But who? Who would kill an innocent unarmed child?

Perhaps, someone who needn't an obstruction in their way, *I supposed.*

Slowly, I sneaked towards the animal. Slowly. Slowly. Slow—

'Dammit!'

The fawn was gone, and along with it, my will. Before I lay on my back and shut out the world, I remember giving one last scan of the misery of Kulla.

I remember thinking: that moment belonged to Dragon Claw.

Was it me? The dead boy I mean. Was it a mere vision of my imminent future?

Minutes, hours, days later? It was difficult to tell, I was found by a traveller named Flir Tomrick. When he discovered me - a broken, one-eyed boy, so near to death - he needn't have thought twice before carrying me to safety. To me, he seemed a saint. Really, he was no different to any other man.

Attainment of sainthood, I believe, is virtuousness; for a person to step away from the normality of their comfortable world and do what is considered morally right.

As the broken, one-eyed boy, so near to death, I ask you, is it not just the unspoken obligation of humanity's very being, and not sainthood, to stop in aid of such a traumatic ordeal? Then, had the wanderer walked on by, leaving me to die, would you still claim him as the same man as he was before it? I doubt it. You would shun him immediately for his actions. You would identify him as a beast.

Don't get me wrong, I was entirely grateful he saved my life that day. But, since it was only his duty as a human to stop at my aid, I cannot call him a saint. He was just a man. Like any other man.

But, is that so bad?

I dove in and out of consciousness as he stitched up my eye. Half of my vision had gone, that brutal fate was to forever be unchanged. White smoke took over my cornea and pupil, yet only black could I see.

Regardless, sleep came easy that night. Whether due to the vast deficiency of rest, else the rich, lavender sheets of Flir Tomrick's guest bed, I cared not to question it.

Sleep took me first. Then, as the nightmares came, the crooked cabin took me soon after.

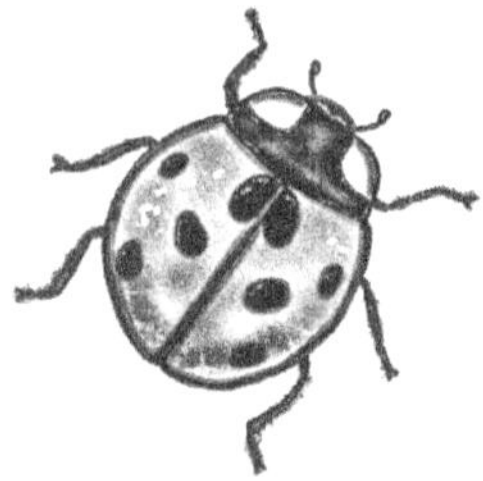

Chapter Twenty-Seven
Pictures of the Past

The cold hit almost immediately for Finn. The temperature reminded him of Hamsville, three winters ago when visiting his cousins. The icy winds had hit as low as minus twenty-one degrees Celsius and the poor boy, whose small body couldn't cope with it, needed to stay inside the lodge for the entire time he was there. It wasn't all that bad. He and his cousins would often play Enchantments by the fire. Because Finn, oldest of the three, prided himself on being much more intelligent than his cousins, he always could work out how to win.

Todd Hampson, youngest of the cousins, would always start the game by playing his Dragon Claw Protection Card – a waste, if you asked Finn, because Todd's older brother, Pip would most definitely play the Demon thereafter, throwing Dragon Claw right into the discard pile. Later, (so as to not rise suspicion of his sneaky tactics,) Finn would play the Matra card, allowing him to bring any card he chooses from the discard pile into his hand. He would always choose the Demon. The three would play the game until Todd was inevitably knocked out first, normally by Pip's repetitive use of Sorcery and Mankarash cards. Pip would then typically be left with his last two. It never mattered what two cards he held, for in Finn's deck, he always saved the best until last. The Medallion Energy card and the Demon. There was no way for him to lose. After all, the Demon is one of the most powerful cards.

The Demon always wins.

***

When Finn climbed out of the tunnel's cover, just above where the well-decorated sewage room had once been, he spotted Eliza standing afar, though, strangely, could still feel her soft touch on his head.

‘H-How did you do that?’ he asked, shivering hysterically. It was the first question that came to mind. If he had taken an extra second to think about what he was going to say, he presumed he would have asked *what* she had in fact done.

What had she done? Merely two seconds earlier, the boy had been stood in the sewer beneath Fortunae Forest, and though it may have retained some awful, stinking mud - *God, he still hoped it was mud* – it had felt very much more comfortable before, much more… *alive*, when compared to where he now stood.

‘I may not have power like my sister,’ Eliza’s voice somehow came from everywhere. ‘But, as unfortunate as it may be, I am still daughter of the Matra and a sorcerer,’

Amongst the brutal blends of white, Finn now stood amidst Kulla Town Centre once more. Only this time, there were no globbers out to get him, nor Ella-Rose by his side. This time, the whole town had turned… red. Though snow paradoxically fell all around him, the sky was on fire; basking in the glory of a disaster that had taken place.

Torn apart town. Torn apart families. The thoughts gave a hot chill through his mind.

'Don't panic, Finn. It's not real,' Eliza told him. The voice still soothed from every direction. 'I mean, not anymore at least. The events you see, in front of you, took place many years ago and though I cannot change it, I can at least show it. Pictures of the past.'

'But— how? H-How am I seeing this?'

'Through the powers of a cold and crooked world.'

There was a burned helping of straw and hay being served near a cabin amid a set of emerald Fortunae trees. A massive cloud of smoke filled the air above. Finn saw only a single soul in sight: a young girl, curled up in the middle of the path leading towards the cabin. Crying. Choking.

Hearing her weep, Finn advanced quickly. He did, of course, have the biggest and sweetest of hearts. One who could find beauty in even the darkest of places.

Understandably, the girl could not see Finn, but he certainly saw her. Shock soon took him. The look in

Finn's face was one of absolute recognition. The girl's appearance was similar – *too* similar - to what Finn assumed a younger Eliza's would have been. In all other ways the two were completely different. How? He couldn't even begin to explain.

Finn could only imagine what horrors had taken place between those emerald trees. He heard a whisper and, at first, assumed it came from Eliza through his head, instead, it was the sad sound of the girl's cry ahead of him.

'It's all your fault,' she whispered, rocking slowly back and forth. 'It's all your fault.'

Finn thought she spoke to him, but it appeared she talked only to herself. He watched a fiery rage take over her entire body and then… a boy… Coccin, was it? He ran rapidly towards her and placed a skinny, dirty hand upon her shoulder. Then, everything around Finn instantly disappeared.

Was there an abrupt halt in the wheels that turned Dragon Claw?

Finn, standing in the cold, crooked realm of nothingness that ought to have been Kulla Town Centre, locked eyes once more with Eliza. 'W-What was that?' he cried, in an almost demanding voice. 'That girl, was that you?'

Eliza offered no reply. Instead, she stared far into the distance. Gazing at something nearing towards them.

'Hey, I'm talking to you. You'd better start giving me some answers lady or—' But there was no need, for when Finn turned to see what Eliza had spied, he felt a sharp pain rise inside his chest.

How could it possibly be?

Covered in cuts and bruises, leg maimed and vision impaired, Ella-Rose hobbled with a small ladybird, flying at her side. Seeing her once again gave Finn a warm reminder of home.

'Ella-Rose,' he shouted as hard as his lungs would give. 'Ella-Rose,' he screamed.

She offered a slight impression that she could hear, but when she turned, she could not see him.

Despite its fierce falling, it was not the snow anymore that trickled down past Finn's brow. Instead, it was the sweat arising, caused by the heat of the sewer. Was it even possible to be in two places at one time?

Finn pursued Ella-Rose's every step through the strange summer snow. Eliza followed closely behind until they all reached the foot of the crooked cabin. Only this time, it wasn't on fire. Time had quickly shifted from the past to the present.

The crooked cabin. The damned crooked cabin. He had seen it at Kulla with Ella-Rose, seen it in his mind when she told him the Legend of Eliza. Saw it burning, only few minutes ago and now… he realised what it truly was. The root of all evil. All bad things lead to the cabin. All bad things came from the cabin. Its very nature was to cause pain.

Finn followed his friend through. Eliza followed shortly after. Both stood left of Ella-Rose. What they didn't know, was that they too were being followed. The sound of scurried, uncomfortable movement came from behind. When they turned back, towards the door, all eyes locked upon the image of a most frightful creature.

A demon.

A crooked smile took over its entire face. Sluggishly and calmly, the demon raised a long claw, not directed at Ella-Rose, but to her left. Directly towards Eliza.

Finn grabbed tight hold of Ella-Rose's shoulders, screaming into her ears, 'Ella-Rose! ELLA-ROSE! Can you hear—'

But once again, everything disappeared right before Finn's eyes.

Chapter Twenty-Eight
Labyrinth is Deadly

Diary Entry #8

The air blew unusually cold for a summer's night in Ramoria. Living my life at Castle Snow, you'd have thought I'd become accustomed to the cold. During my time at Fortunae Forest, before Mr Tomrick rescued me, I found that nature treated me as a friend. I gave my eye to its beauty. Grass so long-grown it practically shared height with the trees. The multi-colour of flowers, contrasting its glow against the dark soils. How beautiful it seemed, yes how beautiful it—

It didn't take long before I realised, I wasn't in Fortunae. There was no surrounding beauty, only a thick, grey fog flooding the area, almost blinding my sight to the carved sign in the distance. As I neared, the letters imprinted in the wood became clearer, displaying only the words: Labyrinth is Deadly.

After the last word reached the end of my lips, the giant bushed maze appeared from beneath a fog ahead.

I realised then, I must have been caught in a dream.

No, not a dream, but a nightmare.

It wasn't because I believed this maze arose unprompted from nothing, but more the fact that I didn't believe the labyrinth to be deadly at all. The fog thinned out and the scent of wet grass tickled my nose. I advanced towards the entrance to ease my curious mind. For long, I wondered what knowledge hid within that strange setting. I couldn't quite figure out the labyrinth there and then. Perhaps if I had, things could have been different.

I shivered as the cold swiped past. How strange. I actually shivered at the ice within my mind. I suppose, being in a dream is like being a puppet. I have no control over my actions, though the actions still belong to me.

I told my brain to raise my hand and my hand obeyed. I told it then to lower three fingers and down they went. This couldn't possibly be a nightmare. No, this was plain old consciousness.

There was a sudden force, much stronger than fate itself, pulling me closer and closer to the labyrinth's entrance. Hours, the length of seconds, would pass until finally, my conscience began to speak to me.

Not inside my head, but from the labyrinth itself. That voice was real. At least, as real as it could be. Soon after came he who accompanied the voice: the beetle.

'Name's Coccin L. Idae,' announced the small, wounded ladybird as it landed upon my palm. Its back appeared partly broken and misshapen, yet along with missing a couple of legs, it did not stop his positive energy. 'Friends call me Co, if it so please yer. Co does always seem to do the trick.'

'Y-You're talking,' I said, astonished, bewildered, you name it, I felt it.

'I am. As are you.'

'But, I don't under—'

'Things may not always appear what they seem,' Coccin explained. 'You'll do very well to remember that.'

The ladybird often flew away during my journey through the labyrinth, returning later with his secrets. I asked where he could possibly fly to in a place as empty as this, to which he told me: 'It is impossible to understand everything, so why waste yer time in trying?'

After infinitely turning the same corner, finally I reached my end in the labyrinth: nothingness. Perhaps the labyrinth was *deadly in a way. It certainly had killed my patience.*

I wanted to scream, to shout, but every possible word eluded me; sticking to the roof of my mouth. I remember the taste of copper, swimming through my saliva, barging against the barricades of my teeth. The words that would not reach my lips soon burst into flames inside my head. "Labyrinth is deadly," it raged. "Labyrinth is deadly."

The ladybird left, once more without warning, but I knew— I knew I was not alone. Might it have been that she was there all along? Was she even there at all? Regardless, I felt her staring at me from that crooked cabin in the distance. Watching me. Hating me.

My mind must have decided, then, that my time was up. Drenched in a sea of my own sweat, I awakened in Flir Tomrick's lavender sheets. My peculiar wake from consciousness.

I never did understand that crooked world then. Though, it is impossible to understand everything, so why waste time in trying?

But I did try.

For years, I studied that world within my head. Studied and searched until at last I could create the very map that lies within this book. It wasn't too difficult to begin with, for the crooked world, in a respect, was quite similar to that of Dragon Claw. Only, many secrets were hidden amongst that cold desert. Secrets, I intend to share in this very diary, in hope that it reaches he who is worthy. In hope it at last leads to peace.

Diary Entry #9

The truth is, sorcery really is a disease. And the crooked cabin? Well, that is just mankarash – a torture. A limbo between life and death.

When waking, I was once again a lost and lonely soul trapped within the body of a broken boy. I arose from those lavender sheets and saw nothing through my one eye. I searched the small house for Flir Tomrick. Not to wake him at all, just to know he was there.

As I walked, I still tackled at the fog in my head, for my sight was now half it had once been. Grey clouds closed in on my mind, scratching deep into my empty socket. I almost overlooked the smeared red writing, on the wall, to my left.

Labyrinth is Deadly, *it read.*

I knew as soon as I saw, that was not paint.

Before finding the dead boy of the forest days earlier, I only ever heard tales of the intolerable smell, oozing from eroding corpses, being the harshest reality of death, though none ever did speak of the horror that takes the eye. Flir's headless body sat coldly on his bed. The knife marks, carved deep into his scalp, looked warm.

Another nightmare, *I assured myself. The lie found my lips easily. A foul taste, poisoning my tongue.* Just a nightmare.

But who? Who would kill an innocent, unarmed man? Why, the same person who would kill an innocent, unarmed boy in the forest, of course.

He had found me. Even days before my arrival at Ramoria, I reckoned. He was there before me. The message he had left, on the wall, was all too clear. Thanisis must have always known we shared the same nightmares. The problem was, we never shared the same morals.

***

Kai-Sal raised his left index finger to the air. 'Read no more.'

Michael closed the book, watching as the monster shared whispers with his masked companions. Immediately, *eerily*, Yolanda and Spider left through the trees.

Sent back for the paug, Michael assumed. Shivers raced down his spine when reality at last hit him. They had both surely witnessed far too much to be kept alive. Though he held very limited understanding of all happenings following his departure from Caesar's, Michael realised he might not live to see tomorrow.

'A-Agarov,' Michael bravely whispered. 'I don't understand, this book – it's just a diary. I thought it was supposed to be a map.'

'A map, aye. However, one must learn to read between the lines, dear boy.'

'Surely no harm can come from it,' Michael shrugged.

'Anything can be harmful when laid into the wrong hands. The book is not *just* a dairy, Michael; it hides every secret of the crooked world; things incomprehensible to the wrong folk. All the words written – if read correctly – reveals the map.'

Michael did not know what that meant, nor did he even wish to, but before he could speak another word, the wolf chillingly shared, 'It was no accident that you were given this book, Michael. I fear sometimes, there are certain truths that are better left unheard. Our time in this forest is running low. I have no doubts of Kai-Sal's plans and where our next destination lies. We must go with the vampire, Michael. I have seen your fate and I fear this is the only path you can take. But know this: I promise you, I will protect you with all of my might. Trust in me. Trust in the prophecy.'

'Hey! Wolf, boy, to me, now,' Kai-Sal cut in, covering his burned and scarred face once more with his mask. 'It's time to go. I believe our destiny tonight is to be decided by the Shadows of the forest.' With a clean swipe of his long sword, Kai-Sal sliced the wolf's chains apart.

'You won't escape,' Kai-Sal assured, landing one hand on Michael's shoulder and the other tightly around Mankarash. 'We will go together in civility and respect.'

Agarov eyed the long sword distrustfully.

'Fine!' Much to their surprise, using the monstrous strength he had inside him, the monster snapped Mankarash in two and threw each part into the forest earth.

Why did you do that? Michael's mind shouted. *Forged by the Matra using blood of angels and souls of demons and you just snap it like a used toothpick?*

'No weapons, no fights. It was fake anyway.'

'What makes you think I won't just walk away?' Agarov asked, his growl more menacing than ever. He knew it would be useless to fight. Even if he could kill Darkness, he would certainly not live to tell the tale.

Kai-Sal let out an ominous cackle, the type you'd expect to hear from a witch who had stubbed her toe. 'Because,' he began. 'You know exactly where we're going. The same place you were headed before you became my prisoner. Regardless of our opposing reasons, we go there together.'

'Go where?' With a mixture of confusion and relief, Michael broke in before Agarov could.

Kai-Sal peered down with studious eyes. 'We leave for the Heart of Fortunae at once,' he said with a grin from ear to ear. 'I believe it is time we paid a visit to Master Jra'bral.'

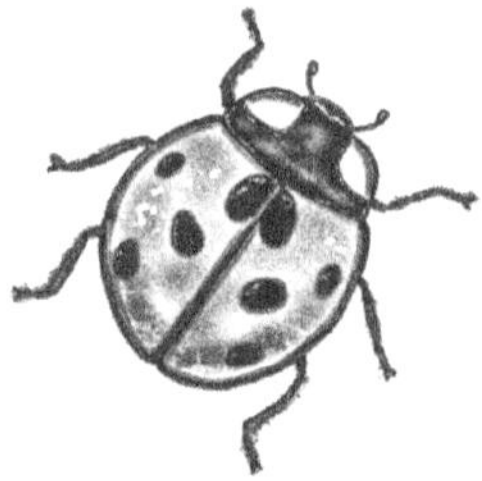

Chapter Twenty-Nine
A Garden of Daffodils

Heading directly towards the row of black mountains in the distance, Ella-Rose stumbled once more across the ice desert longing for warmth, food and help. Perhaps there could be a cave that had all three. But how in this world was she supposed to get there? The mountains belonged to the land of Posre yet appeared so deceptively close. Caesar had told her many tales of the black mountains. Everyone knew of the famous volcano, Mount Hjar, but Ella-Rose's favourite sight had always been Mount Kaah. With its beautiful glaciers atop and the Kaahla Rainforest below, the mountain was filled with exotic animals. Jaguars, sloths, monkeys, toucans.

Michael told her a joke about a toucan once, the memory warmed her caringly.

How many birds does it take to peel an orange? Well, one can't, but toucan.

Her mind cycled from Finn to Michael, Sara to Caesar. She imagined them at the professor's bungalow, peacefully relaxing around the fire with a cup of hot tea. Of course, Michael would plead for a glass of milky cocoa, cramming it with thick pink and white marshmallows. Such a warming image; one she decided to never again allow herself to see, for her tears would surely turn to icicles on their way down.

Instead, her mind drifted straight into the hands of Thanisis Rapture. She knew nothing of him other than the fact that he was a sorcerer.

So was one of his children, Coccin had told her, lowering his own head as if he was afraid to look her in the eye. '*Her name is—*'

Could it be? She didn't feel any different from anyone else. There was no magical, green laser beams shooting from her fingers, no telekinesis, no whizzes nor whazzes.

I'm just a usual girl living in an unusual world, right? Or was it the other way around?

No, I'm an unusual girl living in an unusual world.

Despairingly, she stumbled across the ice desert, occasionally stopping to synchronise her vision with the motionless mountains ahead.

'M-Michael,' she called out with an uncontrollable shivering hysteria. 'Michael, I don't like it. T-That snowman is s-scaring me.' Her body temperature had fallen low. Too low. Causing her mind to escape whatever reality it now belonged to. 'Why is it w-walking t-towards me?' Her heart was stopping and as the unreal snowball hit the back of her head, Ella-Rose fell hard into the white blanket below. 'D-Don't throw, M-Michael! I'm— I'm c-cold. S-So cold.'

In the distance, the mountains were replaced by a blurred blackness. She wished more than anything for Mount Hjar to erupt its fiery goodness and warm her up.

'F-Finn?' Bizarrely, she found herself missing his voice, screeching inside her mind. It had been painful, but at least it was something. 'Finn, d-do you remember the daffodils? Mr S-Sheldon's garden of d-daft-odils?'

Finn offered no reply. Whatever presence of his she had felt earlier on, was no longer there.

Ella-Rose was accompanied only by the tormenting frost. She could practically feel her soul lifting from her body. A menacing pain took her heart. Stabbing. Stabbing. Jabbing. Sharply attacking her slow-beating organ.

Her mouth ran dry, her vision was lost. She knew she was near to dying. It wasn't all that bad, right? Perhaps death truly is a kindness, relieving you of all the pains you have endured in life.

When at last the darkness closed in on her, she closed her eyes and whispered out to the nothingness, 'Is t-this what dying f-feels like?'

When the old man approached from behind and raised her up into his arms, he looked down into her narrowing eyes, sadly, and said, 'yes.'

Chapter Thirty
Joyless Kiss

Black tears filled the bottoms of her eyes. All the happiness Eliza had once known seemed to have vanished completely. They had returned at the very space they stood before travelling through Eliza's visions. She took Finn's hands tightly into her own, yet strangely he could still feel her touch at the sides of his head.

'Joyless kiss,' she said, staring into the sewage void. 'Joyless kiss. It's meaningless really. It was the last gift my sister ever gave to me.'

Finn stared up at her differently. All thoughts and emotions, running through his tiny body, had been muted.

'Words are nothing but deception and lies,' she continued. The smile that once gleamed at her face was now nowhere to be seen. 'They are limited and weak. I doubt words can even exist without an ear to hear or an eye to read. Have you ever witnessed something so beautiful, or heard something so magical that it literally steals the words right from your mouth? Joyless kiss,' she whispered once more. The tears began to steam straight down her cheeks.

'Eliza?'

'I love you, she told me. With tightness in my stomach, water in my eyes and goose-bumps at my flesh, I even believed it. I am as much a friend to love as I am to hate, fear as to calmness, happiness as to sadness. Those feelings were always divided between the two of us,' she cried, 'but the love always belonged to me. She never loved me.'

A cold wind thrust into the sewer then, Finn knew straight away from where it had come: from inside Eliza's body. Could it have been the same force that had pulled him into the tunnel in the first place? A force of fate. Because that was it, right? Fate brought him to Eliza. Why? He was still trying to figure that out.

'Just look at me. Here I am, sharing these words with you and can you sympathise? Emphasise? Perhaps. But could you feel it too? Truly feel it, I mean. *She* could. Everything about me, was her, just as everything about her, was me. I remember our last lie very well: "I won't ever leave you," she told me before the gates to the crooked world were opened.'

I won't ever leave you.
Give me wings that I may fly.
Only warmth lies within my heart.
My tears feel cold when departing the eye.
Now, my soul entwines with my mind.
No light, no darkness, only I.
No, I won't ever leave you. Not as I die.
It is a day like no other.
My final good bye.

'Only, it never was a final goodbye. She kissed me once before imprisoning me within those gates. It was her greatest trick of all; the illusion of love. A joyless kiss.' She took a deep breath.

'Eliza?'

'Stop calling me that!' Another strong force took the sewer, this time much more powerful, pushing the boy into a puddle of waste. 'Eliza's time in this world is finished. You must leave now, Finn.'

Only then did the small boy see the glisten of the medallion shining around her neck and, above that, the cruel, grey eyes of a murderer. What exactly happened when Eliza and Nyla just met within that crooked cabin?

'Leave now, see your friends and your family while you still can, for the Ladybird flies again.' With a magnificent force, she pushed open the sewer cover without even moving a muscle, then beckoned him out with the nod of her head. 'Now begins the true Legend of Eliza, or ought I call it, Legend of Nyla?'

The haunting sound of Eliza's body falling to the ground took his attention first before actually turning to see it, stiff and lifeless in the mud. The blackness, that then shot out of her chest, flew straight out of the sewer's cover and into Dragon Claw.

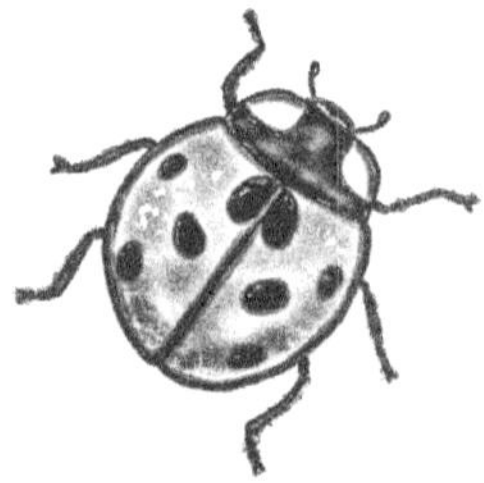

Chapter Thirty-One
The Heart of Fortunae

Some claimed it to be cursed. Others insisted it was haunted by the tortured souls of the dead. Regardless of its status, the very few who knew the existence of Parra Rapture's burial place, knew better than to ever step foot inside. It was always believed that when a sorcerer passes on, their soul lives on through the body of a hawk. However, when this late emperor died, his soul was certainly destroyed alongside him. Rumours spread that the heartless emperor never had perished that dreadful night at the palace gardens. His feeble body still worthlessly roams within the Heart of Fortunae, in hope that he finds that which he most desires: Death.

There once stood a great many temples across Dragon Claw. The *Black Syrath*, once legendary home to sorceress Shai Kalee, destroyed by the hands of Khosi Trajan, now lies empty and alone with its fractured bones. *Cold Flame*, built at Shabrath thousands of years ago, was reconstructed by Adlax Zi Tyrax's construction team after the aftermath of Hjar. Cold Flame was known to once be the humble home of Alura the Ice Dragon, but even she could not withstand the scorching beast that was Hjar.

The Heart of the Fortunae was the only temple remaining in Ramoria, celebrating its hundred and third year of hiding so discreetly amid Fortunae Forest.

The temple's architectural structuring was stolen from Gyra's ancient stoned White Heart Hospital. Its once white-brick, now stained black from pollution and red from war. The poisonous berries, wrapped hauntingly around the sides of its steps, closely spied the unlikely company of three like gazing eyeballs.

Kai-Sal's mind travelled back in time. He had not been at the Heart in a long, long time. It never was an easy place to find; one could only see its stone from a specific spot atop the Dantu Hills. Hiding well behind Fortunae's Scarred Trees, only those who knew of the Heart's placement could visit. Folk travelling through the Scarred Trees were seemingly those who were lost. No-one would ever dare enter on their own accord. It was believed that the trees themselves had a way of manipulating one's mind. Any who mistakenly wandered through, gained an intense thirst for blood and, more often than not, reports were made of folk returning home to murder their family. All with the same tale to tell of the whispering Scarred Trees. Certainly, travelling through with a monster had its benefits; Michael and Agarov heard no such whispers and their minds remained firmly attached to their body.

The three soon reached the hundreds of stairs leading up to the Heart. The moon shone magically down on them.

As Michael began his ascent, he recognised that the air from so high up was brand new; a gift to his lungs. He forced his heavy footwork to keep up with Kai-Sal, who was playing an irritating song of cracking twigs and cackling leaves beneath his feet.

'The moon is alive tonight,' Agarov spoke poetically. 'The light shines bright across Dragon Claw's skies. Tonight, across the four lands, I have no doubt folk will be celebrating the Night of the Betrayal.'

'The what?' Michael asked. All fear, that previously ran though him, turned to comfort when speaking with the wolf.

I promise you, I will protect you with all of my might, Agarov had told him. Michael had believed him.

'It is on this very night years ago that the betrayer was found; on this very night the betrayer was crowned.'

'Who?'

'It's the celebration of Benjamin Syrus' coronation,' Agarov spat. 'Thrown to throne, succeeding the slaughter of Lozari Rapture and his army of the undead.'

Kai-Sal stopped. His ears couldn't help but eat up every word. 'True, Syrus betrayed all that day,' he cut in, sharply. 'Folk were blinded— brain-washed by his play of politics, but I always saw the truth. What good comes from killing the queen bee if her spawn remain? Syrus was a fool to keep Lozari's children alive, let alone raise them as his own.'

'Lozari Rapture had no children,' Michael blurted out uncontrollably. 'Sorry, but I've heard all the tales of war.'

'Your history is mistaken, boy,' Kai-Sal raged.

Agarov nodded. 'Aye, the vampire speaks truly. Benjamin Syrus may have raised Zagan and Thanisis, but he shared blood with none. They are the children of Lozari Rapture and Savanah Fallen.'

'The boys killed Benjamin Syrus with their sorcery no doubt,' Kai-Sal taught. 'But, Benjamin was always to blame. He betrayed Empora and he got what he deserved.'

The three stopped in unison upon noticing the temple's entrance through a mass of clouds. What stood most distinctly from all else was the peculiar mark of a serpent skull, similar to that on Kai-Sal's mask, stained red atop the brick, (with what Michael could only assume was sacrificial blood.) Below, hung a sign reading: *Magicae Mortem.* Michael could tell that the first word meant magic and he was sure he had heard the word *mort* in a different language before from Caesar's teachings. He was certain it meant *death*.

A large assembly of figures spread orderly from the temple's lips. Michael nervously closed in towards the wolf, feeling at light ease at his side. Afraid, and anxiously unaware of what was to come, what worried the boy most was seeing the fear rise in Agarov's eyes. It did not show easily, but fright was clearly there.

'Who are they?' Michael whispered, gesturing his brow to the half-naked, painted bodies, dispersing from the entrance. Each boasted identical marks of a serpent skull in red upon their chest.

'*Shadows*, they call themselves. Radicalised by the Aj'ayahic Testaments to believe sorcery a crime— a mistake in the Great One's plan. Legend holds the mark upon their chests keeps sorcery's energies at bay.'

'Do you believe it?' asked Michael.

The White Wolf smiled; he liked the boy, there was no denying. The dark eyes that stared into his own reminded him of another he once knew. Eyes of a bear. 'I have forgotten much of what I've seen in my years and remember more of what I never lived,' his smile faded. 'I know sorcery to be much more powerful than anything else—' his voice trailed off alongside his stare. He clocked a recognisable face behind the Shadows. A tall, grey figure emerging from the temple and balancing his weight upon a golden cane. 'Michael, be careful in your ways. He who holds the cane, holds the claim of Master Jra'bral Xhea.'

'Who?'

'The *vampire priest.* Worshiped as a God even by the Trajans.'

Jra'bral welcomed Kai-Sal and his prisoners inside with a warm bow. Agarov was first to return the gesture. Michael's gawky effort came next, followed by Kai-Sal's cold offering of a slight nod.

The inside of the temple was seen only by moonlight, reflecting off the pool of water situated directly in the middle. Ruby and sapphire banners hung from the roof, each with a distinct symbol. Tusks of mammoth and skins of tiger hung the walls. Stone-made sculptures of bear and troll lined each side of their walk and, carved into the walls were symbols of ancient scripture that Michael did not recognise.

Jra'bral sat atop a large stash of quartz minerals he claimed his throne, allowing for the company of three to stand in line before him. Michael studied him closely. The priest's skin was flaked and white like a ghost. Bronze rings hugged his ears, from helix to orbital. His teeth were either extrinsically yellow or plated with gold; Michael could not tell which.

Painted Shadows gathered and peered silently from the upper-level of the Heart. They showed nothing of what ran through their minds.

'Before our business is to begin, I ask that you all name yourselves in turn,' Master Jra'bral requested, seriously.

The wolf was first to step forward. 'Agarov of the Aj'ayah,' he growled and the vampire priest narrowed his eyes.

The wolf then turned and edged Michael forward. 'M-Michael of— um, Ramoria, I guess.'

'And I, Kai-Sal,' announced the Darkness.

'Only a true name is accepted within the Heart,' the master stated. His voice was slow and so low it was hardly heard.

Kai-Sal gazed long and hard at the priest. '*Alexander Ezra Fallen*, brother of Raylan Fallen,

Master Jra'bral.' He flinched as the sound of his own name escaping from his mouth. Kai-Sal lost his true name the day he lost his identity as a mage of Posre. The awful memory burst aggressively into Kai-Sal's mind, and Alexander soon travelled back into darkness…

It was Jra'bral Xhea, eldest son of Roland "The Hammer" Xhea first to watch the emerald sky turn grey. Perhaps it always had been and they just hadn't noticed through the thick smoke rising from Quae's burning death. 'Face it, Alexander, we have lost this war,' he hissed, digging his claws into the iron chains. 'Friends and families, dead, and for what? For what? Damn them all! Damn Kraal Syrus and damn Raylan Fallen. There is no denying it, Lozari Rapture owns Empora and Posre now. Lozari Rapture owns us all.'

'Ridiculous, vampire! Burn your words.' The mage forced.

'Didn't you hear them? Kraal Syrus is dead! Raylan Fallen is dead.'

'Aye, Empora is lost, but what is lost can always be found. Forget my brother as I have. He may be

dead, but we are still the United Dragons,' Alexander stated arrogantly. 'I of magic, you of monster, we'll fight with man against the Raptures. Kraal may be dead, but Benjamin will take his throne. Sorcery is our shared enemy in this war, nothing else.'

Jra'bral paused, for he had heard those exact words before, travelling from the heated lips of his beloved Lady Elizabeth. It was the night before he was to leave for Quae; the night he last belonged to himself.

"Liza, how can I possibly fight for a cause in which I do not believe? Further a fight as unfair as this. It isn't right, dammit."

"Fear not, Jra'bral. Let the Testaments speak your actions. Good against evil is all it is," Lady Elizabeth assured. "You fight not for war, but for peace my love. Protect our home. Sorcery is our shared enemy in this war."

Jra'bral shot Alexander a questioning gaze. 'Do you have a lady, Sir Alexander?'

Alexander grinned. 'Why, I've had many a lady in my time and many a lady at one time.'

Jra'bral noticed there was a secret pain hidden in his eyes. 'That's not what I—'

'I know exactly what you meant, Jra'bral. Aye, I had a lady once. Just once. Most beautiful bitch I ever did lay my eyes on. Hair as dark as my heart and long as my cock. Her freckles, her voice, her eyes—' he trailed off and for a second Jra'bral thought he'd shed a tear. 'Xhea, do you know the one thing a fella needs to stay sane?' The mage didn't give chance for an answer. 'Hope,' he sighed. 'Everyone in Dragon Claw needs to hold onto some hope of a perfect life. Doesn't matter whether they'll ever get to live it. Most folk don't, but that's beside the point. You might get beaten near to death, your valuables stolen, your heart torn in two. You might get lost, hungry, lonely and yet you still hope for a perfect life. It is a comfort to hold onto; a goal to strive towards; a thing to live for. So, what do you suppose happens when all hope is taken from you?'

A long, comfortable silence was offered in return.

'Aye, I had a lady once,' he hesitated. 'And forever she will hold my heart.'

A long, comfortable quietness took the air, broken once more by the lips of Alexander. 'If we lay our trust in the new Syrus emperor—'

'Trust? The boy is thirteen-years-old.'

'Aye, but still a member of the United Dragons by blood. While we fight for Syrus, we fight for Trajan. Khosi remains strong.'

'Strong you believe? Then, you're ignorant to the truth. Khosi has gone mad with power.'

'Aye he has,' Alexander laughed. 'Is it not the very duty of an emperor to do so? We are the United Dragons,' he said once more.

Anger started to burn deep through Jra'bral's divided heart. 'What damn loyalty you keep,' he spat. 'To turn so quickly on your own emperor, nay, your own brother—'

'I speak well and true. Raylan is dead, Kraal is dead. Strong leaders, aye, but weak fighters,' he admitted. 'What use has loyalty to war? Loyalty's what gets folk killed. There ain't no place for right and wrong when it comes to choosing sides. I'll tell you this for nothing - you'd do well to not speak again in that tone, less you want your throat cutting.'

'Another threat?' Jra'bral scoffed. 'My, that's got to be seven in the same hour if I count correctly.'

'I wouldn't make light of it. After all, we only met just two ago.'

'Only two?' Jra'bral stretched his foot as far as the chains would reach. Shackles of three-inch-thick dragatus trum; a Sebastian Steel. He parted his hands as far as the cuffs would allow, dropping them behind his head upon which to lean. 'Feels much longer.'

'Soldier, I'm afraid it ain't just these chains tying us down,' Alexander sighed, raising the shackles attached to his own wrists and ankles. 'We're all just slaves to time. Chained to a world of politics.'

'Is that right?'

'Aye,' the mage replied. 'I wouldn't worry too much. See, chains are meant to be broken.'

Jra'bral shook his head. 'They're literally built for the opposite reason. You're saying you can free us?'

Alexander offered a confirming, 'Uh-huh.'

'And you know all this from experience, I'll wager?'

'Else whenever I wish to spice up the bedroom,' he winked, waving the chains attached to his hands. 'Chin up, Jra'bral. They say time flies when you're having fun. But do you know what happens when you're stuck with an arrogant prick like you?' Though he did not see, Alexander assumed Jra'bral shook his head and rolled his eyes. 'It damn right breaks.' And at his final word, Alexander broke the chains that imprisoned his wrists and ankles.

'How did you—'

'A simple trick of magic,' Alexander lied.

'Could you not have done that two hours ago? My wrists are killing me.' Jra'bral smiled, holding up his chains for request of freedom.

Alexander nodded his head towards a tall man in the distance. Their captor: Joje Sebastian. 'You see that man over there? Had I escaped hours ago, I'd have been killed immediately. You must always choose the right moments.' He glared at the vampire in distain. 'Why should I to help you?'

'Don't be foolish now, mage. You said it yourself, we are united.'

'True, we are. But that does not change the fact that vampire are the scum of this world,' Alexander spat.

As the mage turned to take his leave, Jra'bral threw the chains, still attached to his wrists, at the mage's feet, knocking Alexander to the ground. The vampire pulled Alexander and positioned the chains to take a tight hold at the mage's chest.

'Off me, dirty bloodsucker!' Alexander Fallen raged.

'You must always choose the right moments,' Jra'bral mocked. 'You damn me to die. Then, I will damn you to live.'

In mere seconds, Jra'bral's teeth sunk deep into the mage's neck and instantly, Alexander felt the change of flow in his blood.

Chapter Thirty-Two
An Unlikely Friendship

The Ladybird flies again.

The four words had not hit Finn's mind even once in the first few minutes since leaving the sewer. His mind was gone; stolen and he didn't know whether it would ever return.

The boy had not paid much attention to his departure from the tunnel. The night sky shared a much dimmer shade of grey than before. Opposing the exotic flow of incense bursting throughout the luminous sewer, what he now encountered was the dirt of Suud Swamp, shooting up his nostrils.

Suud Swamp was nothing less than a damp and dark desert of dirt. A forest in reverse. Rather than a golden path surrounding itself by rich and powerful oak, there were only fields of green, gunged ponds with flopped, black willow lazing into it.

The clouds above bowed their bodies before clearing the sky for the moon's re-entrance, allowing a slight white light to bounce off the sludge beneath him.

Finn kicked a couple of branches as he walked and threw some rocks at the trees. It was not sadness which overwhelmed him, but anger. Anger for being alone, anger for remaining clueless still as to Ella-Rose's whereabouts, but mainly anger at himself.

I saw her, he thought. *Saw Ella-Rose in that cabin and I didn't help her. I couldn't help her!* A chill soon took his entire body. *The cabin! That's where she is! But I don't remember the way.*

Finn released a weakened shout from his lungs. He knew that to make even the slightest of sounds could summon a range of dark creatures, but he did not care. His problem was not that he was lost within Fortunae, but that he was lost within himself.

Reality soon hit him and it hit hard. Finn's mind returned, displaying the dark image of the demon standing— no, floating at the cabin's door. The exact same image he saw escaping through Eliza's motionless body and out into Dragon Claw.

Then it was true. The Ladybird flies again.

I must find Ella-Rose! What would she think of it all?

Finn stopped, suddenly. There was a groan in the distance. 'No, no! Not again.' It wasn't loud, but it was unmistakably there. A groan, followed by a voice which spoke so exasperatedly: 'Oh for goodness sake! I must be going round in circles. I'm sure I was here not so long ago.'

'Who's there?' whispered Finn.

'Ah yes, I remember this tree, oh and of course that tree. No wait, wasn't that the other tree? Oh dear, I do believe I'm lost.'

Finn soon spotted the owner of the afar voice. It was a strange-looking creature, oddly, even smaller than himself, treading its tiny-toes into the muck of Suud. Its little legs had become an empty canvas to a chestnut shade of brown. Warily, the small creature prodded along the wetland of waste, followed by the soft sound of squelching slop between Finn's toes, as the boy closely followed behind. Each time the creature turned to check his surroundings, Finn would rush behind the nearest tree where hundreds of orange-lit eyes sat heavily on him. Their silent scrutiny teased.

'This wretched place makes me so nauseous,' the creature sympathetically moaned to himself. 'In the name of Jra'bral, won't anybody point me to the nearest exit?'

Finn continued to pursue the creature, assuming that something so little could not offer a large threat. He tried to pluck up the courage to ask if he knew the direction of Kulla Town Centre, all the while knowing it would certainly be useless, for the creature appeared to be lost too. He couldn't help but feel sorry for the small thing. It's not easy being the size of a dwarf; he couldn't imagine being smaller.

The creature continued through the swamp, stopping at every small mud mountain that spurt warm muck from its peak to rub the smooth texture over its body.

'Ah, what does it even matter if I'm lost?' It spoke again. 'When nowhere is home, everywhere is home. Especially for a paug.'

The paug was more than accustomed to travelling Fortunae alone, it was all he had known his entire life. Abandoned by his family literal seconds after his birth, who knew whether they even realised he had been born amongst his hundreds of brothers and sisters in the litter? He recalled only a single memory from the day he was shot out into the world: the four words that defined him: *You are a paug*. From then forth, the only thing he could possibly confirm was his own existence. All else, he had uncovered either through stolen literature or the wild experiences he had faced.

In the distance, the creature clocked a large pile of bricks, disguising themselves as a bridge. The space was open and dry, the mud more solid than liquid. Its construction was similar to that of a child's playtime activity; disarranged and unbalanced. *Cosy enough to take rest though,* he supposed. Until hearing the crack of a twig and spotting the boy behind him. 'No,' the paug cried painfully, backing away from

Finn through the mud of Suud. 'No, no, no not again. Not another cretin-boy, I beg of you, leave me be!'

Quickly, the paug dove into a pond of algae that Suud tried to pass for water. He kept his head underneath for as long as his lungs would possibly allow before popping it back up to see Finn's inquisitive face staring right at him.

'Sorry to bother,' Finn said, 'but do you know which way I would find Kulla Town Centre, sir?' Of course, when addressing one you didn't know, a Hampson must always use proper terms, like sir and madam.

The paug looked at hi, perplexedly. 'Didn't your parents teach you *not* to speak to strangers? I've heard they can be… well, quite strange.'

'I don't think you're strange.'

'I beg your pardon. I wasn't talking about me,' the paug huffed, pushing himself out of the green pond and shaking himself dry. 'Might I ask what a man, like yourself, is doing in a swamp at this time of night? Seems awfully um, what's the word? Strange.'

'Man? You must need those eyes testing.'

'Excuse me?'

'Sorry, nothing. I'm here because, well— it's a long story. I guess I don't really know why I'm here, but I know where I'm heading.' Finn explained, trying his best not to recall the events of the day. What exactly had brought him to that swamp? Was it Ella-Rose? The globbers? Eliza?

'Well, if you know where you're going, you don't need my help.'

'No, I mean, I know the place – I just don't know where it is.'

'Hmm.'

'All I know, is that I need to make my way to Kulla right away.'

The more the two talked, they found that they oddly trusted one another. They may have even found that they *liked* each other.

The paug accompanied Finn on his journey to Kulla, told him that his name was Creep and explained about the hectic day he'd had. Starting with the "gigantic tree" that had fallen atop his leg.

'I'm lucky to be alive,' Creep explained.

He went on to share his tale of a cretin-boy who had stolen his favourite book and ran into the forest with it, causing them to be captured by a masked clan.

'Wow, what a bully! Let's hope we don't run into this cretin-boy! Oh, the things I'd do to him,' Finn blurted, punching his little fists out in the air. 'Sorry, I'm not usually like this. It's been a long day.'

Finn shared his tale of the sewer and the demon that had escaped into the world.

Creep, however, thought that his tree and cretin-boy story was much worse. 'I mean, you were trapped in a sewer with what sounds like a beautiful woman who gave you a head massage, while I was tied to a tree with a group of masked idiots for company. I think I'd very much prefer your day to mine, Mr Hampson.'

'Oh please, do call me Finn.'

The short boy's lips reached a wide smile and Creep couldn't help but return the expression.

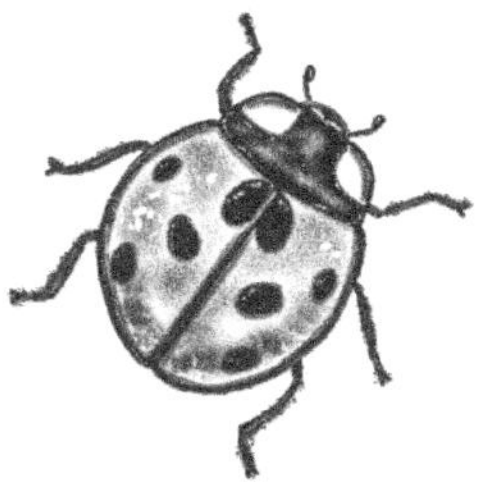

Chapter Thirty-Three
Resurrected Death

Like a strong rumble of wind, the sound of Master Jra'bral's sullen laughter took the walls heavily, releasing Kai-Sal back from his dark past.

'Alexander, I welcome you and your prisoners to the Heart. I do not doubt that the spirits of fate has led you to enter my door.'

'Please Jra'bral. Bypass all the pleasantries,' Kai-Sal threw the small, leather book before the vampire priest's throne. As the opened pages of sorcery hit the sacred grounds of the Heart, all eyes surrounding spread wide. Stares rougher than Agarov's claws surfaced from the Shadows. The air became tasteless. A shout of silence roared fiercely across the hall as time came to a halt.

'What, pray tell, is this?' asked Jra'bral, leaning slowly forward for a better look.

'The map of the crooked world,' announced Agarov.

'The very one,' Alexander agreed. 'Brought to us by this boy.'

Jra'bral concentrated his charcoaled gaze now on the book's blank pages. 'Now, I see quite well.' His words, much like a savage swipe of a sword. Both his eyes and soul gripped hard on Michael. 'Alexander,' Jra'bral said, through the side of his mouth. 'Do you see me a fool?'

Kai-Sal pushed forward like a soldier readying for war - not battle, but war. 'I see you as nothing other than my master. Myself, your most humble servant.'

Although the temple's jaws were permanently agape, Michael could not help but feel trapped in its gut.

When the vampire priest turned his black, scrutinizing eyes onto the boy, he would not dare move a muscle. 'Then, is it you, Michael, who sees me a fool?' he asked. 'Something ghastly has been brought into my temple, you see, and it is not this book of which I speak. I cannot deny that I smell Rapture blood.'

Agarov shoved Micahel behind him. 'Assumptions are but daggers against trust, Jra'bral. The scent you smell must be Zagan's upon that book.'

'Aye, there is no Rapture here,' Kai-Sal reluctantly agreed. 'The only living Raptures are Zagan and Thanisis, and they've both been hiding since the Fall of Snow.'

'I care not for your words. It *is* the boy. His scent is an insult to my nose.' Jra'bral paused judgingly. 'The boy dies here and now.'

'What?' Michael blurted.

Die: a mere three-letter word that once belonged to the characters in Caesar's books. Never had Michael dared to give it any true meaning until this day. To die is to have lived and to have lived is to die. But Michael hadn't lived long enough to die.

I have seen your fate, the wolf had said earlier. *And I fear this is the only path you can take.*

The path that leads to death? Michael trembled.

An insane, thick drool slipped between the wolf's sharp teeth. 'You will bring him no harm,' he warned. The fear, within his eyes, showed Michael that Agarov must not have anticipated for this to happen. 'There will be no killing tonight. This boy has no further purpose to you.'

'Perhaps none to me, but he who shares the blood of sorcery is no friend of the Heart.'

At his last word, a group of Shadows gathered around the company. 'Jra'bral, one ought to be careful with their tongue when proof is lacked,' Agarov growled.

A loud clanking of machinery disguised as a laugh scraped loudly from the master's throat. 'You are a prisoner of the Shadows and you would forge threats against me, within my own home? Courage is not absent with you, that much I see.' His smile was as dark as his heart. 'If it is evidence you require, then evidence I shall provide, lest we go further down a most unforgivable path.'

The melody of brushing footsteps, performed by a young, painted woman came from the stairs left of the throne. The bases of her bare feet shared colour with the dark ground, though the rest of her body was ghostly white. She strolled royally down the stoned staircase with an elegant grace, holding admiringly-good posture. Two older painted men, eyes bluer than the seas of the Aj'ayah joined behind, each holding onto a single arm as they dragged behind a broken, beaten man.

Down a most hostile path, the decaying man approached the bench painfully. Hauled like a raw piece of meat, ready to dance between Jra'bral's golden jaws. It was not surprising that the musky aroma of resurrected death did not faze Michael even once, for far too much had the boy seen this day to not be believing in ghosts. Instead, what grew demandingly nauseous through Michael's stomach was the sight of a respiring scar which ran deep across the dead man's chest; a lazy sewing job it would seem. Pulsation of the unfit organ within his chest was slow, though as it retained its unsteady melodic beat, the dead man's chest weakened and shrunk in at his every daunting breath. A charred blackness burned deep within the man's eyes; his arms and his legs were both either broken or had just completely given in.

Forced like a beaten animal before the White Wolf's paw, this skin-tight skeleton reached out with hope in his soul and recognition upon his face. 'Agarov, my old friend,' he gasped unhealthily between words. 'I beg, I beg you to end my suffering.'

The stillness of Agarov's mouth spoke much more than any word could. The Shadows surrounding may have been ghosts in their cold white skins but, in this man, everyone within the temple truly saw resurrected death. Agarov looked not to the praying corpse, but instead to Master Jra'bral who was laughing at his throne. 'Misdirection is a trick of magic, Jra'bral,' he half mocked. 'When here, I understood, that magic wasn't your desired game.'

The wolf growled loud in horror and disgust as the dead man grabbed loosely at his fur. 'Broken man, I do not know you and therefore owe you no favour.'

'You know me, sir, you know me well,' he groaned. 'Please, give me… mercy.'

'False wolf! Agarov, I name you a liar,' Master Jra'bral rose alongside his accusation. 'You know this man, as he knows you. Behold Parra Rapture, broken emperor of the Ramorian Empire. A dead man living. Resurrected death. A new man with the beating heart of his son, Thaddeus.'

'I share no lie. I once knew a brave man who held the name Parra Rapture.' Agarov almost choked on his words. 'This *thing* lay before me is nothing but a pet for your games.' He kicked the dead man aside with his colossal paw. 'What reason do you have for throwing him at my feet, other than for your own amusement?'

'Rapture,' Jra'bral spoke scornfully. 'Tell our dear guests what it was you told me the day I saved your pitiful life from the Demon Mother.'

'P-Please, Master. Please, sir. I do not—'

'Dare not deny me!' Fire burned in Jra'bral's eyes.

Sweat poured down the dead man's forehead. *Was such a thing even possible*? 'My son, L-Lozari Rapture,' Parra began. 'Had t-two children, Z-Zagan and Thanisis, it is true.'

The vampire priest rushed onto his feet. 'But the sorcery line does not end there, does it?' A boasting smirk took to his lips.

'N-No priest,' Parra spoke with an apologetic tone. 'For, it is also true that Thanisis had t-two children of his own— A-Agarov, I'm sorry.' His words sank into him, just like his chest.

'Name them.' It was Kai-Sal who gave this order, sharing an identical look of curiosity with Michael. 'Name them!'

'Ella-Rose and M-Michael Rapture—'

'Enough!' Agarov's roar shook the entire temple.

The broken man offered apologetic eyes to the wolf. Dark, thick, sorrowful eyes. Eyes of a bear.

For two minutes, Michael had counted the dangerous silence, not daring offer a word from his mind. Michael and his sister had lived their entire lives having not known, nor cared about their true parents. Not that this changed anything. His knowledge of Thanisis Rapture still remained unknown. Yet, there stood his alleged broken Great Grandfather. Purposelessly, Michael clenched his fists, squeezing tightly onto the hard rage growing within.

For the same two minutes, Agarov too had counted the dangerous silence. Preparation was crucial. He needed to be careful in his ways. To be ready. To be quick. While several lightened eyes locked onto the wolf from the Shadows' gazes, his own stuck heavily on Master Jra'bral.

If he went, he went to kill.

Chapter Thirty-Four
Man

As they continued through the darkness of Fortunae, Creep started to recognise parts of his surroundings. Everywhere they wandered appeared different at night. The paug soon sensed the tree in which he was tied to earlier that day.

'What makes you think it's the same tree?' Finn asked dubiously, to which Creep scurried behind the trunk and rattled some chains. Of course, he had wished to pull them out and drop them before Finn's feet for dramatic effect, but when it came to lifting the chains the paug struggled far too much.

'Right, okay, this is where you were tied. Now which way to Kulla?'

Creep pushed his lower jaw out and made a noise that sounded like a snake hissing inward, mixed with the sound of boiling water sizzling out of a pan. 'Yeah, I seem to have forgotten to mention that I was dragged in a sack. I don't actually remember the way.'

Finn released another agitated cry and kicked at the leaves beneath his feet. 'Typical. Just my luck. Of course you wouldn't know the way, why would—'

His speech came to an abrupt stop at the sound of a loud *clank* beneath his shoe. He had kicked something - something that would have gone straight through his foot had it not been lay flat on the soil. For that, he was very thankful.

The small boy bent down and raised the shiny, glistening object at his face for closer inspection. It had clearly been broken, but the part he held had a thick, golden handle and one word carved deep into the side of the blade.

MAN

By the look of it, it could have easily once been a long sword, only for some reason it had been snapped in half. There must have surely been more to the writing on the other piece of the blade, but that didn't matter to him one bit. Strangely, the half sword, fitted at his grasp, felt right. Certainly, for Two-Feet-Four-Inches-Finn the half sword appeared much larger than it would in the hands of a proportionately sized man.

'What have you got there?' Creep asked. The Paug eyed the half sword up and down, yet no recognition of the sword entered his mind whatsoever.

'I just— I found it laying here, buried beneath a pile of leaves.'

'Suits you,' Creep smiled. 'You look like a warrior.' The paug read the writing across the sword aloud, 'MAN. Rather fitting, wouldn't you say?'

'How do you mean?'

'Well, it's half a sword that says the word *man*.'

Finn looked at Creep curiously.

'Half man for a half man.'

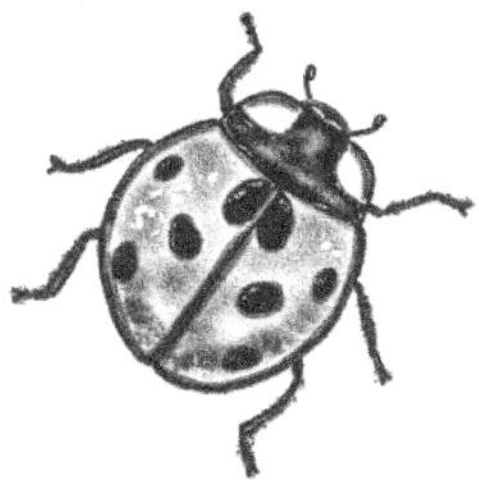

Chapter Thirty-Five
Monster

Through a fierce burning rage, Agarov pounced, only not towards the vampire priest, but instead forcing Parra Rapture to the ground. 'Here is your mercy, old friend.' The wolf ran his claws into the dead man's throat, ripping the nothingness his skin had to offer out of him and onto the floor.

Four. The deaths your soul will face.

Master Jra'bral forced the wolf's halt, or rather that which he grasped so tightly within his hands forced the wolf to stop. How he could have snatched the boy and brought him close to his throne so quickly when he had stood next to him mere seconds ago was amiss to the wolf. The power of a vampire always astounded him.

'Let the boy go, monster,' Agarov demanded. 'Else I'll kill every last one of you.'

But it was too late, for the vampire priest had already sunken his teeth deep into Michael's neck and tossed him coldly aside, like a toy he no longer wished to play with.

Agarov sprung immediately to attack Jra'bral, the fur around his face glowed a harsher red than blood. However, Kai-Sal was quick to strike, leaping from where he stood and taking the wolf to the ground.

'No,' Jra'bral forced hoarsely. 'Alexander, he is not yours to kill.'

'Then whose—' but Kai-Sal knew he needn't waste anymore breath, for everyone's stare within the Heart directed towards Michael's blood-filled eyes as they opened aggressively in the shadows.

'Our young monster will be hungry.'

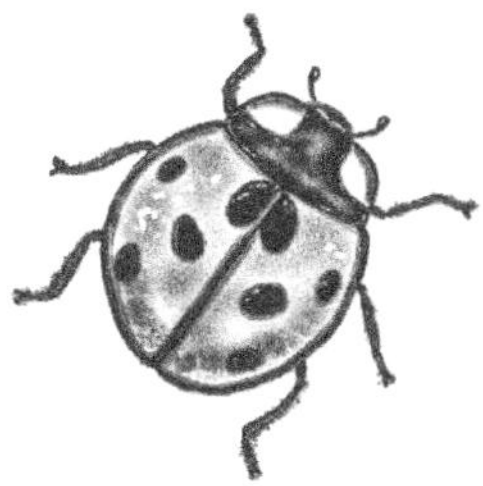

Chapter Thirty-Six
Magic

Only by the hands of Eliza can peace forever be restored throughout Dragon Claw. Was it true? The snow-covered charred sign on the front of the crooked cabin, could it possibly have been words of Dragon Claw's destiny?

From miles away, near the Black Mountains, Zagan had stood and spied through the broken windows of the crooked cabin, just as Nyla had done to him not so long ago. Zagan had watched the small party enter the cabin, and the exchange between Nyla and Eliza, with anxiety taking hold of his every nerve. Nyla had trapped Eliza within the crooked world, taking the complete medallion right from Ella-Rose's reach. The demon had awakened in Dragon Claw. The Ladybird flies again.

Good, the old man thought to himself. *The prophecy has spoken truly after all.*

'Thank you Coccin,' he said aloud to himself, as he carried Ella-Rose away from the cold nothingness and back into the warming hands of Fortunae.

Zagan allowed his mind to return to the nights he had met Mr Coccin L. Idea in his youth. The small beetle had shared many secrets within that deadly labyrinth. After all, it was the beetle who told him the prophecy that would decide the fate of Dragon Claw.

First, the ladybird had instructed Zagan to create a diary with a map for the crooked world, meant only for a Rapture boy named Michael to read.

'You must send someone that you wholeheartedly trust to Shayam Village to watch over three very important children.'

Joje Sebastian. Who else could he have chosen? For Joje has been a trusted friend to the Raptures all his life.

'Yes,' Coccin had agreed. 'Perhaps it would be best to send his granddaughter, Alena, too. She can care for them like a mother.'

'I'll make them hide their true identities.'

'Good,' Coccin nodded. 'These children will need to be protected at all cost.'

Zagan had agreed.

'Pass the book to Joje and he will give it to Michael.'

'When?'

'You'll know when the time comes.'

Next, Coccin explained that the boy will be captured after retrieving the book and forced to read the first nine entries to confirm its true worth. 'Only you and I will know, the first nine entries of your diary will share no secrets of the crooked world, for you will write the first nine only to stall for the prophecy.'

'Stall how?' Zagan had asked.

'By sharing only fragments of the truth.'

'How do you know it will be only nine? Not ten? Not eleven?'

'Trust in the prophecy, Zagan!'

Then, the beetle had told him that he would need to sacrifice fifty years of his life within the crooked cabin, gaining knowledge of its powerful energies to be able to teach Ella-Rose.

'Could I not just go to her?' Zagan questioned.

'Don't be so silly. Though you're young now, age will take you, as it does all things. It would be unwise for a strange, old man to tell a young girl that she was born to defeat a demon in crooked world, don't you agree? You must let her find this world of her own accord. In order for the prophecy to hold, there must be no alterations. Understand?'

He did.

Next came Finn.

'Finn Hampson is no relative to the Raptures,' Coccin had taught. 'Though he plays a huge role in the war to come.'

'War?'

'The War of Four will end, but a greater War of Man, Monster and Magic will begin. The prophecy states that Finn Hampson, a boy the size of a dwarf will meet Eliza and allow her to guide them both into the crooked world. It is then that the demon will trap Eliza within and be released into Dragon Claw.'

'You mean, the prophecy wants the demon to be set free into Dragon Claw?'

'I'm afraid it is not what it wants, but what must be.'

'What happens to the children?'

'Finn will discover a broken sword named *Mankarash*. A most powerful sword that disguises itself as a fake for any who are not worthy to hold it. This broken sword is meant only for Finn to possess.'

'But—'

'Trust in the prophecy Zagan! The small boy will fight for the men and women of Dragon Claw. Michael will become a monster at the hands of Master Jra'bral Xhea. He will grow into a most powerful vampire and will fight for the monsters.

'And the girl? What of Ella-Rose?'

To this, Coccin had given a long, sad sigh. 'The girl will die within your arms,' he said solemnly. 'But she will rise anew. Ella-Rose has a most powerful magic inside of her. The beauty within her soul holds more energy than the Ladybird itself ever could. She won't be aware of it. You will teach her the ways of the sorcerer. Together, it is written that the three of them will destroy the demon, close the gates and at long last, bring peace to all races of Dragon Claw. Man, monster and magic will come together as a unity.' Coccin had stopped then. 'Of course, only if the prophecy holds true.'

'And Eliza?'

'Only by the hands of Eliza can peace forever be restored throughout Dragon Claw,' Coccin recited. 'She serves a purpose more crucial than you'll ever know.'

***

'But for now,' Zagan said to himself, looking down at Ella-Rose in his arms. 'Legend of Eliza is over.'

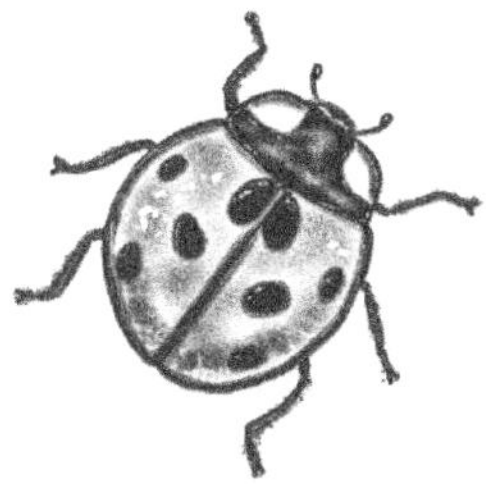

Epilogue
Death's Door

Lurching past the Shabrathian cells, whilst basking in the sinister cries of the helpless prisoners within, the cruel man headed towards cell D1-3183 with a matter of urgency.

The prison known to most as Death's Door was divided into four separate wings, ranging from A to D. Ground floor is meant for all convicts from Posre, second for Ramorian, third Emporan and of course the top floor is given to the most dangerous criminals of all – the monsters of Danjin.

Though no-one else probably could, Yara Trajan heard the footsteps advancing towards his cell, D1-

3183. Heard them all the way from Jimmy Ferdinand's D1-3172 about a mile away from his own.

But were the footsteps real?

He often found himself asking the very same question every minute of every day. *Was the sound actually there?* Behind the advancing footsteps, he heard only agonising screaming, though even their existence became doubted after having heard them non-stop for weeks.

Yara Trajan glanced down at the puddle mere inches from the bars that closed him into his tiny jail. He took his reflection as he always would when needing to remind himself of his identity. Ah yes, the distressing look of death; a most fitting appearance for a prisoner at Death's Door. The sight of a dying man was one he had laid eyes upon many times before, but never had he seen it in himself.

Before the footsteps arrived at Trajan's cell, a black-pebble eyed raven had beaten the cruel man to it. The tips of the raven's horned jaws were covered lightly in golden flakes of sand and the rest of its beak was scratched white.

Was the raven real? Was he himself real anymore?

Just like his soul, the eyes and hair of the approaching being, who was dressed head to toe in the darkest shade of black, was filthy and ruined. The blood, running fiercely through his veins, belonged to Rapture. With great and crucial purpose, Thanisis marched past cells made from iron and bone, beside him, a woman dressed all in white.

When, at last, the two arrived at the foot of cell D1-3183, the sight of the decayed vampire came only from the violent fire burning from the outside torches. No life remained within that cell. Only torture. A limbo between life and death. *Mankarash.*

Thanisis had insisted the prince ought to be treated as fairly as any other prisoner, which explained the unforgiving burns and scars covering his entire upper-body. Albeit through lack of food there was not much body left to damage.

'Ravenna, to me, girl.' The raven landed gently atop Thanisis' shoulder, causing a light breeze to waft through his dishevelled hair.

The familiar scent of the Shabrathian Sea quickly ran up Yara's nose. 'Is that you, Death?' Trajan asked. His voice pleading.

'Worse,' the cruel sorcerer answered. 'It is your chance of life.'

Yara moved as close as his chains would allow. 'What if I care not to live?'

'Unfortunately, there are certain things in life that lie out of our control. I find that what we want and that which we have control over are often two most different and painful things.'

The woman in white studied the cell closely. The only time the cells were ever opened was to allow entry; the bones within were never removed. 'Do you remember the child who once owned this very cell?' she asked calmly.

'Many have died before me and many will die after.'

'True enough,' Thanisis agreed. 'Yet, the child with whom she speaks never did die within this cell. Just a boy was my father, less than half the age I own this very night and even I can admit, I'd be unable to endure such punishments as he.'

Yara Trajan smiled. 'Ah yes, Lozari Rapture; famous prisoner at Raylan Fallen's hands—'

'Khosi Trajan's hand,' he corrected. 'Come on, let us not play games.'

'And here I was thinking it you who were playing the games, for unlike your dear brother, I am not blind. I see it true that the woman in white beside you is Mia of the Aj'ayah, so I ask, what is it you both want of my life?'

Mia entered into the light for the first time since entering the doors of Death; her body appeared red from the torches. Such exquisiteness could never be described using words; her beauty shone. 'The Ladybird flies again,' Mia elegantly spoke. 'You, and you alone, are to deliver this message to Divina Syrus, Empress atop the Orca Throne.'

Yara let loose what should have been a laugh but was actually a most painful cough. 'You're a fool if you think Divina would trust me!'

'Oh, but she will trust you. She will trust the fear in your eyes. The very fear I just witnessed when delivering the message to you. Share it with Divina. Only then, will you be granted death.'

Through a powerful inexplicable force, the chains of Cell D1-3183 unlocked themselves and burst inward against the back wall.

Yara was quick to crawl out, squirming away from Ravenna as she squawked loudly into his ears. He could have sworn the bird was repeatedly screeching the word *die die die.*

Then again, how could he be certain when he couldn't even hear his own mind anymore?

Yara scurried across the wing's walkway, past Jimmy Ferdinand's D1-3172 until finally reaching his freedom door - a thing he never knew existed, but was most certainly real.

***

When the ruined son of Khosi Trajan escaped Death's Door, Mia noticed a figure, hiding in the darkness, at the other end of the walkway. How he'd passed the guards outside, she could not say.

As the figure slowly approached the two, Ravenna flew aggressively near, screeching and clapping her wings to quickly force the figure into sight.

'Sorcerer!' the Darkness called out.

'Alexander,' Thanisis replied. 'My my, you look terrible. What happened to you? You've more scars upon your face than an untrained lion tamer. How long have you been hiding there?'

'Long enough,' Kai-Sal returned.

'And here I was thinking you were no friend to sorcery,' Mia smiled happily, enjoying the moment.

'Oh dear, Thanisis. I was once a mage myself, don't you recall? My line of work stands much simpler when I am friend to all and enemy to none.'

'And what line would that be?' he asked.

A thick smile cut across the vampire's lips. 'Exchange.' Kai-Sal threw a small, leather book, frightening Ravenna as it crashed onto the dust at the ground. It fell wide open and though Kai-Sal still could see no words, he could read the amazement upon their faces.

'Exchange you say?' Mia questioned. 'For what Alexander Ezra Fallen?'

Kai-Sal gave a sly wink to the woman in white and again, a shark-like smile cut from cheek to cheek. 'Survival,' he announced before beginning his decent back down the wing's walkway. 'I wish to be one of the few who live to see the aftermath of the Ladybird's forthcoming destruction.'

Ravenna brushed past Mia and sat atop Thanisis's shoulder, once more squawking *die die die.* Then, the three of them watched as Kai-Sal disappeared back into the darkness of Death's Door.

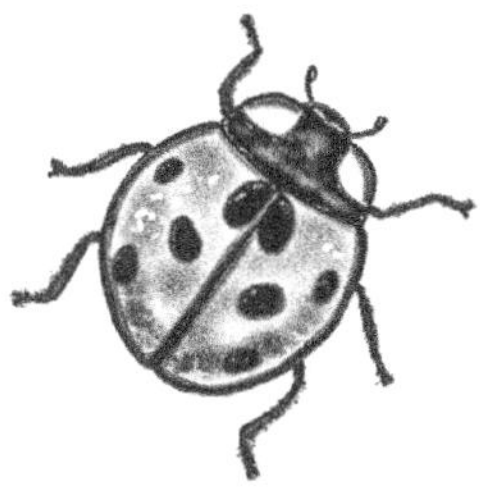

Dragon Claw Chronicles: Legend of Eliza

Timeline of Key Events in Chronological Order

---

1. At the beginning of time, Dragon Claw is divided by two lands: Luminous and Aj'ayah.

2. Mount Hjar erupts and divides Dragon Claw into four lands: Ramoria, Empora, Posre and Danjin.

   Kraal Syrus's reign upon the Elephant Throne in Empora begins.

3. The Wolves of the Aj'ayah discover the three Testaments of Man, Monster and Magic.

4. Young Parra Rapture and Yakub Sebastian visit the Heart of Fortunae.

    Parra is met by a young girl who shares his prophecy.

5. Khosi Trajan's Reign upon the Devil Throne in Danjin begins.

6. Parra Rapture and Korine Sebastian marry and have two children named Thaddeus and Lozari.

    Parra Rapture's reign upon the Orca Throne in Ramoria begins.

7. Raylan Fallen's reign upon the Bear Throne in Posre begins.

8. Yakub Sebastian is murdered by the Trajans upon discovery he was a sorcerer.

9. Agarov of the Aj'ayah meets with Parra to share the news that Lozari Rapture has been captured by Raylan Fallen.

10. Thaddeus is poisoned by mistake by an order sent from Kraal Syrus for Gabriel, (the servant boy,) to murder Parra Rapture.

11. The Matra visits Joje Sebastian in his dreams. She speaks Thaddeus's name.

12. Joje Sebastian sends his soldiers to invite the Matra to the Siren Palace.

13. The Matra meets with Parra Rapture, removes his heart and becomes pregnant with his child.

    Parra Rapture's reign upon the Orca Throne in Ramoria ends.

    Lozari Rapture's reign upon the Orca Throne in Ramoria begins.

    The War of Four Officially begins.

14. Nyla/Eliza is born and discovered by Clementine, Mr and Mrs McArthur's maid.

    Lozari Rapture removes the head of Raylan Fallen.

    Raylan Fallen's reign upon the Bear Throne in Posre ends.

    The Bear Throne is destroyed by Lozari Rapture.

    Lozari Rapture and Savanah Fallen marry and have two children. Their names are Zagan and Thanisis.

Savanah Rapture dies during childbirth.

15. The Battle of Quae begins.

    Kraal Syrus's reign upon the Elephant Throne at Empora ends.

    Benjamin Syrus's reign upon the Elephant Throne at Empora begins.

16. Nyla steals the medallion from Mrs McArthur's neck. She runs away and meets Coccin in the sewer.

    Nyla burns Kulla and the gates to the crooked world are opened.

17. The Matra visits Lozari Rapture in his dreams and instructs him to visit the crooked cabin.

    Lozari Rapture becomes the most powerful sorcerer ever to exist and raises an army of the dead.

    The Devil Throne is destroyed by Khosi Trajan.

18. Benjamin Syrus slays Lozari.

    Lozari Rapture's reign upon the Orca Throne in Ramoria ends.

Benjamin Syrus raises Lozari Rapture's children as his own.

19. Thanisis Rapture kills Benjamin Syrus.

    Benjamin Syrus's reign upon the Elephant Throne in Empora ends.

    The Elephant Throne is destroyed by the people of Empora.

    Wyrell Syrus's reign upon the Orca Throne in Ramoria begins under the protection of Khosi Trajan.

    Zagan Rapture runs from Castle Snow and travels to Ramoria. At Ramoria, Zagan enters the gates to the crooked world through his nightmares and meets Coccin.

20. Khosi Trajan betrays and kills Wyrell Syrus.

    Khosi Trajan's reign on the Orca Throne at Ramoria begins.

    Divina Syrus secretly conspires against Khosi Trajan.

21. Eliza gives Zagan her half of the medallion and explains that the other half is Coccin.

Zagan gives the medallion piece to Thanisis.

22. Zagan Rapture spends fifty years of his life within the crooked world to take care of Coccin and abide the prophecy.

    Thanisis finds Nyla and gives the medallion piece to her

23. Divina Syrus slays Khosi Trajan.

    Divina Syrus's reign on the Orca Throne at Ramoria begins.

    Khosi Trajan's reign on the Orca Throne at Ramoria ends.

    The War of Four ends.

24. Nyla finds Zagan within the crooked cabin in search for the other medallion piece. Zagan takes her piece and disappears.

    Ella-Rose rises from her nightmare.

    Michael arrives at Caesar's to listen to stories of the War of Four.

25. Ella-Rose and Finn travel through Fortunae Forest to Kulla.

Ella-Rose discovers the Amethyst Cavern.
Ella-Rose receives the medallion piece.

26. Michael leaves Caesar's and meets Creep.
    Zagan visits Caesar.

27. Ella-Rose and Finn become surrounded by globbers and run for it.
    Ella-Rose collapses down a hill and awakes in the crooked world.
    Michael and Creep are captured by the Masked Clan.

28. Finn escapes the globbers and is forced down a tunnel leading to a sewer where he meets Eliza.
    Ella-Rose meets Coccin and they both travel to the crooked cabin together.
    Michael is taken to the Heart of Fortunae.

29. Finn and Eliza follow Ella-Rose to the crooked cabin.
    Nyla switches consciousness with Eliza, imprisoning Eliza in the crooked world and releasing herself into Dragon Claw.

30. Finn leaves the sewer and meets Creep. He then finds the half-sword Mankarash.

31. Master Jra'bral, the vampire priest, turns Michael into a vampire.

    Zagan finds Ella-Rose and takes her back to Dragon Claw.

32. Thanisis Rapture and the Matra visit Yara Trajan at Death's Door and force him to deliver the message: *The ladybird flies again*, to Divina Syrus.

    Kai-Sal gives Thanisis the book which shares the map to the crooked world.

33. The War of Man, Monster and Magic begins.

Main Character List
Glossary

RAPTURE FAMILY

Harlam Rapture – Father of Parra Rapture / Emperor of Ramoria prior to the War of Four

Parra Rapture – Son of Harlam Rapture / Father of Thaddeus, Lozari, Nyla and Eliza Rapture / Emperor of Ramoria in the beginning of the War of Four

Thaddeus Rapture – First son of Parra Rapture

Lozari (Harlam) Rapture – Second son of Parra Rapture / Brother of Thaddeus Rapture / Husband of Savanah Fallen / Father of Thanisis and Zagan Rapture / Emperor of Ramoria during the War of Four

Nyla Rapture – Daughter of Parra Rapture and Mia of Green Sands.

Eliza Rapture - Daughter of Parra Rapture and Mia of Green Sands.

Thanisis Rapture – Son of Lozari Rapture / Brother of Zagan Rapture / Father of Ella-Rose and Michael Rapture

Zagan Rapture – Son of Lozari Rapture / Brother of Thanisis Rapture

Ella-Rose Rapture – Daughter of Thanisis Rapture

Michael Rapture – Son of Thanisis Rapture

SYRUS FAMILY

Kraal Syrus – Father of Benjamin and Wyrell Syrus / Emperor of Empora during the War of Four

Gabriel Syrus (Gross Gabriel) – Nephew of Kraal Syrus

Farah Syrus – Brother of Kraal Syrus / Father of Gabriel Syrus

Benjamin Syrus – Son of Kraal Syrus / Brother of Wyrell Syrus / Emperor of Empora during the War of Four

Wyrell Syrus – Son of Kraal Syrus / Brother of Benjamin Syrus / Emperor of Empora during the War of Four

Divina Syrus – Daughter of Wyrell Syrus / Empress of Empora after the War of Four

FALLEN FAMILY

Raylan Fallen – Brother of Alexander Fallen / Emperor of Posre during the War of Four

Alexander (Ezra) Fallen (Kai-Sal / Darkness) – Brother of Raylan Fallen

Savanah Fallen (Rapture) – Daughter of Raylan, Wife of Lozari Rapture / Mother of Zagan and Thanisis Rapture

TRAJAN FAMILY

Khosi Trajan – Father of Yara Trajan / Emperor of Danjin during the War of Four

Yara Trajan – Son of Khosi Trajan

SEBASTIAN FAMILY

Yakub Sebastian – Father of Joje and Korine Sebastian

Joje Sebastian (Caesar Azerius) – Son of Yakub Sebastian / Brother of Korine Sebastian / Father of Francis Sebastian

Korine Sebastian (Rapture) – Daughter of Yakub Sebastian / Wife of Parra Rapture / Mother of Thaddeus and Lozari Rapture / Sister of Joje Sebastian

Francis Sebastian – Son of Joje Sebastian / Father of Alena Sebastian

Alena Sebastian (Sara Azerius) – Daughter of Francis Sebastian

AJ'AYAH

Agarov – The White Wolf

Mia (Matra) – Mother of Nyla and Eliza Rapture

ADDITIONAL CHARACTERS

Finn Hampson – A friend of Ella-Rose Rapture

Mr Coccin L. Idae (Coccin) – A friend to many

Creep – a paug

Master Jra'bral Xhea – Vampire Priest

Wallim McArthur – Carer of Nyla and Ella-Rose / Husband of Penny McArthur

Penny McArthur – Carer of Nyla and Ella-Rose / Wife of Wallim McArthur / Cousin of Clementine Hunter

Clementine Hunter – McArthur's maid / Cousin of Penny McArthur

Val Adamou – Village butcher

Zebu – A globber

Tonzil – A globber

Rump – A globber

Sarajai Sharjal – A sorcerer, friend of Lozari

Yolanda – Member of the Masked Clan

Spider - Member of the Masked Clan

Phillop Roman – Dismantler of the dead / Creator of the dead

Mr Farash – A rude man

Flir Tomrick – A saintly man

Walter Fitzgerald – One of Joje Sebastian's men

Acknowledgements

There are so many people I wish to thank for encouraging me over the years and helping to get Legend of Eliza to where it is today.

I wish to begin by thanking the magnificent Michael Cummings, who has spent many years of his life reading and re-reading this book prior to its publication. Without him, Legend of Eliza may have only ever remained locked away in a drawer.

A massive thanks to Jemma Bunce for being ever so patient with me whilst I got the book right. She has been just as important to finishing this book as I have.

Thank you Kate Roberts for always pushing me to finish the story. Thank you also Rachel Glover for your support with my writing and publishing business. And, I guess, thanks Liam Gilbert, so I don't miss you out.

Thank you Kevin Dunne and Marion Dodds for the support of Ray-Sparkles. It will forever remain in our hearts.

I wish to share a huge thank you to everyone at the casino I used to work with for pushing me to finish my book. Although I can't name everyone, you all know who you are. A few special mentions are, (first names only), Daniel, Elvis, Elliot, Dom, Sarah, Justyna, Charley and of course, a very special mention to Swamp Rat.

Thank you Nik at Book Beaver (UK) for the Cover Art.

Thank you Diane Maguire and Angela Roberts for waiting eagerly for Eliza's release.

Thank you Maguire & Cummings Publishing House for this first publication.

Finally, thank you all the readers of this book. I hope you have enjoyed it and are looking forward to the next installment of Dragon Claw Chronicles.

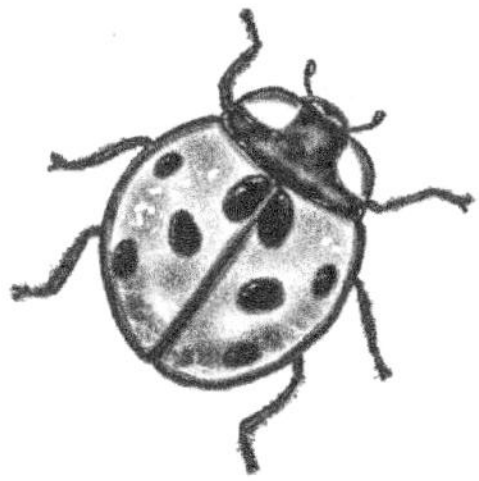

About Legend of Eliza

Legend of Eliza is the first novel I have ever written, although it has held many titles and many different stories prior to what it is today.

The truth is, Legend of Eliza was originally a children's story named 'Ray-Sparkles' where the main characters were fairies who searched for a map.

Legend of Eliza has taken many names, including: 'The Magical Adventure Saga', 'The Light of Conqulass' and 'The Turnings of Dragon Claw'. However, the more I wrote over the years, the more the story arranged itself to what it became.

I find it strange now thinking about how far Legend of Eliza has actually come. You see, I would write thousands upon thousands of words, then disregard and scrap 98% of what I had written. It was all those 2%s that amounted to the book you read today.

For instance, I wrote of a wolf named Agarov meeting a witch to search for a map that had been buried years ago, only to keep the wolf, Agarov in the actual story. I wrote of a girl named Alena sneaking into a meeting of her father's, only to use this for young Zagan, sneaking into Benjamin Syrus's meeting.

I think the message here is this:

When writing, don't force your story to go in the direction that you have planned. Instead, let the story decide who it is and who it wants to become. You are a parent to your writing. Watch over it, provide it with the foundations, but let it travel along its own path, (or in my case – paths).

Thank you for reading Legend of Eliza. I am looking forward to sharing the next instalment of Dragon Claw Chronicles with you.

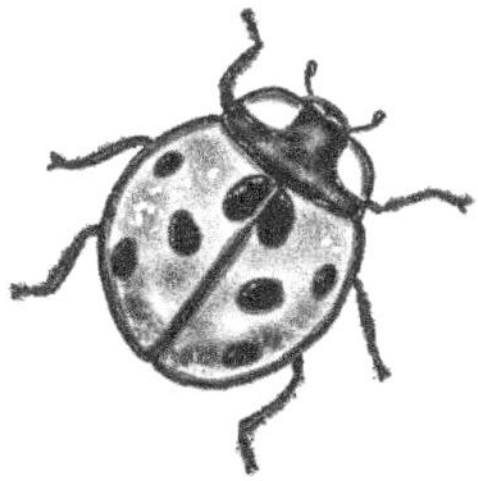

Legend of Eliza Blurb

When Ella-Rose has a recurring nightmare of a demonic presence in a crooked world and a sorcerer who tells her she must search for answers within Fortunae Forest, she meets up with her best friend Finn to explore the mysteries between the trees. However, they must keep their wits about them, as dark creatures hide behind every shadow.

Meanwhile, her twin brother Michael is stuck listening to old tales of war and battles. Little do they know, the war between man, monster and magic is about to begin.

Join Ella-Rose, Finn and Michael on their adventures through the magical forest of Fortunae as these three characters play a huge role in defeating a demon and closing the gates to the crooked world.

DRAGON CLAW CHRONICLES

Legend of Eliza

Printed in Dunstable, United Kingdom

74544991R00221